BLUE ROCK

Jeremy Reed

Blue Rock

JONATHAN CAPE
THIRTY-TWO BEDFORD SQUARE
LONDON

First published 1987
Copyright © by Jeremy Reed 1987

Jonathan Cape Ltd, 32 Bedford Square, London WC1B 3EL

British Library Cataloguing in Publication Data
Reed, Jeremy
Blue rock.
I. Title
823'914 [F]   PR6068.E3418
ISBN 0-224-02434-5

The extract on pp.123–4 is taken from the 1965
edition of G.R.S. Mead's *Orpheus*, published by
John M. Watkins.

Phototypeset by Falcon Graphic Art Ltd
Wallington, Surrey
Printed in Great Britain by
Ebenezer Baylis & Son Ltd
The Trinity Press, Worcester and London

To Martyn

'A hard night! Dried blood smokes on my face,
and nothing lies behind me but that repulsive
little tree! The battle for the soul is as
brutal as the battles of men; but the sight
of justice is the pleasure of God alone.'

Rimbaud, *A Season in Hell*

1

Things happen. I don't believe there are beginnings; by the time you're conscious of the thing, it's you anyway, it's happened as something you have to own up to, you may not even wish the change that's occurred.

It was the summer of 1968 or 1970. I could hear Bunny standing in the bathroom, saying to me, 'You won't ever be the same again after that, both men and women will treat you with detachment, we'll be outlaws in a world our parents despise.' But I had to go on with it, the articulation of lipstick, the red lips given the flourish of a bow; the transformation was simple, and I went face up to the mirror and left a petunia pink signature there. I could see the fibres of my lip tissue minutely defined, and in between them pure silver. It was like the translucency of a flower; you lose consciousness of the fact that the poppy is substantial, it appears more that the light has crystallised into a red nimbus. It's only when you finger the black seed heads that your hand registers the shock that it's material, and by then the flower's shed two or three silk petals.

We had the bathroom window opened wide on to the honey-suckle; the little white stars of jasmine were a cascade of scented moths. Bunny said their musty perfume smelt like the barn in sunlight, except that straw and sunlight weren't scented, but you could give them the scent of jasmine. And honeysuckle, well that smelt like rose and vanilla and lilac, only it wasn't any of those; it smelt of the powder on moths' wings, but that was because we'd seen moths constellating the jasmine. We weren't doing anything that day; we both stood there with carmine lips, fascinated, wondering how the world would respond to our change if we went out like this. Bunny thought he'd scare Louise and Rachel, but what of the adults? Wouldn't I be sent away again to Dr Moravia and the shaded green desk-lamp alight all day even in summer? Dr Moravia smelt of tobacco, his mind tried to enter yours, and he'd do this by paying no attention at all to you; you thought he'd lost the subject whereas all the time he'd been anticipating exactly what you didn't wish him to know. He was like a bathyscope; he went into your head and looked out at the shoals of brightly coloured fish flickering in lightning zig-zags through the green opacity of the depths. He used to say, 'This will hurt, but by the time you're my age you won't even remember it.' He had a map of the world on his wall, and all I could look at were the sapphire spaces, the land masses didn't interest me. When he asked me where I lived, I'd say I hadn't discovered yet, I was out on an ice-floe of consciousness, I inhabited a mental space he could only partially fill with his own inquisitive suggestions. I used to guard this illimitable territory; it was all I had, and it was me. My parents used the word co-operate, I should co-operate with Dr Moravia; he would dispel the huge fear that eclipsed the mental territory in which I cowered. Sometimes I would detect fear in him; the space that he couldn't conquer in me was a diminution of his powers. Each time he advanced he was forced to retreat. He would manoeuvre to get me into his sights, and just as he was about to squeeze the trigger I wouldn't be there. My imperceptible shifts to left and right startled him. He'd say, 'Why don't you allow me to help you, why don't you come out of your hiding place?' as though he would shell me like a lobster, remove the blue carapace and examine the interior. Bunny knew things about me that Dr Moravia didn't. Perhaps it was this that irritated him; there was a leak in my circuit, but the current wasn't fed into his reservoir of knowledge about me. I'd say to him, 'If I throw the lights on inside my head, you'll see what you don't want to see – the dark room in which the cine-film never stops, not even in death.' But Bunny knew. There was that day out in the barn when we confided in one another; it was a weird chemistry, stepping out of the light into the dark and then making that dark into light by retinal adjustment. It happened like that. A flash, and you knew everything about yourself and about others, only you couldn't always keep the light on, life came at you from too many improbable angles.

It was hot in the barn. The rafters smelt of dry sawdust, the incandescent July sun beat at the thatched roof, but the stone walls kept us cool. Touching them was like touching moss. No one used the barn now; what had once been a goat-stall was now

10

littered with rusty farm machinery – old forks, old hoes, a defunct ploughshare, slatted flower caskets, empty fertiliser sacks – but old and musty as it was we could smell jasmine. We lay back looking up at the chinks of light that stabbed through like gold needles, and the bigger weight of light that came through two small rectangular windows and mellowed in the dust-white straw. Bunny said that you could eat silence, you could fill yourself up with it like snow as a protection against adults. If you ate enough of it you'd go as quietly through life as the flight of an owl or bat. We lay still and listened to what went on inside our heads. When Bunny spoke again, his voice could have been pitched from a neighbour's garden. It came out with the big thudding bounces of a windfall, something too large for his mouth, a sort of swallow's sticky ball of insects that it would jam into its fledglings' beaks. He said, 'The reason girls don't like us is because we're more beautiful than them; Louise said that make-up was for boys who didn't like girls, and I said it was for boys who liked girls so much that they wished to look like them.' We each listened to the silence that succeeded his words; it went on and on like a meadow-lark crossing a field. Then I knew it was my turn to speak, and I said, 'Dr Moravia wanted me to confess, he asked me if I knew Yeats's poem that begins "If I make the lashes dark/And the eyes more bright/And the lips more scarlet" . . . but I said I only write poetry, and never read it.' The lie jumped out of me, I could see its conspicuousness glaring in Moravia's hand like a red dice. But Bunny knew. He said, 'Words are traps, people lay them out in the way you bait hooks on a trot-line. They want to get you through the lip, and when you can't find the words to fight them, they reel you in.' I looked down at the straw; it was like firelight, red and gold in the furnacing air.

Bunny lay face down in the straw. I could smell the saltiness of his flesh, his brown arms protruding from a black singlet. 'Why don't we bring Louise and Rachel out here?' he said. 'You wouldn't guess what I heard; Louise puts on lipstick to kiss boys in the dark. I saw Louise lying in the high grass with Stephen Bartram. It was odd. You had to look hard to find her; all I could make out was her arms pulling his head down, and her bare legs sticking out beneath him. Stephen Bartram shoots rats; he nails them to his shed door. There's a red twist in his eye like the spiral in a marble; my father says it's conjunctivitis, but I know

11

it's cruelty. He beat his whippet until the dog winced and its eyes turned. My father said I was to avoid him; he lights fires on the heath and smokes in front of girls.'

We lay there each turning over the image of Stephen Bartram's red eye-twists. The heat was unbearable; when you breathed in your nasal passage nettled with cinders. It was like inhaling smoke; we were addicted to summer. I could hear the insane yatter of a green woodpecker ululating across the countryside, then the raucous scream of a jay. We were free to take in nothing but the air and light; we'd brought ourselves to this barn to give our thoughts boundaries, to test our ideas against walls and not the sky. I said, 'All right, try and arrange to get Louise and Rachel here on Thursday afternoon, I'm too shy to ask.' Bunny lay savouring his superiority. For a brief moment he was an invincible feudal lord, he could summon people. At his word, Louise and Rachel would stand in the blond light of the barn door. Only, unlike the silver oval in the flower petal Bunny had imprinted on the mirror, they'd be tangible. I said, 'Bunny, do you know what I see when I keep my eyes closed? A red poppy disintegrating into small silken wings. Are girls like that? Do they lie down like scarlet petals in the gold corn-ears?'

We were listening. When you're that quiet something always intrudes; it may be the consciousness of your own heart-beat or the imperceptible noise of a cloud shadow crossing the stone floor. Bunny was thinking what I couldn't know, in the way Dr Moravia said I wouldn't show him my thoughts face up like a hand of cards. And if you stop thinking, you're nothing, just an inner hum of rhythmic noises. If we were where we should have been we'd be miles away at Tommy Smith's place. His mother was expecting us, Tommy would have pilfered cans of his father's beer, we'd drink it and feel our heads turn light by the pond. We'd come here instead of going there, and Tommy's mother was sure to telephone and say we'd gone missing. Then there would be lies to make up – Bunny lost his shoe in the high grass that smells of sunlight and green juice; when we looked for it, we found an adder and took fright. You could do so much more by not going somewhere; you could imagine the red love-bites on Stephen Bartram's neck after he'd spent the afternoon with Louise. You could imagine the kingfisher dra-gonflies on Tommy Smith's pond, the saw-flies, the clouds of sweat-flies buzzing the lazy cows, the flick-flack of their tails.

Flick-flack like the windscreen wipers of Tommy's father's car when he drove us back from the party on a night of driving rain. The rain stomped on the car roof, it was like popcorn spitting out of a pan, but my parents said it was just rain. When the sky cleared in the morning you could see everything in double, the trees stood on their heads, leaves painted themselves into water. It was through this that I learnt how my face could be an object of focus. Dr Moravia said that a face is like a map, it expresses human emotion even if you don't always want it to. And that afternoon when Bunny and I painted our lips red in the bathroom, it was the mirror that wanted this, or rather we wanted to look out from the mirror at faces that weren't ours. They'd be looking out at us and we at them. It was weird; my mother called it putting on a face, there was this part of you you could put on or rub out. But when I escaped from Dr Moravia I had to keep the same face only go backwards, I could be anywhere, and he would be searching for me.

Bunny rolled over, and said, 'What are you thinking of?' I was thinking how I'd like to die and come back, I'd like to become invisible when I didn't want to do things, and then carry on living when I did. That way you could avoid punishment. If I could have been invisible when I was up Tommy Smith's apple tree, his father wouldn't have hit me with a stick. They have so many trees, each one emblazoned with fruit, *a red blush on the green apple globe.* I told Bunny that I was drifting, just pushing out on a raft into the azure. I didn't want to say I'd seen the red love-bites on Stephen Bartram's neck, or Louise's pink gym-shoes discarded in the grass. I said, 'If I keep on looking I end up seeing myself. Not my face, but something that lives inside me, something you could search for for ever and never find. It's like light, you see by it but you can't touch it or even know what it is.'

The gold sunlight lit up pretzels of straw; we could hear a tractor's rackety shift of gears in the lane next to the field. They'd never know we were here, and even if they did they wouldn't find us, for we would be anywhere, out at Tommy Smith's pond, or just sitting here ignoring the intruder, looking through him on an invisible beam of imagination. You could be safe for ever like that. They could cut your head off and you wouldn't know.

Bunny looked at his watch. He said, 'It's 4.20.' *See how the light begins to loop on the floor; it makes itself into a necklace, and later on it will be like the skin of a nectarine.* 'We'll have to get back by 5.00, so let's make one more journey. Tell me where you're going; I want you to go into the pond or into Louise's bedroom, you can go right down where the pike and eels are, or you can stand in the room while Louise undresses, and she'll never know you are there. Go on, tell me where you're going.'

I shut my eyes. It was red and black inside the cave of my head. Tiny lines wavered back and forth like dots on a radar-screen, then I went down to the bottom of the pond. It was olive-green and murky. I could see a great ram's-horn snail, its antennae projected like elongated bull's horns, the grass-green carapace of a diving beetle flickered past, there were the blue and orange markings of a crested newt, a minnow's pink and green translucency, a stickleback and a pin-thin water stick-insect. In a tangle of weed I could make out a water-spider, its bulbous sack looked like an astronaut's helmet, and all the time I wasn't conscious that I was in water – I just went on breathing while a frog stretched its mottled orange and green body and flippered to the surface. I was safe here. It was like what Bunny said about being invisible; you only had to think yourself somewhere and you were there. Bunny was saying, 'Now tell me what you see on the surface, are there dragonflies?' *Their bodies are like Egyptian mummies inlaid and speckled with turquoise.* I said I could only see damselflies – there were red ones and blue ones, they were sitting on water-lilies, waiting like fighter planes ready to lift off and intercept the enemy.

Bunny's voice grew tremulous. There was a shake in it, as though he was drinking and trying to speak at the same time. I could hear him steadying his voice before he said, 'Now pretend you're in Louise's bedroom when she undresses at night. Tell me what you see. Isn't she pretty? Don't go too fast or I might miss something.' But I said, 'I've never seen a girl undress,' and he rolled over and over in the straw as if he was escaping running firelight, his black singlet was corrugated and cross-hatched with white straws. The light was looping now, a deep gold; it was the colour of untrodden sand in a cove. It moved when the wind did, it branched into fibres like strands of gold hair selected for pink ribbons. Bunny said, 'We'll go back in ten minutes, but let's try and make ten minutes seem like two hours or two days.' *If we had Tommy Smith's father's beer here, we could hear it fizz and go whoof in a cream lather as it escaped through the tadpole-shaped aperture of metal. Beer goes up in a mushroom from the stomach to the head, that's what they call getting high; you can kite over the trees with all of those bubbles popping behind the eyes.*

I was thinking of Dr Moravia. The way there were six or seven white hairs on the tip of his eyebrows, they looked like they were painted on. They were stiff like a paintbrush when you don't wash it out. He wore a green tie with white horizontal stripes. I used to try and make them stand up vertical, to see how he'd look with his neck resting on thin stalagmites. His suit was a sandy grey, it had four tabby buttons on each cuff, and the ice-blue cuffs of his shirts were starched and fastened by rectangular jet cuff-links. His shoes were snakeskin, you couldn't hear him when he got up to leave the room, or when he came back down the corridor. I used to think he did it to surprise me. To see whether I'd open his Havana cigar-box, or try to read the scribbled notes he took in royal-blue ink. He never stained his fingers; his pen was streamlined like a jet's fuselage, an aquamarine Parker with a thin gold nib. He used to hold it as a point of balance and look away at the green desk-lamp, hoping that would bring me out. He used to act shy to try to make me bold, only I'd retreat, and he'd lay his pen down and scan the incomprehensible squiggle of his notes. When he left off thinking, he'd train a question at me that seemed to come from nowhere at all. He'd say, 'Mr Finch tells me that you need to mix more at school,' and he must have been nurturing that for days, only now it swung out from its orbit behind an obscuring planet and hit me in the face. And how long had Mr Finch been observing me? There were eyes everywhere; people had eyes like the swivel control towers of spiders – even hidden in this barn someone would be sure to be watching. They'd see the straws zig-zagged on our clothes, they'd smell the sunlight on our bodies; you couldn't rub that gold light off, it dusted the skin like pollen.

Bunny said, 'Another five minutes and we'll have to go back. We might see an adder or a grass-snake or a frog down by the pond. I once saw a crow scrag a frog.' *It was sunning on the green dinner-plate of a water-lily pad and the crow came down like a ragged bolt of storm, all beak and talons, and lifted the wriggling bulb of mottled skin into the air. It happened so quickly. The frog's eye never saw the crow, the shadow fell on it at the same time as the crow. And when the bird dropped it in the rush-scrub it went down*

15

again ferociously, shook the frog like a terrier a rat, and flew off with it. 'That was by Heath Marsh. I've seen crested grebe there, and snipe, and coots and moorhens, and once a big heron flapped up out of the reeds and stroked into flight. When it lifted, the power of its wings fanned the air.'

I said, 'I once saw a raven chasing a barn-cat across a field.' *It kept lowering on the cat as though it was going to sink its claws in, and then at the last second it would gain a little height. When the cat slipped into a hedge the bird went off, raucously hoarse, gaining height by staggered lifts, and going right on up to the crown of an oak. You could hear it for ten minutes barking at the blue air.*

The light was beginning to withdraw from the barn. It was pooling. It reminded me of an ebb tide, the light being drawn back leaving a fox-russet pool stained with gold. If you dipped your finger in there you'd be touching the sun's eye; it would warm the nerve-ends in your finger-tip.

Bunny said, 'It's 5.00. We're going to be late home.' There was some pull from which we couldn't disentangle ourselves, a magnetic field that induced lethargy. We were heavy with sunlight and barn mustiness. If we could have suspended ourselves like bats from the rafters we would have stayed there, swooped out at night and returned with the first cinnamon streak of dawn. Adults couldn't catch bats; they whizzed by frenetically, they picked off insects spotting the air like polka-dots on a blotter. They dived the cow meadows at twilight and lurched through the orchard trees. I used to go out in the sooty blue dusk and watch them hunting with swifts. Bunny said that he preferred owls. A barn owl had roosted at Tommy Smith's; it was piebald, like white snow through which lichen still shows. Sometimes its cry went through you like a razor-blade forced into a U-turn on tissue paper: it snowed the flesh with goosepimples. Tommy Smith used to collect its pellets. He said pieces of vole and field mouse and sparrow had dried in them. There were pellets everywhere, like the dried rabbit droppings we found littering sea-pinks and harebells on the cliff-path to the sea. Little blond miniature cannonballs. They dusted between your fingers.

Very slowly we let ourselves out of the barn. It was like disbanding a conspiratorial cabala, the secret ritual of two enacted by gold light. The heat walked into us, it beat up out of the grass where it had lain supine all day long. Burs stuck to us,

mauve thistle flowers were mobbing the field; they'd taken it by
purple rule – soon they'd grow grey and fluff their luminous
seeds into the wind-stream. Cuckoo-pint had acid green berries
in the lane. They'd turn blood-orange and then garish scarlet.
We walked back, hardly speaking as each tried to fabricate a
bullet-proof excuse. Bunny said, 'We'll say that we set out for
Tommy Smith's only we went on to the heath to watch birds. We
saw swallows and swifts, a willow-warbler and a chiff-chaff, the
black and red markings of a stonechat, and the lime-speckled
crest of a cirl bunting. We wanted to find the heron, so we ended
up by the pond, my watch stopped and we had to guide ourselves
by the light.'

We walked on. 'Don't forget,' Bunny said, 'we'll invite Louise
and Rachel out to the barn next Thursday. If we mention the
barn our last outpost of privacy is gone. They'll forbid us to go
there, they'll say we might set fire to it accidentally.' We walked
facing into the sun, it was red warpaint on our features. I
remembered the lipstick in my pocket; I said, 'Bunny, will we
paint our lips on to surprise Louise and Rachel?' He kept silent
for a while, then said, 'We can use it for other things, it's our
secret phial to the future.'

We kicked our way through the tall meadow-grass, picking up
the cartridges intended for rabbits, inhaling on the secrets of the
day in the way that my father savoured the sweet lilac smoke of
his cigar. He'd touch his taste-buds with it like the bouquet of
wine. There was nothing and no one on the road. Not a car, not a
person; a blackbird became shrilly panicky under a hawthorn
hedge. We felt guilty without having done anything of which to
be found culpable. Guilt is like that – it makes you own up to
things you've never really done. And then when you've owned
up to them you go ahead and do them.

Bunny left me at the crossroads. He'd found a stone to dribble
down the centre of the road; he scuffed it from hedge to hedge,
finally breaking into a run. I could hear his gym-shoes go
flick-flack, only much faster than a cow's tail, and then he'd
gone.

When I got in, my father and mother were arguing upstairs. I
could hear their voices slap the walls with animation. My father
was saying, 'Why would Karen have stolen the lipstick? There's
no reason for it.' I sat down in the quiet of the house and pinched
the lipstick phial between my thumb and forefinger. It was safe

17

as long as I believed I didn't have it. I sat and waited, listening to a thrush's melody grow higher and higher, its untiring notes turning liquid on the air. When my father came downstairs he went straight out of the front door. My mother quietly said, 'You're back then.' I nodded; soon it would be the hour for bats, a blood-red moon would fire the blue meadow-grass.

2

A wet day on the road. His ties were candy colours, someone had once remarked at a party, and ever since then he'd gone on indulging himself, picking them up on his travels, selecting them for their aesthetic and tactile qualities – pink and white, blue and red and white, turquoise and white, endless silk permutations. They had become a part of his identity; it was reassuring to run his fingers over the silk in times of stress, it had become an unnoticeable but habitual idiosyncrasy.

Dr Ernst Moravia was of German Italian extraction. In 1920, the year subsequent to his birth, his mother had separated from his father, a jeweller, and taken Ernst to live with her in St John's Wood, London. They had relatives; someone who owed money to Mr Moravia suggested, as a means of surrogate payment, that his wife avail herself of the big second-floor flat with its balcony of white scrolled iron overlooking a garden dense with the foliage of cherry trees. It was here the child nurtured the gift of quiet. He had learned early on to interpret people by listening and observing. People invariably used speech to disguise the thought behind the thought they were expressing; if you really listened, if you got into the habit of determining their method of compensation for half-truths or lies, you could penetrate their camouflage. You could duck in under the smoke-screen, and then it was guerrilla warfare, except that thought is so elusive you can't ever pin anyone to a position whereby language is cognate with it. The child had made the garden a springboard for the precocity of his inner dialogue. He had little patience with his mother's love of flowers; the rust-orange and canary-yellow fiesta hybrid lilies, the pendulous mauve of Canterbury bells, the mauve flowers of hosta, the purplish-crimson scabious, hollyhocks, and luxuriant pink and white peonies. And there were roses, Boule de Neige and Mme Lauriol de Barny, white and pink rosettes exquisitely scented. Outdoors, he avoided them, but when his mother cut several and arranged them in a crystal glass beside his bed, he would take pleasure in their fragrance. He would sniff them before retiring to bed; that special hour when he could put on the bedside-lamp and island himself in the gold pool suffused over his open book. He was reading Balzac's *Seraphita* and the next week Jung's *The Psychology of the Unconscious*. He would keep the books locked up in his bedside cabinet; reading was an act of secret ritual and to have his books known would have been to invite dispute or ridicule. He learnt to deposit the knowledge he gained from reading in the manner that a bank secures gold bars in its vaults. The habit had stayed with him a lifetime; he'd gone on authoritatively hoarding library after library – his mental archives were fat as a harvest granary. When his mother tried to distract him with things more becoming to his age, he'd complain of migraines, he'd say his head felt as if it had a glass chip embedded in it. He'd lie on his bed with the blinds drawn in the green shade of the summer afternoon and savour the luxury of his solitude. It was then that he'd review both his own and his mother's lives. He couldn't know why this practice began, it just did. He wasn't doing the thing and then suddenly he was. You couldn't explain it any more than you could say who you were, lying there with the shadow of an acacia tree fingering the wall.

If he looked back to why he was motoring across the city, occasionally glancing down at an immaculate royal blue and silver striped necktie, he'd have to acknowledge those silent afternoons of childhood, a wasp like a fighter plane needling from wall to wall, the house silent, and his mother three streets away visiting a friend, her anxiety over her son's migraine showing in lapses of concentration, while he dreaded her return, and imagined himself living on independently in the house: an adult's mind in a child's body. He used to make believe that no one would ever find him, he'd educate himself, live off his mother's income, and then surprise the world one day by appearing in it. They wouldn't notice, they'd think he'd always been with them, only they hadn't paid enough attention to his being visible. In his perfect life he'd appear and disappear at will; many of his patients had expressed a similar desire to have absolute control over their psychophysical bodies.

Those long afternoons stretched back to a green cave in which he hid. His nurse would be reading Flaubert or Tolstoy; she never intruded, she realised intuitively the boy's need for

20

solitude, the way he sheltered beneath those afternoon silences like a tent. When he wasn't reading, his eyes lit up with the narration that he continued to expand – fiction had become his fiction. The variations on each thought were as many as the leaves on the plane tree outside his window. When the wind agitated the leaves his mind followed that cool green sibilance. He used to wonder what it would be like to have a father. Would he sit and smoke and toy with a jeweller's eyeglass; would he rest his masculine tobacco-scented hands on his son's shoulders when he left the house in the morning? Would he arbitrate over his son's interests, and discourage a passionate devotion to the colour markings of moths and butterflies? Ernst used to draw mental pictures of the father he couldn't remember. Sometimes his father would be a man lazily flicking an aquamarine trout fly into the eddies of a stream; at other times his father would be a thin man, heavily mackintoshed, walking the streets at night, stepping out of the showers and sheltering under awnings, his gold spectacles taking on an amber tint as he cupped a match flame in his hands. His face would disappear into a myopic's blur with the blue smoke he expelled.

But those pictorial fantasies were for twilight, that slate-mauve hour in which the phantasmagoria of the boy's mind showed like slides from a magic-lantern. He would drift with the flow, either startled by faces that menaced him with their unfamiliarity, or entranced by their intangible beauty. It was like peering into the prism of a rock-pool. All kinds of small aquatic fauna were to be discovered only by looking. It was the green and maroon and prune-brown seaweeds that compelled him to go on seaching. He would discern the pink turban of a hermit-crab, the rock shrimps whose darting bodies were as translucent as the water, the staring eyes of a green crab looking out from under a stone. At twilight these shapes assumed forms he could no longer recognise; they became gnome-like faces encrusted with lichen, or they were monsters of the deep, pot-bellied globe-fish nosing down-current in that endless flux of mental imagery we seem neither to control nor create. His twilights were kaleidoscopic; jewel-fires flashed on the eyebrows of harlequins, figures ran towards a smoke-screen on a battlefield, he seemed to be falling down a well-shaft and then soundlessly and with no impact on hitting the water he'd be asleep.

He checked his rear-view mirror; driving still made him

nervous, he valued it only for the insulation it afforded. When he applied his brake-pads at the warning of a scarlet light, he still thought, as he had done in childhood, that it was the eye of a cyclops or gorgon. For a full minute he would remain transfixed by that red eye-lens. In the inclined seat of a taxi alongside, he could see a pretty blonde girl hastily checking her face in a cosmetic mirror. She was holding a black pencil to a linear eyebrow. Each time she raided the mirror her glossy red lips pouted.

He was slow to get away from the lights; his twin-cylinder Jowett Bradford, with its anemone-red bodywork, threaded conspicuously back into the traffic flow. A 1952 two-seater sports model, its dashboard had a big clock-faced speedometer. When the needle twitched clockwise, he could feel the nerves in his body thrill. It was his one indulgence; most days he used a utility Honda, a car he could thug into the grinding circuit of London traffic without fear for its bodywork. There was reassurance too in sitting beneath the convertible sports canopy; when it rained the sound was detonative, the big drops ruckled across the black convex surface. He felt safe here; it was like the green afternoons of childhood, a cave or a sea-shell. In thirty minutes he'd face his first appointment, a country boy from Norfolk whose parents considered him to be too dissociated from his companions. Nervously agitated by his fellow beings, the boy had come to identify only with animals and to adopt nocturnal habits, disappearing at night and sleeping fugitively by day. He was isolated and knew things that either he hadn't experienced, but thought he had, or else he simply wouldn't communicate. It was as though he'd carefully determined the formulaic answers to most questions, and had skilfully devised a manner of answer that evaded the question which was about to follow on from the one he hadn't answered. Either the boy was playing games or he was answerable to an inner world that he wasn't going to allow anyone to encroach on. Moravia was baffled; he'd failed to satisfy the parents' anxious telephone calls, and had ended up by devising a means of screening the boy's behavioural patterns from his parents. Moravia's meetings with his patient had devolved into conspiratorial games of mental chess. For a boy of seventeen coming on eighteen, David, with his sand-blond hair, his luminous sea-green eyes and high cheek-bones, was possessed of an extraordinarily rich inner life. His quietness, the fragility of

22

his slight body, his manner of ducking as he walked, and his inaudibly light tread, all suggested that he was intent on listening to an inner music. He didn't want this exquisite balance of nerves intruded upon; he seemed to want to hear his being note by note. He listened to himself in the way that a thrush stands stock-still listening for a worm.

When Dr Ernst Moravia arrived at his consulting rooms in Harley Street, he felt a pervading sense of apathy. This state of apprehension, of fear that he wasn't going to be able to fill his thoughts out to encompass a lifetime, had become a recurring feature in the last year. He did what he always did at times of crisis; he went over to the mirror and adjusted the knot of his tie. He kept altering it, allowing the coolness of the silk to bring relief to his agitated sense of touch. He'd come to rely on this ritual much as other people fix a drink to assuage their exhaustion. He must have stood there for a good five minutes, tracing out a thin gold line that was almost imperceptible in its bordering of the royal blue, when he noticed a pink envelope propped up on his desk. The cleaner must have placed it there; it was unstamped and had clearly been delivered by hand. He stared a long time at the dusk-pink rectangle, with his name and professional address typed in italics. Although he couldn't account for the caution with which he viewed and handled the letter, a feeling of deep disquiet began to spread through his body like cuttlefish ink clouding clear water. Simultaneous with his apprehension, his mind flashed back with alarming and immediate clarity to the summer of 1960. He'd foolishly accepted the invitation of an attractive former patient Mme Claudette Duras to visit her apartment in the Rue du Bac. Even after a decade he could feel the burning confusion suffuse his skin. What had ensued was what he had hoped for and anticipated; she had, as the evening wore on, grown progressively more amorous, the slash in her tight lavender silk skirt had inchingly revealed her black stockinged legs to the thigh, until in a moment of incandescence he had found himself moving in on her, hungrily searching out the mad insect of her tongue, and then both fighting for breath like two divers come up for air. She had slipped into her bedroom to change. He remembered toying with the stiletto shoes she had discarded; their wine-glass-stemmed heels had felt sensuously abrasive to his heated palms, and when she'd slowly opened the door, peeking round half face, then ducking back into cover, wiggling her red painted toenails, he couldn't have suspected how this insane taunting was to end. Impatiently he rushed the door and, as she sprang back and somersaulted head over heels on to a luxurious pink counterpane, she had exposed, beneath the black wisp of a transparent nightie, the genitals of a man. He could still feel the thud of his heart; it sounded like someone was repeatedly kicking a football against a yard wall. But in the heat and the impassioned confusion he had not felt repelled; all manner of contradictory and guilty thoughts had flashed through his consciousness, but his desire was unabated. He wanted to feel revulsion, but instead he felt excitement. When he left her apartment in the early hours of an oppressively hot August morning, he was changed for life. He had sought the palliative of his tie, but it wasn't there; in the confusion and in his anxiety to leave suddenly before remorse set in, he'd hurried from the apartment leaving Claudette cat-drowsy in the ruckle of silk bedclothes. He had turned round once; the pink counterpane looked like a red lake disturbed by a wind at sunrise. His distraction was such that he'd left his life-stabilising tie coiled beneath the moulded eddies of a rose pillow. When he'd got back to his hotel, he'd checked his body all over. He wanted to know if it had changed, if the release of a potential he had suppressed for forty years had in any way altered him. He imagined at first that the transformation must be visible to others and invisible to himself. He would catch himself turning round abruptly in the street to find that the head-turned aghast stare that he so feared was not there. What had changed had done so internally, and his own fear that he would wake to find himself a woman had disappeared by the time the scarlet and yellow autumn leaves splashed colour on to the London pavements. What had occurred was a shift in his sexual propensities; an aura had developed in his quiet moments which was not dissimilar to those hours of intangible well-being he had experienced in childhood. It was the glow on the peach you never picked, the red and gold sheen you could hold on to all winter against rain and wrist-bangles of blue ice.

Somehow the envelope recalled Claudette's apartment. He knew it was from her even before he nicked a crisp edge with the paper knife, and anticipated the contents of the letter. The note was a brief one. It read, 'I saw you in your favourite candy-stripe and I thought you might be missing the bottle-green and pink.

Think of flamingo sunsets, my dear Ernst. I'm near you at Claridge's.' He hadn't realised that there was a partition between himself and the light; he found himself nose up to the window, attempting to pass through it but meeting with an obstruction. For the first time in his life he discerned how deeply dirt ingrained itself in the corners of glass – crow's-feet of black patina had rimed the otherwise impeccably polished window. When he returned to himself he automatically checked his watch. He still had fifteen minutes before his first appointment. The shutting of a door in the corridor told him that his secretary had arrived. So completely had he been overtaken by the note and the memories it evoked that he had imagined himself back in childhood with all of the interminably long afternoon at his disposal, a green light filtering through the plane trees outside.

He went into the adjoining office to say good morning to Sandra Vince. A quiet, discreet girl with studied hawthorn-red lips, she was plugging her typewriter lead into the socket. Her thin white cotton blouse showed just a hint of her white bra straps, her sapphire silk fantailed skirt was too elegant for day wear, but was worn with such unassuming grace that it drew attention to her slim hips and long legs rather than to the design of the skirt. Dr Moravia liked to discover each night the two strawberry-tipped white St Moritz filters that she left in the ash-tray. There were always two. He would place them in his palm rather as a detective might study a clue that he had previously overlooked. The cigarettes were always half-smoked, the tobacco above the gold band was unburnt, the tips were like daisies with their strawberry eyes. He handled them like small change, and savoured an intimacy with her in these moments which was analogous to moments relived through the prism of memory. That rock ledge above a blue cove in Aegina ten years ago, the water crystalline, and high above him a girl picking cornflowers immemorially framed against the sunset. The salt of memory; you could run your tongue over it and relive it all.

She turned round to face him, her eyes twinkling through blue-tinted glasses. They never spoke much, just as much as was necessary for a business relationship, but this time she volunteered more. In a voice that wavered, but which was perfectly natural, she said, 'I do like your tie, Dr Moravia. The blue and silver stripes look super against that ice-blue shirt.' He thanked her, complimented her on her skirt, and walked distractedly back into his office. In ten minutes, David Thompson would insinuate himself into the room, with muffled feet hurriedly cross to the chair opposite Dr Moravia's, and there take up his habitual stiff position, legs tightly crossed, fingers joined together as though in prayer, his brown animal eyes seeking shelter in the world of imagination he so richly peopled. You could feel the knots in his muscles, the anatomy welded together by an unmitigating tension, his nervousness causing him to take big fish-gulps in between pauses in the dialogue.

Dr Moravia got out the boy's manila file and browsed through the notes. In six months there had been twelve appointments; during that time nothing of any signal note had been divulged. He had felt like a crab side-stepping instead of going forward. The boy's mind was the elusive shrimp which forever darted beneath a stone. But, try as he would, his hand kept feeling for the pink rectangle he had fitted into the inside pocket of his suit jacket. How well the pink fitted in with the oyster silk lining of his blue silk and mohair suit. To satisfy his curiosity he brought the letter out again and stared abstractedly at the laconically phrased but barbed message it contained. Was there not a veiled intimation of threatened exposure in 'I thought you might be missing the bottle-green and pink'? Why had this attractively hybrid creature chosen to insinuate herself into his life again after a lapse of a decade? Would she still be as beautiful, or would silicone treatment have erased the natural beauty of features indeterminate in their gender?

He tried to recollect her, but could only do so by returning to that night of love he had tried so hard to bury and forget. By some perverse instrumentalisation his mind returned again and again to the blinding moment of discovery which had done so much to trouble him in later years. When he had walked home that night, with a lilac streak in the sky already premonitory of dawn, he had felt like a snake or toad that sheds its old skin. So distracted was he by thought that when he had placed his room-key into the door-lock, he felt his strength would break the slender serrations of metal. He had emptied his thoughts into a sleep which was as busy as an aquarium tank.

When the intercom sounded, Miss Vince announced David Thompson's arrival. 'I'll buzz you when I'm ready,' he replied, and returned to the unyielding notes that comprised the boy's case. There was clearly some sexual disturbance, distrust or

26

misadventure, he reflected. The boy's obsession with his father's habit of often returning late at night, and, in an unguarded moment, his admission that he loved to bury himself in straw and lie face down in its heat, could be no more than a slightly retarded adolescent syndrome, if it were not for his ability to find advanced associations between the senses. Everything reminded him of something else: the fragrance of a peach-skin was like opening his stamp-album, the chack-chack of the wheatear not only recalled mist on the hills, but also reminded him of foxgloves, droplets of rain tapping from the mauve bells on to a dock leaf or fern. Ferns reminded him of his mother's soap, the luxurious tan-coloured lozenges that came to her in a box each Christmas and birthday, and other scents too, the yellow of oriental jasmine, the pink of tea-rose, the green of mimosa. For all of these scents he could find a correlative within the spectrum of his own experience. The boy must have handled each of these intimately. Did he wait until his parents were out, and then open the soap-boxes, his sexuality awakening to an essence that corresponded to a desire he couldn't properly focus?

Dr Moravia buzzed for David to be shown in, and waited for the soundless steps suddenly to announce themselves at the door. The boy's tap was hardly audible, and Dr Moravia found himself rising from his chair as the door opened. Something about the boy disquieted. As usual his head was slanted on one shoulder like a violinist, but today with his quiet black blazer and grey trousers he sported a livid purple tie. Dr Moravia made no comment on this ostentatious acquisition to the boy's dress, and busied himself with poring over the boy's file, fingering an unlit cigar, and preparing himself for an introductory gambit which would also serve as a reassessment of their last meeting.

'Well, how are things?' he said, perfunctorily. 'Have you managed to meet new friends, or do you still feel that there's nothing inside people and, if you touched them, you'd find there was nobody there? Isn't that possibly the fear that you're not properly in touch with yourself?' It was an opening deliberately designed to make the boy drop his defences, to have him meet the challenge with aggression, or violently refute it. But instead, he countered the question by anticipating Dr Moravia's next line of enquiry.

'People do unexpected things,' David said, 'and I suppose you are wondering about my choice of tie. When I was five or six I

27

used to paint pansies – the deep purple ones with black interfaces which my mother placed in a jar on the kitchen table. The other day we found purple loosestrife by the pond,' *if you closed your eyes the colour became the wash in a child's painting book.*

'Who accompanied you to the pond, David?' Dr Moravia sneaked in.

'I used to have friends,' the boy said, 'but that was before the shapes started coming at me across the fields. Now I prefer to be alone.'

Dr Moravia toyed with the cigar he had no intention of lighting, and manoeuvred for another line of ingress. 'Have you met someone who shares your interest in searching for wild flowers?'

'Even out walking in solitary places, you meet people,' David said. 'It could be a heron or school-friend.' *When the sunlight's on the water it smells of red iodine.*

'How is your school work progressing?' Dr Moravia said.

'It's better to be alone; that way you can think,' David said. 'You can hear the silence forming words inside you.' *It's then you know you can do things, it's like sunlight pooling in a dark space.*

'You seem to spend a lot of time observing things, David. Is that because you set out to discover them, or because they are pointed out to you.'

'Most days things are made known to the eye,' David said, 'it's like we are blank screens on which things come to register.' *You can be looking in a pool of water and suddenly it's made into a paintbox by a rainbow, and you'd have missed it walking eyes down in the grass, looking for butterfly orchids, with the sky not even apparent.*

'And are you sleeping more regularly?' Dr Moravia enquired. 'Your parents were anxious about your night excursions into the countryside. Don't you think it would make life easier if you adjusted to a more accommodative cycle? If you live irregularly, it makes it hard for others to have access to you.'

'I saw a badger the last time I was out at night,' David said. 'I lay down very still, and watched the white tip of its nose sniffing a way out of the set. I couldn't have seen that by day; most nocturnal creatures avoid man or their enemies. If you wait up in a tree hide you can see deer pass.'

'But you have to establish their tracks by day, don't you?' said Dr Moravia. 'Otherwise you wouldn't know what paths they

28

frequented with regularity.'

'I like to be in the dark by day,' David said.

'So you build hide-outs, do you?' said Dr Moravia.

The stone coolness of the barn darkened inside David's head, the musty sacks, the straw smelling of jasmine; it went on and on building itself into his consciousness until he feared he would have to decompose it by words. Only language could dismantle this structure; he could feel the pressure of the walls against his skull. Bunny would be lying there in the blond straw, saying, 'Tell me what you see when you close your eyes. I can see an aborigine running through a grass-fire with a woman over his shoulder. The grass is blazing like a hayrick – I can hear the scarlet and yellow flames beating the grass. Can't you see them, David?' And he could – he could see the fire run like a molten wave; when it met with an obstacle it grouped around it on all sides like surf pushing round the barrier of a submerged reef. He was staring off, not answering Dr Moravia's question, just floating, buoyed up in his own light, so he said, 'Everyone has to conceal themselves from danger.'

'What sort of danger, David?'

'Things come at you, buildings grow up inside your head, there isn't room for everything that crowds in. One's head can be so full that light can't get in; if it did the inner pressure would explode.'

'But aren't you describing a form of anxiety? In other words you feel compelled to shut off people by the build up of thoughts they can't penetrate.' The conversation was devolving into its customary inconclusiveness; the boy simply wouldn't allow the ice to crack. He would lean on it in areas where the sunlight hadn't reached. It was strong there, it would secure his weight. 'Apart from your studies of nature,' said Dr Moravia, 'what else do you find to occupy you in your night walks? Don't you ever wish for a friend to accompany you on these rambles?'

'When you're out in the dark,' said David, 'you're free. I used to try and identify moths, but I never got beyond the most obvious – the emperor moth which the nightjar feeds on, the swallow-tailed moth, the lappet, the large white plume . . . sometimes you see them on honeysuckle and jasmine.'

'You once said there was honeysuckle by your bathroom window,' said Dr Moravia. 'Do you spend a lot of time in there at night?'

'Mirrors show you the wrong way round,' David said.

Dr Moravia toyed with this intimation at some narcissistic propensity, but he knew he could only use it as a weapon of extreme subtlety, otherwise David would rush back into thickets that no sunlight could penetrate. 'We all need some reflective surface,' he ventured; 'some of us find it in the lives of others, or else one can search for self-identity in modes of inner revelation. But appearance is important too; we learn things through our features.'

David wasn't going to be drawn. He said, 'Water reflects the sky when you look for eels and frogs. It paints itself in by hand. Sometimes you think the water's sky-blue but it's clear when you cup it in your hands.'

Dr Moravia tried to look thought through the needle's eye, got out his cigar cutter, momentarily killed the image of Claudette, and said, 'What would you do if you knew someone was looking through the key-hole when you were in front of the mirror?'

'People look through key-holes to see whether you're different from them,' David said.

'And also because secrecy permits us to act out the inner dialogue,' Dr Moravia established. 'We are all dual beings, we present the face of the coin and live on its obverse side. It's only when we're alone that we become the unrepressed instrument of our inner selves. The self is like a musical instrument, David; most of the time we can't hear its chords, but when we're alone we listen, we hear something which is uniquely our own.'

'It's like that when you hear the cry of the water-rail or lapwing in the winter fields,' David said. 'It goes through you, but something stays there.'

Dr Moravia glanced at his watch. He could account this session a breakthrough; never before had David's answers responded even remotely to the questions put to him. In five minutes' time the boy would slink across the ivy-green carpet and disappear into Sandra Vince's office. 'David, I could prescribe something mild which would assist towards more regular sleeping hours,' said Dr Moravia, 'and there would most certainly be no side-effects, no morning drowsiness.'

David averted his eyes; he wasn't here anymore, perhaps he'd never been sitting in the mushroom velveteen armchair, and straight away he saw the mental image of a yellow-hammer flexing its wings on a field wall before diving into the grass. In

30

three hours he'd be safe again. He was too late for afternoon school, he would be able to go out to the old barn alone and watch the sunlight make quick magnesium thrusts over the floor. Bunny would be at school, he'd be able to savour the taste of being alone, he'd be free to place his eye through a spider's web and watch the sunlight become a fractured prism.

'Would you make an appointment to come again in two weeks, David,' Dr Moravia said. 'Just see Miss Vince on the way out. And next time, if you'd like to bring some of your writings to show me, I'd be grateful to read them. Poems, nature notes, whatever you would care to have me read.'

David got up and left without saying a word; he inclined his head, took a deep breath, and felt as though he was being propelled to the surface after too long an interval underwater. If only sunlight was blue; it was in the few seconds before you bulleted your head through the pane of water and exploded into the air. As you did so peacock-blue splinters of light detonated over your shoulders. Things rectified themselves with oxygen; you cushioned your head on the wave and craved the hallucinatory colour bands of flickering weeds, the belly-flash of blue-sequined mullet. Up there was a blue sky snowed with cumuli – an afternoon so still it could have been a photograph. It was as though the blue was taking a picture of you; in years to come you'd find yourself framed in black swimming trunks, one foot on the ochre flat of the beach, the other still trailing in the wave's hem.

Dr Moravia closed David's file and glanced at the notes for his next patient. John Swanson LLD, a member of the Inns of Court, a highly successful practising solicitor suffering from what appeared to be prolonged rather than temporary sexual impotence. Repressed homosexuality was a salient feature here, along with an abnormally fastidious hygiene complex. Dr Moravia still had ten luxurious minutes at his disposal to recontemplate the enigmatic note from Claudette Duras. Each time he touched the flamingo-pink paper he felt himself projected into a syncope of recollection. He remembered the way her black silk stockings bunched on the floor had resembled cocoons from which exotic spiders might pupate. He recollected her scent; he had subsequently met with it on a lady patient, and admiringly, but with considerable reserve, asked her its name. It had turned out to be Shalimar by Guerlain; he kept a bottle in its

31

black and white lozenge-pebbled box in his bathroom cabinet. Memories crowded in like pollen drifting downwind; his skin was dusted with the seeds of the past. Claudette and David; and had the boy not disquietingly parodied his own manner of dress? That violet silk necktie was not so much a splash of ostentation as a conscious desire antagonistically to imitate.

On the underground on the way to Liverpool Street David's panic had begun. Big drops of sweat stood out on his forehead. They were a mint of black fear. He'd felt himself losing his awareness of self-identity, in his mind was the terrifying image of someone forever lost and patrolling the labyrinth of those corridors in a state of amnesia. He wouldn't be able to ask for help because he wouldn't know who he was any longer, or where he lived, or where he should go. Several times he took the elevator back upstairs to the turnstiles, and then, fearing the incessant ant-chain of street faces, took the stairs down again to the graffiti of the underworld. He wanted to be back in the cool of the barn, to be striding with the wind in his face towards an oak wood with the blue and lilac wash of a watercolour sky on every horizon, a sparrow-hawk hanging its red fuse in the wind, rooks squabbling as they lifted into yew tops by the village church. On a frosty day last winter he'd seen foxes at dawn; just when the sky was flushed camellia-pink against the blueblack, a dog-fox and its vixen had come through the wood and, seeing him, cut a red dash for the brake. If only he could have calmed them, brought his dimension into attunement with their own plane of consciousness, he would have felt part of things and not separate from existence. And by remembering those foxes he was able to calm himself sufficiently to squeeze into an asphyxiating tube compartment. When he connected again, people were looking at him. Everyone was manoeuvring for eye-space, trying to find a fixed location wide of the human face, but one man kept staring right at him as though he could reappraise David from the inside as well as the exterior. The man's suit was polished to glass at the knees and cuffs, his blue eyes missed their co-ordination in blinking; it was as though he saw things flickeringly and couldn't fix them. It was, David thought, rather like having the shadow of a moth playing over one's face. Contact was like this; people could use your face for anything, it became a protean mask to be worn and reworn. There can be so many

32

yous, David thought; Bunny might be thinking of his face now, as he was thinking of Bunny's, but it wouldn't really be either of them. It would be an image or a simulacrum, and that was how he imagined his dead aunt – he would think of her as embodied with the same face as she was buried with. Perhaps people could do that; they came to know their own features so well that when they lost them they reassembled themselves through memory.

When David got to Liverpool Street, the man who had been staring at him so fixedly, followed him out. He was small and nondescript, his eyes shivered to clear their focus; then he hurried away, frightened, once stopping to glance anxiously round, and was finally swallowed up by one of the reverberating corridors. David felt his heart beating to explode; in a hallucinatory flash he saw scarlet and yellow flames, his body melting down to a glue-pot of fat. When he slammed the door to on the carriage of his Inter-City overhead, he found an empty compartment and settled into its comparative dark. He needed this dark; he thought of the blue mole, the hedgehog, the vole, owls – they would all be hiding out of the sunlight waiting for twilight. That hour when the hobby soundlessly raked the hedgerows. He was so vulnerable. How did people travel? At any moment a stranger could come into his compartment, overpower him, and take him off into the big city where he would never be traced. His heart was beating fast again; it was like someone was knocking to get out, it was an importunate drum, the rhythm increasing to the turbulent thunder of hooves. In panic he got out the green cloth-bound notebook in which he kept a diary of nature observations, and prepared to steady his mind by writing of recent discoveries. The book had marbled endpapers, they were pink and green and blue whorls escaping into shell-spirals, into nebulae and frost-flowers; the effect was like the paisley pattern on Dr Moravia's tie, it was like the pastel rainbow you saw when you cracked open an ormer-shell. He tried to concentrate. His sketches of hazel catkins, the three lobed wings of hornbeam clusters, a slightly tilting field maple by a cow-gate, and of the long earring-shaped catkins of alders; all had the fine detailed articulation of things observed in serenity. His mind was too confused to sketch; he felt the powerful impulse to write down his feelings. He would begin a novel, he could read it to Bunny out in the barn. His thoughts were slowly becoming crystallised; they were like droplets of rain studding the underside of a twig –

he had only to tap the branch and they would fall. He uncapped his fountain pen and began.

Chapter 1

When my aunt died, Bunny said we should look for her in the spaces between the clouds. The big white clouds which labour across the summer sky and float their shadows over the grass. Sometimes you really believe that you can step on clouds, or you can feel them brush you lightly when you lie on the hillside. It's nothing, there's no weight at all, it's like thinking, thought doesn't weigh, you don't even know it's happening when it is.

I've never told you about my parents; the first time I recognised my father his face was soaped up like a clown's, he was fish-eyed in the mirror, concentrating, bringing a line of contour back to a blue jaw. My mother was upstairs crying over my aunt or an altercation with my father. He said, 'Hurry off, David, you may see a robin if you go outside,' but I remained watching him through a crack in the door. He had a pale blue towel around his shoulders; a cherry spot of blood appeared on the last snowdrift of lather. He poured an aquamarine lotion into his hands and splashed his cheeks. He stood a long time looking at himself; I could feel my eye watering with the strain of focus. He had his black wallet open, the one that smelt of oil that has leaked on to a garage floor; he was fingering the photograph of a woman, holding it up to the light, scrutinising it from every angle. I knew he wouldn't do that if it was my mother; he returned to it several times in the course of dressing, and then concealed it beneath the miscellanea that wallets carry. I know it was a woman; I stole into my parents' bedroom early one evening, that blue hour when the air crackles with swallows, and took out my father's wallet from the cherry-red silk lining of his inner suit pocket. I watched as my warm finger-balls left vaporous imprints on the soft black leather. I could feel him watching me although I knew he was not there. The rectangular black and white photograph was concealed at the back of the note compartment, hidden behind his miscellaneous credentials. The woman was black haired, black eyed and was wearing a black skirt which she had fluffed up to show off her black-stockinged legs. Her lips were articulated into a dark bow. I stood there looking at the photograph for a long time; a ray of sunlight came through and striped the carpet. It made the

34

unapparent dust-motes seethe. I hurried out when I heard my mother moving in the room below.

When we came back from the woods behind Stephen Bartram's place, our hands were ingrained with the dirt from a badger's diggings. We'd found fewmets from a deer-trail, and Bunny said we should sit and think by a gap-holed granite wall in a field. A painted lady was circling over the lilac-blue flowers of ground ivy. I started to sketch the squarish heads of the mauve flowers, my mother called them ale hoof, and Bunny cracked open a can of Nastro Azzurro lager that we'd taken from Stephen Bartram's hiding place in the woods. He said, 'Rachel likes you; when you go out with a girl it's like there are three of you. There's you and your double and there's her. You have to let go of your double in order to reach her.' I let his words sink in the way a raindrop darkens and diffuses when it settles on stone. I said, 'No one missed my aunt at the funeral; they were all looking to confirm that they had survived, that their feet were square on the earth, while she floated between the clouds.' I lay there feeling the warm light tingle on my skin; I wanted my life to be like the narrative of a novel. Things would happen without my being there, and when the book was closed they'd still go on happening inside some-body's head, late at night, propped up on pillows, reading by lamp-light. And in that way you wouldn't have to die; someone could open the book in a century's time and the narrative would still be going on. I could still hear Bunny's voice interwoven with my own thoughts before the pictures began in my head. I had only to find a rhythm for them. Bunny was saying, 'Why don't you go out with Rachel?' but the inner dialogue was clarifying. I closed my eyes; shapes were coming out of the red-black of inner space, the narrative was coming clear.

It was after midnight. Stephen Hudson sat listening to the rain tap on the veranda roof below his bedroom window. A gust and another gust; the apple trees flurried with sparkling droplets. Outside was a blueblack flying October storm sky. He was fully dressed, his thin shoulders fitted into a black double-breasted jacket. A carnation-red silk handkerchief formed a casual over-hang from his breast pocket. He flicked the numerals on his watch as you might activate a fountain pen. In an hour a car would call for him. The driver's white gloves would accentuate his slim fingers in the chink of amber light that came on when the car door opened. The chauffeur's heavily painted face was like a mime artist's; the cheeks whitened by powder, the lips scarlet, the eyes blacked into shape by Egyptian kohl. They'd begin their usual drive downtown towards the coast-road. Rain dazzled the bonnet; it split into coronets and jewel fires. Ed was high on cocaine, talking too fast, saying, 'Your words are lit up like dragonflies, Stephen, I can see them tapping against the windscreen.' When the car swung into a side-street, Cherry was waiting, her high heels clattered over the streaming asphalt. She jumped into the car and said, 'Quick, let's get the hell out of here, I'm in trouble.' Ed's eyes were chestnut-sized, the white streamlined shark of a police car with its blue bubbling klaxon cruised into the rear-view mirror. He slammed his foot down; Cherry was shouting, 'I never got the stuff, Ace was lying face down in a pool of blood, someone had shot him. His shirt was a heavy red platter . . .'

David looked out of the train window. They were pulling out from Diss; in half an hour his father would collect him at Norwich station. On the platform a boy was doing a headstand on a green painted bench. David knew that if he was on the other side of the glass he would hear birdsong. He closed his writing book and drowsed for the remainder of the journey.

3

Claudette scrutinised the features that had been a lifetime's obsession in the breath-frosted oval mirror that she travelled with. Its rococo gilt frame was spiralled into bell-shaped flowers; mignonettes intertwined with asphodels snaked from a dolphin's mouth into the tracery of a cupid unleashing his arrow. She had made the bathroom into an artist's studio of cosmetics. Her vanity case contained a litre of liquid silicone, disposable syringes, a cache of vermilion and carmine Dior lipsticks, eye pencils, blue and aquamarine and gold dusted palettes of eye-shadows, a bottle of Oscar de la Renta, poudre parfumée, and a large black and gold egg of Crème majeure by Yves Saint Laurent. She smoothed the cream gently into her face, feeling the activating micro-circulation that this brought about, the exciting introduction of hydroreflectan into her pores. It was her habit to test whichever new cosmetics were introduced into the competitive field of beauty care. She would look for the transformations in her face, a translucency she hadn't been aware of before, an erasure of the hairfine crow's-feet that veined the skin beneath her eyes like the tendril-branching in an ivy leaf. She pencilled on two mauve linear eyebrows; it was like recomposing a face she thought. Neither her mother nor father could lay claim to her new birth; she was the child of a skilled surgeon. Claudette? She tried to picture her mother's baffled surprise if they were reintroduced, she with the big peasant's hands, moulded and chapped from years of working the land on an impoverished farm in Brittany. Claudette's only holidays as a child had been spent on the Ile de Houat in a whitewashed granite cottage, the roof slates oranged with lichen; the outside water-pump cranked in the morning to get the day's supply of drinking and washing water. She used to get up before her parents and cousin, and look up at the pink and green ice slivers of stars which were visible above the horizon. Even then, she hadn't felt right as she was, a frail young man with bewitchingly high cheek-bones, already drawing attention to himself by refusing to wash in cold water, or to swim naked in the ultramarine shallows. She had guarded the privacy of her body, she had a secret to keep which she could never let out. She didn't want things to be as they were; that swinging, mushroom-capped appendage between the thighs was too external. She wanted to be retractile, intimate with herself, concealed as the eye of a rose in the convolutions of its petals. She used to lie in the stiff marram grass and watch her cousin hurl boulder after boulder into the sea. He would balance an angular granite block over his head and smash it into the water. A white cauliflower head of froth boiled on the sapphire for an instant and then subsided. All of his latent aggression, all of the as yet unpronounced masculinity in him tested itself against the elements. Daily he grew more sun bronzed by the wind; when Claudette showed him the blue harebells and sea-pinks and corn-salad that she had found amongst the rocks, he mocked her. He said, 'That's for girls, boys don't pick flowers. Why don't you come and flip pebbles on the flat of the wave?' He could make a stone jump six times like a swallow skimming the wave. But Claudette would walk away. When she was alone she was safe. She could integrate with her true self, she could soliloquise, and there were always the sea-stars at night or a moon anchoring its pearl in the navy-blue bay. She learnt to make the rhythm of her breath correspond to the ocean. Each time a wave dragged its white swash over shingle she breathed in. The sea could enter her like that. When she exhaled the wave was chasing back through pebbles that jumped like dice across an uneven surface. She would become entranced like that. Flux and reflux, systole and diastole, the incessant movement of the sea.

One morning she awoke when the farm cocks were issuing their madrigal to the false dawn, and went outside and looked into the old stone well. The water was a jet film with a moonstone of light superimposed on it from the sky. As she looked down, and a cloud obscured the moon, she was conscious of her own transformation. She didn't know what was happening, only that she knew she was staring at the image of a pretty girl's face. That image was never to leave her; when she stared into the cracked, defaced mirror in the cottage hall she was furious at what she found. The change hadn't really taken place; she still had the features of a boy, only that she surprised herself by pouting and tracing admiringly explorative fingers over the contours of her cheek-bones. If she stared long enough, she believed she would see the transformation occur; the old face would shed its skin and in its place would come the translucent twinkling highlights in a young girl's face and eyes. How she wished the skin would be of the finest gold, the eyes violet, the lips so dark as to give the impression of having been deepened in tone by the application of an imperceptible lipstick. She went back to her room, lay down on the coarse-blanketed bed and waited for the daylight. All of those secret dawns had affected the mutation; the urge she had felt to expose her body to radiant starlight, to lie face down in white clover and smell the earth and sea, had somehow resolved the conflict within her. She had been fascinated by myths, by the element of metamorphosis, a god turning into a swan, a girl into a tree, a man into a stag or hyacinth, and then there were the hybrid creatures, centaurs and satyrs, the bloody lacerations of the bacchantes crowned in ivy and coupling with a fabulous leopard on the hill's wooded slope. But mostly it was the myth of Narcissus which obsessed her; if she stared long enough into a pellucid sea-pool, she might dissolve her old identity and assume the permanent mask of beauty for which she longed.

That summer was one of excruciating pain; her parents could detect an alteration in her but their simplicity prevented them from perceiving what it was. She began to lose weight, to go missing on long solitary walks; they found cigarette butts in her room, and glossy fashion magazines that she had stolen from a neighbour's house. At sixteen she had run away to Paris and taken a room in the Bois de Boulogne. The neighbourhood was full of transsexuals, she felt ugly for still being incomplete, but Honey-Baba had taught her how to use cosmetics, they had made her face up to look like Billie Holiday's, her hair was dyed cobalt, her magenta lipstick was defined by a black lip pencil. They stole clothes for her and introduced her to silicone boosts; she had black candles in a squalid room and read Jean Genet curled up on a counterpane of silk scarves, the braiding of black and purple and emerald into a mosaic of waterlights. She was happier here, she didn't have to pretend any longer; she could give birth amongst friends to the mental image she had perceived that summer night in the moonlit well-water at the Ile de Houat. And piece by piece that image became a reality; her voice grew

39

quieter, it softened with the imminence of conception. She knew that one morning she would awake to the same joyful surprise with which she greeted the first mauve crocus each spring. One day there was frost and the next the tiny earth-bound transpicuity of a lilac crocus veined with deep purple.

The year was one of somnambulistic entrancement for her. She would never forget the moment her diminutive feet stepped into black stilettos. For days she had practised walking around the room and then Honey-Baba had walked her through the flickering neons of a night alley. Only briefly had she panicked when a man with a watery vodka eye had homed in on her, only to be beaten off by Honey-Baba's authoritative protection. Honey-Baba was South American, over six feet tall, her shapely body moulded by the briefest and tightest of black dresses. Once when she'd returned at dawn, and her theatre cosmetics had thinned out to an archipelago of peeling flakes, the blue stubble had shown on her cheeks. Claudette was terrified. If you changed, did it mean that you would have forever to live behind a cosmetic mask? If you lost that, you would lose your identity. It would be endless, she thought, the daily ritual of assuming a face, then the secrecy of the face one hid in sleep. But what had begun as an obsessional fear had developed into a routinal pleasure. Today, with the accomplished finesse of a cosmetician, she could transform her face according to the mood her inner life adopted. If people perceived in her the slightly heavier bone structure of a man, a wren with a blackbird's body, she had learnt to deflect their hostility. Money had afforded her protection; it was easier to face unvoiced affrontery through the sedate tick of a champagne glass than it was through a lipstick-stained rum glass in Pigalle. At first when she had run away they had beaten her in alleyways. She had come in time to project her own psychic defences, to illuminate her face with absolute belief in her sense of audacity, and in that way you unnerved the potential aggressor. To look away was fatal; either you fixed into a man's eyes or you didn't look at all. She had walked along the Champs-Elysées with the downturned stare of someone seeking for a seed pearl or diamond chip displaced from a ruby. She had dared to look at no one. Gradually she learnt to look at every third person, then every second person, and so her confidence had accumulated. Eventually she learnt to look right through people as though they were of no consequence at all. Intuition told her when she met with a sympathetic glance, or the light brush of a hand on her shoulder in a late-night café.

She worked a holly-red lipstick into her nether lip and brought her lips together. It had all begun with the American in the Blue Orado bar. The one from Detroit who looked like a professional snooker player, but was the chief shareholder with Wills & Texas Oil Investments. There were hazel rings in his sea-grey eyes; his check button-down collar shirt was threaded by a black knitted tie. His suit was a double-breasted mint-green. Taciturn, reticent, he possessed the innate morbidity of one whose sexual obsessions are not easily or often accommodated. Ince Martin Jnr; he spoke with the hesitant drawl of someone who listens to his pronunciation of each syllable. He seemed to dangle his words on a spider's thread, he would retract and release them with alternating volume; Claudette had found herself following the rhythm of his speech rather than the words. In public Ince always appeared to be less than himself; he shivered inwardly like someone engaged in the art of making himself invisible. When he registered interest in a topic, his eyes lit up like tiny fish coming out of a cave. Unlike most of the men she had met, the night wolves hungrily prowling the streets, Ince had manifested no immediate desire. He had talked to her like one who was listening for the moment when his words would strike bottom. Only when that little cloud of sand was shaken from the sea-bed by the plummeting of a particular resonance did he glow with the radiance of one who felt himself to be understood rather than isolated. His sensual inventory was inexhaustible; he was a man who, having found satisfaction in neither sex, was seeking the anatomical anomalies of the bizarre. And if his physical desire was not easily assuaged then his mental curiosity was unappeasable. The photographs he had taken of her, dressed and undressed, were sufficient to form a small archive of transsexual records. He had paid her 100 dollars for each; the wedges of notes lay on her bed like books discarded from a student's rucksack. Ince used to lie back propped up on silk cushions reading Burroughs. When he wanted to be deep inside himself he would read. At such times it seemed that nothing else existed but the space between his eye and the page, and at first Claudette had felt disquieted by his absence. Only through long acquaintance did she learn that such periods of withdrawal were a prelude to his manic sexual activity. With Ince it was always a question of

41

finding levels, of browsing down on the sea-floor, then, without warning, bursting back to the surface in an explosion of white spray. Over a period of four years, punctuated by his returns to the States, she had grown rich. She had never revealed this secret, she continued to live in the same squalidly decadent room, but already she was planning her escape from a world of remorseless social ostracism. She dreamt of encountering another starlit well, of realising a new image, although she had exhausted the possibilities of physical change. The last time she saw Ince he was walled up inside himself. He couldn't get out this time; it was as if he had entered a cupboard of personal vision and someone had locked the door. When the letter from America arrived six months later naming her as one of the legatees to his will, she was free to embrace the solitude for which she longed. At first she had gone into hiding; there was that winter's afternoon in a country lane when she had stood stock still and listened to a robin singing from a holly bush. The moment was silver with clarity. Another time she was caught out in the rap of a big shower; she watched it smoking across the bare fields from the shelter of a fir wood. The sky was lovat and grey, the rain looked like bright needles on the horizon, lancing verticals that beat the countryside to the dull colours of a hedgehog's back. For two weeks she had gone without make-up and female clothes; she had come to recognise her incompletion. The stubble stood out mole-blue on her cheeks, grape-mauve along the line of her jaw. She lived in between states, neither man nor woman and not desiring to be either. Exhaustion had brought her to this; she slept like an animal prepared for hibernation. Cocooned under blankets in the cottage she had rented, she would sleep all afternoon, drowsy as a bat, and then at twilight walk across the fields. The cold made an anvil of her forehead; she walked face up to the stars counting them like suspended snowflakes. At night she curled up like a cat before the red and blue hissing flames of a wood fire. These were weeks of half consciousness, the uncertain period between hibernation and waking. She reverted to a primal state of consciousness; things whinnied in the dark of her sleep, there was a smell of peat fires and bog moss, hooves thundered a trail towards a cyclopean red sun. She would wake bathed in sweat; the fire would have sunk to a peach grid beneath wood ash, a sky the blue of ink would be resting outside the window-pane. Wrapping a fur over her blue bleached denim jeans, she would walk out beneath the early stars. They twinkled like diamond fireflies against the blue backdrop. Chestnut and plane leaves rattled tinnily along the lanes; once she met with the headlights of an oncoming tractor, and hid behind a hedge. She, who had lived all of her life in a state of overpronunciation of her body, flinched from the thought of any human eye making contact with her in this state of sexual uncertainty. Ravens would batter back to roost at twilight, black stringy festoons of birds beating across the winter sky. She would like to have followed them back to the wooded fir slopes on the hills. But gradually, day by day, a new clarity returned to her as it had done all of those summers ago at the Ile de Houat. One afternoon she was walking down a tortuous hill flanked by holly hedges when she heard water in the ditch by the roadside. She stopped and listened to the trickle. A small stream was winding its way downhill. She burrowed through the hedge and knelt down. The water was clear from the recent rains and carried a cargo of dead leaves and sticks. She placed a finger in it, and then immersed her entire hand. The cold closed around her, it was pure and glacial, her numb hand had turned to liquid diamond. She felt the act was one of purification. She lay down flat and placed a second hand on the bed of the shallow stream. After a while she couldn't feel her hands at all, and when finally she withdrew them her fingers were red and blue with cold. She buried them in the pockets of her fur and quickened her pace round the side of a farm and on across the fields. A dog was barking somewhere, but she didn't care. She was revitalised; she ran and called out to the rising moon. From a fir grove she could hear the first goosepimpling shiver of an owl's cry. When she got back she heaped logs on the red embers, drank whisky from a flask, and felt her fingers tingle with the radiance of heat which had succeeded their numbness. Another week and she would be able to resume life; she was no longer dependent on using her body as a sounding-board for the propensities of others, she was free to live according to her own dictates. From that moment she evaluated every small thing that entered the field of her con-sciousness – the wiry hoar-frost before sunrise, the thumbnail of ice on the window-pane, the grey piping around the robin's scarlet breast, the pinpoint of silver in the starling's black eye. On the day subsequent to her rebirth by water, she had discovered the first snowdrops. Greenish-white, bell-heavy, they had brought themselves to light in the darkest hour of winter. They corresponded to her own awakening; she picked two or three and placed them in a glass of water beside her bed. She lay awake watching for the dawn's bullfinch-pink blush to show in the east. When the sun came over the ridge it was blood-red against the stark black tree-line. Then the unexpected happened; she found herself wishing to reclaim her misidentity. With cold fingers she brought out her mirror, and spent three hours restoring her face to the cosmetic beauty she had come to think of as her own. By noon she was ready to leave. A cold winter sun intermittently broke through the grey massed clouds. As she walked over the fields towards the station she could hear the peewit of lapwings. She looked back; the cottage was desolate in its setting by a bare hawthorn tree, crows cried stormily in an adjoining field. She bumped her luggage down in the cold provincial waiting-room, and the ticket collector joined the thousands who had accepted her identity without questioning. By the evening she would be back in Paris, and in a week's time she would book into a first-class hotel in London. She knew no one in London, apart from a man who had given her his professional address in Harley Street. Or had she stolen it from his wallet? She couldn't remember. In her former life, survival had been everything, you needed to be one card stronger than your partner in order to acquit yourself in the event of physical threat or psychological manipulation. Dr Moravia's professional card was one of hundreds she kept as a tenuous assurance against violent recriminations. When she mailed her brief note to him on arriving in London, she had no idea whether he was dead or had long ago changed the address of his consulting rooms. The telephone directory had failed to reveal his name; she had paid a taxi-driver to deliver the note to the Harley Street address.

She zipped up a tight, black rayon ruched dress, and snapped the black straps of her suspenders on to black silk stocking tops. The oval mirror gave her face back as an ivory heart-shaped locket. In a vase beside her bed she had placed blue and pink cornflowers, punctuated by an occasional white or maroon one. She had already rejected the exotic bird of paradise lilies that an anonymous admirer had delivered to her suite. In flowers she loved natural simplicity – the harebells and sea-pinks and strawberry-headed clover of her childhood vacations on the Ile de Houat. These remained with her, together with the smell of salt

44

and the incessant outwash of surf. She had begun to keep a journal which she interleaved with poems; something in her nurtured the secret prospect of literary success. She hoped to surprise people, to come out of the dark as Jean Genet had, with a book that would fulminate like a gold shooting-star chasing across the black of the night skies.

She lay on the bed and made believe that she was counting the pinking of raindrops from the underside of a sycamore branch. When the internal telephone mutely intruded on her reverie, and asked her whether it was convenient for a letter to be delivered to her room, she had to come back from the Ile de Houat in order to connect. Even before she saw the ivory Smythson's of Bond Street envelope, she knew the letter had come from Ernst Moravia. His spiky Gothic handwriting corresponded to his predilection for secrecy. She took out the letter and met with two sides of double-spaced writing. His response must have been immediate.

Dear Claudette,

I cannot believe that, after a decade's silence, you and I could find any good reason to meet. Memory is surely the bottle one uncorks in the cellar, imbibes its essence, and then returns to the rack. My work is my consuming preoccupation, and my limited social life an extension of it. I imagine that your life too is a series of mirrors that converge on a singular focus. When I think of Paris I recollect the green shade of plane leaves, the avenues of poplars. One must have trees; for me they formed an important part of childhood. Trees help me remember the things I would otherwise forget. Balzac, Tolstoy, Proust, Jung; I remain an inveterate reader. The night sky for me is constellated by the great minds of the past.

What is it that brings you to London? One can't live here; one's work is here, and one's life is elsewhere, in the heart of a forest, or on a mountain summit that expires in clear blue air. I expect my years in the city are numbered; I long for the anonymity and quiet of a country retreat. One cannot go there soon enough.

By the way, how did you get my professional address? I'm ex-directory in case you have not already discovered that. I prefer to keep potential clients at bay. But if it's consultation you seek, then perhaps I could recommend a colleague. In view of our acquaintanceship, it might not be wise for me to act. Let me know if I can be of help in any way.

With best wishes,
Yours sincerely,
Ernst Moravia

Claudette placed the letter on the bedside table and imagined how he would have been altered by a decade's persistent silvering of the hair and eye. Would he be conscious that he had changed? No, he would meet her from behind a smoke-screen of defences that assumed he was as vulnerable as the moment in which he had met her. Men, she reflected, were like this; they seldom realised that events had changed with them. Rather, they demanded that the two were contemporaneous; it was a means of perpetuating youth, of repudiating the downward gravity towards death.

She checked the lineation of her lip-bow and lay back on the bed. If her life was unreal it was because she had consciously allowed it to become a part of fiction. Those who met her would disseminate the myth of her sexuality; in that way she became the protean protagonist of a novel without an author. She was both as real and insubstantial as Hyacinth, whom the god accidentally killed with a discus and then caused a mauve scented flower speckled with blood spots to grow in place of the dead youth. She was news in Paris, Cologne, Amsterdam, Berlin, Chicago, London; wherever men talked of her she existed in a different embodiment of words. And this was how myth was perpetuated; it blew across the waters like gold thistledown, men gave it the names of flowers, or stars or birds, the symbol lived in its variations while the source died. But in order to inhabit her own myth she must give it the structure of language, it must become a novel; how otherwise would people 'really' believe in her existence?

She would reply to Ernst Moravia. This man, whose letter intimated that his sexual curiosity overcame his professional circumspection, who wrote of the loophole of retreat, and yet demanded the immediacy of action, was a catalyst to the formulation of the novel she wished to write.

Dear Ernst,

It was good of you to reply to what was intended as no more than an enquiry about your well-being, and most certainly not a letter seeking an introduction to professional consultation. We seem to be living on different planes.

What I remember of Paris is its confusion, my own misexpenditure of energies, the tense night streets of Pigalle, and of course the Bois de Boulogne. I'm sure you remember the latter. But people change; I feel that we would prove strangers to each other should we decide to meet. I'm writing a novel called *Gold on Black*, and I suppose that most of my friends will feature in its extraordinary plot. I'm hoping that, in this way, my inner life will find enrichment by externalisation.

Do you never feel that life's all a big mistake? I'm a stranger to London, I'm viewing things with caution.

With best regards,
Claudette

She placed the letter in a pink envelope and addressed it to Harley Street, London W1. Instinct told her that he would reply; his vanity was a silver wire, it would never become tarnished. She took out the stationery she had intended for letters, and began to scribble down the first sentences of *Gold on Black*.

Chapter 1

It begins with nothing. For a long time you don't even know who you are, and then suddenly you're called Andy or Andrea, and there's a red ladybird cupped in your hands in the sunlight. Who it was that called out Andy from the garden gate is irrelevant. The word went up like a red ball and was caught unquestioningly. At the same time the identity of the ladybird became manifest. An older voice named it and there was no need to question. Andy and the ladybird. It was spotting with little silver sparks of rain; he had to go in and play with his imaginary sister Andrea.

Andy faced the mirror. He was thirty years old, and yet that connection of memory remained as real to him as if he had just heard his name for the first time. He could still see and feel the weightless red and black speck of the insect in his hands, and when it had surprised him by flying away it left only the remotest

47

tingle on his skin, as though two disparate thoughts had connected and jolted him into the reality of being alive. For a long time he had lived outside society; he felt constantly that he was on the edge of self-realisation, that the seed he had nurtured within himself since childhood was about to germinate – it was the gold eye in the white fringe of a daisy.

He lay with his pillowed head to the wall, and his feet facing the window primrosed by sunlight. The cycle of history was intermeshed with his nerves; he would make big things happen, not by turning the soil beetroot with blood, but by a sign, secret as a bird's voice in mist, or a kingfisher's feather dropped by a pond. At midnight he would leave his room and join the fraternity that had grown up around him. Ten of them would gather in a rooftop flat in Knightsbridge; each was adjured to wear a mask, a black cut-out with gold eye-slits and a gold mouth. On the right-hand cheek of the mask was painted the gold caduceus of Hermes with two interwoven serpents in opposition. Each of the initiates carried an ear of wheat and a small mirror in the shape of a cross. By ritual they prepared themselves for the initiation into a deathless rebirth. They called their order Gold on Black; they were the sun kings who would preside over the black marsh of death.

Andy dragged on the acrid smoke of a joint, and watched the sunlight form a luminous frost-flower on the window. A jet was lifting into the pink and blue sky-lakes of the evening sky. He could feel the power generated through his body. For months now he had practised astral somersaults. It was not only that he could project himself out of his body, but that once in a state of levitation he could choreograph his movements. He had learnt consciously to think and imagine without his brain. With the dilation of his astral eye he could telescope into a suprasensory spectrum; what was out there was so brightly coloured that each atom pulsed with the eye of a microscopic sun. He lay back; his head was really buzzing. He didn't hear a knock at the door, or, if he did, he wasn't quick enough to rise. When the door opened he wasn't sharing the same light as the intruder – the man was looking into his face while he was looking through him into a crystalline spider's web in which gold and emerald and scarlet stars scintillated. He must have stood up and faced the door, for the shot took the back out of the window. And what had been the constellated spider's web was his own psychic body; he was looking at the man from the centre of the web.

48

4

The sun put a gold fire in the cornfield. Stephen Bartram's mother had put green and red Guy Fawkes masks on the faces of the scarecrows. Four of them deployed strategically, showing from the waist up their threadbare dark jackets. On the first day they were there one took them for real – why were they watching, these immobilised sinister figures? It reminded Bunny of the day men had walked the fields, beating the hedgerows; they'd gone out looking for Timothy Adams who'd been missing for two days from his home and school. They never found him; even today his parents lived in expectation of his return. It had been a hot reconnaissance; the men's foreheads were runnelled with sweat as they returned, wearily grouped in the field, drinking cider from the bottles that a neighbouring farm brought out. That was the day that Bunny and David had discovered a natterjack toad. The details of its gold and green back and the green irises of its eyes, and its almost smooth skin surface, had all been entered up in David's nature journal. They had found the toad basking in the sun beside a pool on the heath. David knew it was a natterjack from its fast gait over land. It flopped into the pool as Timothy Adams probably had done up on the moor.

'The girls are coming out to the barn on Thursday night,' Bunny said.

'But what if our parents insist that we stay in to study,' David replied, 'what will we do then?'

'We'll just go missing,' Bunny said. 'I've already told my parents that we've been invited to go over to Stephen Bartram's that evening.'

It was a day of high-flying clouds; another week and they'd begin the harvest, combines would thresh the bronze fields that stepped off on to the horizon. Thousands of mice and voles and rabbits would break from their hiding places in an exodus of alarm. David imagined the tiny, frightened lives, the spiders and

49

ants, the metallic shields of beetles; everything would be hurrying to get free. And the fields would be levelled, baled and stooked; a red stubble would turn the colour of a fox's coat under the gibbous harvest moon. 'We'll need some drink,' Bunny said. 'Girls are always wilder if they have some alcohol.' David lay back and cradled his head on a sack that was puddled by sunlight. He had never been with a girl, shyness had withheld him; his absorption in nature had provided a surrogate for his strong sexual desire.

The barn smelt of musty apples. From the hide they could watch magpies undeterred by the scarecrows; the birds were invisible in the corn, and when they rose once in alarm they pursued a wide arc and planed down in an adjacent fallow field. David could hear two of them engaged in an alarm rattle, a heckling ratchet of gutturals that devolved after minutes to silence. They flew off again rapidly, beating towards an elm clump, dropping speed above the trees, and effortlessly coming to rest in the topmost forks of the trees. From there they could shout at the horizon.

David selected a straw and ran it sensuously over his tanned forearm and wrist. No matter what one does in life, he thought, one is constantly irritated by the need for distraction. Something within him craved the minute action of straw tingling over his skin, *you went on needing something else until there was nothing and then you died.* He didn't communicate this to Bunny. His visits to London to see Dr Moravia were a guarded secret, so too were his disquieting nocturnal rambles. He said, 'I think I can get hold of a bottle of Bacardi. There's one in the back of the cupboard that no one has touched or mentioned for two years. I'll bring that with me.'

Bunny said, 'I think they'll destroy the old barn next year, and then we'll have to establish a tree-hut in the woods. This place is like a sea-shell, it hums with our thoughts.'

'And what if we go away after we've left school,' David said, 'where will we hide then? Rooms are communal. The same sunlight will be playing over the fields only it won't meet with the obstruction of stone walls.'

'And our words will be in other places,' Bunny replied, 'but nothing ever again will have the same sanctuary, the same conspiratorial air of privacy.'

50

David spent a long time brushing his hair. In an hour's time he'd set off for Stephen Bartram's, make a detour in the lanes, and double back in the direction of the barn where Bunny would be waiting for him. Globules of light or moths were dancing in his stomach. He was nervous; what if Rachel sensed his shyness and rejected him? What if she made advances that he couldn't reciprocate? He had the lipstick phial in his pocket as they had agreed that they would both dress up to surprise the girls. He placed the bottle of Bacardi and his new pink and blue striped button-down collar shirt in a carrier, and hurried out of the house. The sun was a red fireball on the horizon; an ash-blue twilight would follow, then there would be bats. He lost his sense of nervousness at the thought of bats. Their aerodynamics allowed them to be free; if only he could achieve similar results with his inner life, no one would ever hurt him. He'd simply shift territory inside before they could home in on a vulnerable spot. He kept thinking of that all the way out to the barn. When he got within range of the old building and its lonely site away from the farm, he screened himself by a hedge and sat down. It was his custom to take refuge in inner silence before he committed himself to any situation which might involve change. Would he walk back home tonight having conquered Rachel, or would he be locked deep in his own anxious thoughts, his ear listening for owls or the occasional nightjar? The ten-minute respite he allowed himself was magic time. He could slow things down. There was a white hooped ruff on the chocolate poker-head of ribwort, a cygnet-grey plume on the thistle flower. Once when he had looked through a microscope at the seeds of henbane he had discovered that they were kidney-shaped; now he emptied a poppy's black seed-heads into his palm, and rubbed them to a graphite trail. Bindweed was everywhere, the white trumpet-shaped flowers he had learnt to call convolvulus. He looked at his watch; he had five minutes. He touched things for reassurance; a sparkle of green glass, a feather of timothy grass. The sunlight was peach-red on his wrist; he got up and crossed the field to the barn.

Bunny was already waiting. He was dressed in a black shirt with white trousers and was smoking. He'd greased his hair back, and David could smell the scented pungency of Paco Rabane or Givenchy. Something had changed in Bunny; David saw it in his eyes, and in the assumed confidence of his mannerisms. Could going with a girl do that? David didn't want to change; he thought of the noctules which would be flipping into their unpredictable orbits. He thought of the kestrel's surety, the crow's unchanging obduracy, and all the time Bunny was saying, rushing his words, 'Did you bring the drink? Let's taste it before the girls arrive.' David produced the bottle, and Bunny uncapped it and drank unceremoniously from the bottle-mouth. The alcohol must have laid an unexpected blaze-trail in his stomach, for his eyes went huge, and he gagged on a spilling tilt of the bottle. The light was going; a blueness as of chalk-rubbed slate set in over the quiet of the fields. 'You wait and see what the girls will be wearing,' Bunny said. 'And by the way, did you bring the lipstick? I've got a pocket mirror so that we can make up.' Bunny's movements were fast and overadrenalised; there were metal rims on the heels of his pointed boots and these grated on the stone floor of the barn. 'Another five minutes and the girls will be here,' he said. David felt a calming influence in the cool scarlet lipstick blade that he inexpertly applied to his lips. Bunny stood back, his hands on his hips, exclaiming, 'That's incredible, that will turn Rachel on. Now it's my turn.' He dabbed spots of lipstick on to his lips and spread the texture with the ball of his right index finger. For a moment they were like accomplices dressing for a secret ritual known only to themselves. For the first time that evening there was a common sympathy between them, but David still felt that he was watching not Bunny but a stranger, and that, if he were to go outside and come back in again, Bunny might really be there.

David tried hard to remember whether there had been an interval before there was a knock and girls' voices giggling on the other side of the door. The copious gulp of spirits that he had taken to give him courage had engendered the feeling that a red ember was dilating in the pit of his stomach. What if it kept on glowing and grew to a blinding sun-spot in his head? Would he incinerate; would his breath set fire to the harvest the day before the machines moved in?

Bunny lifted the latch on the old timber door, and verticals of light chased across the floor. The girls came in, whispering, not looking at anything but themselves, jostling together, and David watched Bunny mentally appraising Louise's short skirt. When he interlinked his arm with David's, they could both feel the girls taking in the shock of seeing them dressed in lipstick, seeing for perhaps the first time in their lives the grained scarlet gloss of cosmetics on masculine lips, and all the time Bunny was holding the bottle out like some apologetic enticement, saying, 'Have a drink, girls,' then laughingly, 'This stuff has the blaze of a bush-fire.'

David glanced at Rachel. Less overtly pretty than Louise, she was dressed in a figure-hugging scarlet jumper, and skin-tight white jeans. She'd tied her hair up in a white chiffon bow, her lips were softened by a muted coral glow. She looked at David in surprise, not with the deprecatory or disparaging stare of one who was offended, but more with the sympathetic complicity of one who understood, and quietly smiled through the green lights in her eyes. 'Aren't the poppies beautiful?' David said. 'Their petals have the silken feel of a moth's wings.'

She looked away and said, 'Yes, they're so fragile a hailstone could dislodge them.'

Bunny was splashing the liquor into paper cups, saying, 'Can't you two talk about anything else? When I last got drunk, I was over at Stephen Bartram's. We ran through the trees clapping our hands and scaring wood pigeons into flight.'

Louise sat down on the straw and arched her legs. 'Give me a light, Bunny,' she said. 'Why don't we tell each other stories while we wait for the light to go?'

'That's a good idea,' said Rachel. 'I'll begin, and then you can each add to my narrative; in that way we'll compile a joint story.'

They sat around in an imperfect circle; the embered sunset seemed to solidify in a gold bar on the straw-squiggled stone floor. They were silent, and when Rachel's voice began to circulate, it was as if it didn't belong to her. Her mouth had become mysterious, it was a filter through which wasps checked out of a hole in the earth; you could feel the words come out of the depths in her.

'When it was dark a man used to come into a clearing in the woods and light a fire. In his sack he'd carry a quail or pigeon for roasting; its flesh would drizzle or spit in the bubbling flames. By daylight he would move across country. In his youth they had called him the bird-boy on account of the facility with which he could name or handle birds. For a long time he had kept a pet crow called Topsy; it ate gobbets of cheese from his hand and archipelagoed the floor of his hut with droppings.'

'You've read this in a book,' said Bunny, canting his hair back into an overhanging strait.

'Carry on, Rachel,' said David quietly, and you could hear them settle back into themselves as she resumed her story.

'This man's name was Branden. He laired up in a tumbledown keeper's hut, and when he could afford or steal the materials he would draw birds. The big black members of the crow-tribe – the indigo and black body of the rook, the sleeker blueblack of the raven, the ragged plumage of the crow. Or brilliant coloured spotted woodpeckers with their beady red eyes and scarlet headcrests, the tulip-red that splashes the underside of their breasts. Or a goldfinch, or the shy redstart with its orange tail that it forever lifts, the inquisitive nuthatch scaling the bark of a tree for termites, baleful owls with their white facial disks, kingfishers in their iridescent dart of flight, the vigilant wren, the brown autumn-leaf coloured dunnock shyly emerging from under a hedgerow. Or it might be a big spotted thrush, a bark-dappled sparrow. He came to know the voice of each bird; he would imitate them when alone. Although he was uneducated, he began to write down his observations. He shunned human company, and once when a poacher met him in the dawnlight the man dropped his sack and ran. What happened after that lived on in the clawed lacerations of the poacher's face. He attributed his scars to a man with the piercing face of a kestrel, the meditative eyes of an owl, and the quiet vigilance of a heron. The taloned fingernails that had slashed at the poacher's face gave rise to the story of Branden's being a bird-man, half hawk and half human.'

David looked across. Bunny had his eyes shut and was preoccupied with tracing a finger from Louise's knee to the back of her thighs. She offered no resistance, and David thought that perhaps Bunny had done this often, and that it wasn't the same Bunny who shared in those timeless afternoons in the barn, but a Bunny that divided himself into two beings. David felt a flush of heat kindle his body as Bunny's hand disappeared for longer intervals. Then Rachel was saying, 'It's your turn, David, you have to resume the narrative where I left off.'

David took a sip of white rum from his cup, and looked out into the dying light. 'It was the dead of winter. Branden sat huddled in a greatcoat before a fire that wouldn't catch. Blue smoke drizzled from the green sneezing logs that were too wet to

54

crackle to an orange blaze. His body had grown haggard, he was thin as a starved starling; he buried his hands deep in the holed lining of his greatcoat pockets. How much longer could he hold out? The severity of the winter was unprecedented; birds froze on the branches and dropped stiffly to the ground. The frost was an iron lid on the earth. When you cracked your heel on the earth's crust it was solid and unyielding. The furrows were sculpted into snow-powdered waves of a frozen sea. Something inside urged him to go out and seek company. With the heel of his boot he extinguished the recalcitrant fire; it went out in a snuffle of acrid smoke. He crashed through the dark wood and across the dry brake; he was headed towards the perimeter road. He didn't know what he was going to do, only that he would flag down a car. He was compelled by an inner momentum that he couldn't oppose. His breath steamed on the blue crystal of the night. The stars were green twinkling ice-daisies, the cold threatened to freeze him into upright rigor mortis; he ran rather than walked, bear-hugging the warmth to himself whenever he slackened his pace. He must have been nearing the road, for he could hear the hum of a car waver on the hill's ascent, and then zip off into the blackness, its gold headlights floating across the asphalt. He manoeuvred through the bare hawthorn hedge and on to the road. Not a sound. Farm lights stood out across the fields in perfect clarity. A dog was barking in a courtyard; it must have heard his strong blundering movements force a gap in the hedge. He listened. Far away he could hear the midge-drone of a car approaching; it was clearer now, he could see its headlights playing over the fields, its reverberations growing louder, and then it was coming face towards him, assertively fast on the trafficless straight. He got out almost into its line of flight, waving his arms desperately, but there was no hint of recognition that the driver had even seen him. Or if he had, he had no intention of slowing on a dark country road; his foot remained squat on the accelerator, the car receded into the buzz of an electric-razor, and then it was gone, a projectile with two gold eyes bulleting towards its destination through the frost-rimed night. Branden jumped up and down to increase his circulation; it was so cold that each breath seemed to crystallise into a snow-flower. He imagined that he had left a trail of stars all the way back to the hut. He started walking. If he kept his back to the oncoming car, the driver wouldn't be able to see the state of dilapidation to which he was reduced. He pulled up the collar of his coat; in that way he could half disguise the spiky fox-red stubble that bristled on the weather-creased rugations of his face. He must have walked for half a mile on the unlit road, when he heard a car beginning the approach of the hill whose summit lay parallel to the hole he had forced in the hedge. His heart pumped at the anticipation of the unexpected. For years he had isolated himself from human discourse; where could he say he was going, and what account could he give of his actions? He started walking briskly, quickening his pace in order to place himself strategically in the line of the driver's vision for a clear stretch of road before the car drew level with him. He half turned round, swinging his hand out in an importuning gesture, and heard the sudden squeal of brakes as the car slowed ten yards in front of him. He could see the red brake-lights stand out like coastal beacons on that black road. Everything was silent but for the puttering engine with its thin discharge of blue exhaust smoke. The car was a white Triumph Spitfire, its chassis low to the ground, and Branden had to stoop, half averting his face, in order to confront the driver. The latter was buttoned up against the cold in a brown leather flying-jacket; he wore a cap and scarf and, without properly looking at Branden, he said, "I'm going to the Lamb and Flag at Buxton, if that's useful to you." Branden mumbled his thanks and crumpled himself up into the low bucket seat. The man hardly looked at him, put the car back into gear and accelerated into the night.'

David sat back; 'Your turn, Louise,' he said, and waited for the response. The light was blueing to black; soon they would light candles. When he looked across, disentrancing himself from Branden's story, he could see Bunny pinning Louise to the floor. His hands were beneath her jumper, and when they finally broke off their kiss, Rachel said, 'If you don't want to join in we'll complete the story ourselves.'

'I'll go last,' said Bunny, 'but Louise doesn't want to be involved. You carry on, Rachel; we're listening, even if we don't appear to be.' Louise was dabbing small kisses on Bunny's neck as he spoke; his shirt had come free of his jeans, and Louise was tickling the small of his stomach. Rachel smiled at David, imperceptibly brushing his thigh with her leg, and looked off into the distance that was opening up behind her eyes.

'Branden screwed his eyes shut against the white undipped

lights of an oncoming car. Speed unnerved him; he watched the green needle on the illuminated dial stand still at 90 mph. Then it quivered at 98 and resettled on the apex of 90. The driver casually glanced at the big moonface on his watch. "Another ten minutes and we'll be at Buxton," he said; "do you live there?"

' "Uh, no," Branden said, unaccustomed to finding himself in the assumed role of an interlocutor, "I'm from the other side of the woods."

' "You mean, sort of Frettenham way," said the man; "I don't know that part although I motor through it sometimes."

'The needle went vertical at 100 mph. Branden was shivering internally with fear; he could feel his stomach caving into a vortex. They slowed to meet the solitary, red cyclopean eye of a road repairs light. The man lit a cigarette; his lighter's snap of blue and orange butane magnified the hollow beneath his right eye. There was a scar worked into the skin, a red matchstick-sized incision that stood out like print on a page. That scar would stay there until it rotted in the grave, thought Branden. "Do you smoke?" the man said. "By the way, I'm Graham." Branden took a Marlboro from its crisp red and white box, and dragged heavily on the smoke.

'After a period of concentrated silence, the man said, "I'll drop you here. I hope it's got you nearer to where you're going."

' "Thanks," said Branden, as he manoeuvred himself out into the cold of a huddled village high street. He blew on his fingers, the red cone of the cigarette eating its way down the rapidly singeing paper. He stamped on the ground, cracking a thin film of ice that had congealed in a rut in the road. He had come this far; it was a long way to hike back, even if he took a short cut across the fields. He had to act. He heeled his cigarette into extinction, and shrank back into the shadows.'

Rachel ceased, and cradled her head against David's thigh. 'It's your turn,' she said, 'unless Bunny wishes to take us to a sensational denouement.' The light had gone completely; the dark was blank like the silence, punctuated only by the periodic gasps that David could hear, coming from the corner in which Louise and Bunny had wedged themselves. 'Light a candle,' Rachel whispered, 'then we can see what they're doing and finish the story.' Rachel had already assumed an understanding between them that David accepted as having always existed. He trembled a match-flame on to a candle, and lit a second one from the first. His eyes ran to the corner. Bunny and Louise were oblivious of the sudden muted light. Louise's short black skirt had concertinaed to her waist; they lay side by side, interlaced, and hungrily exploring each other's bodies. 'Go on, David,' Rachel said, 'although we can't let them have all the fun.'

David felt the red eye of a cyclone centring itself in his head, his voice trembled as he began to narrate.

'Branden stood for a long time looking at the windows of the Lamb and Flag. The car ride had unnerved him. Instead of being able to hear his own thoughts resonate across a black lagoon of inner peace, he felt disoriented. It seemed an interminably long way back to his hut in the woods. He listened for the familiar shriek of a long-eared owl, but there was only the sound of voices on the other side of the whitewashed stucco walls at which he was staring. But now his compulsion was returning – he could feel the inner dynamism, that had propelled him out on to the road in search of some indefinably elusive experience, return like the crossing of two red wires. For a moment he felt empowered with the strength to walk in and out and in and out of the bar doors, until the community slunk away, terrified by the silent pacing of this fierce man. He would stand there and roar for all of his frustration, all of his bitter isolation, his retreat into a world of primitive survival. He looked down at his blackened, split fingernails, his hands charred with wood ash. He would have to go inside or make a vigorous march across country in order to keep himself from freezing. The warm air of the bar hit him. He swung back from the mirror in which his reflection detonated. Who was this rabid, unkempt, lupine figure, his big hands thrust out from his body, his baggy coat torn at the shoulders, his eyes red streaks in the glaze of a white china marble? Something had happened before he realised that he had the weight of a man over his head, the tiny effete struggling of someone he would break like firewood over the bar counter. There was an abrupt clatter of glasses, tables scraped chalkily over the wooden floor; he could sense the paralysed stare of the barman, the cowed, complacent retreat of the village regulars. Someone broke for the door and started screaming. He couldn't bear that shrill, nerve-tunnelling cry; he cracked the man over the sill of the bar counter, and flapped him loose. Only when he recollected the warm brown leather of the man's jacket did he recognise that the man he had cracked over wood was the driver who had stopped for him on that deserted strip of country road. But, by then, everything was a blur; he was running over frozen furrows, the village was alive with dogs barking and the momentary hysteria of voices. He ran into the cover of a wood, his breath loud and steaming, his head rocking with the numb barbiturate-packing of shock, his body racked from the prolonged exertion of flight. When he slowed down, he heard an owl's cry searching the cold. He came face to face with a gibbet of dead weasels, crows, jackdaws, and rubbed his face against the leathery frozen fur and feathers. He dropped down into the crackling leaf-litter. Something was sniffing around his legs; the hot, panting breath of a dog-fox, he smelt its fur and stared into the liquid jet of its eyes. When it turned heel and flashed away, he felt dispossessed of the cyclonic anger that had welled up in him. It was the keeper who found Branden's dead body stiff in a ditch, and who came across the dead fox a mile further on in the woods. The winter was excruciatingly severe; the pond froze for six weeks. Men said the ice-age had returned, and they meant it, as they recounted the story of Branden. They hung the fox up on the barn-door; it was a warning to keep inside by the roaring hearth, to leave the creatures of the night to search out their own dark ends.'

David let the last of his words die down like embers in a fire. 'Where do these things come from?' Rachel puzzled.

'We know everything,' David said, 'it's a matter of finding a key to the door behind which it's hidden. I'm writing a novel at present, so I may have incorporated some of my themes. Once you begin to test the surface of the subconscious you're faced with limitless possibilities that you never realised existed. It's like pack-ice exploding on the Danube in the spring thaw, jigsaw-pieces of ice jockeying for the right current.'

Bunny and Louise had taken themselves up to the timber floor beneath the rafters. The sporadic creak of their movements overhead had regularised into a rhythmic pattern. 'It sounds like they're making love,' Rachel said, and David listened, astonished at the accelerated motion overhead. He could hear Louise unsuccessfully trying to repress cries that broke out again and again in long sustained gasps. Suddenly it was dark. Rachel blew out the candles, and said, 'Find me in the dark.' His last recollection before submitting to her body was that of an owl's scream. The creatures of the night were searching out their own dark ends.

59

5

The Givenchy aquamarine silk would offset his lilac shirt, but not the blue. He took down a scarlet silk tie with the faintest hint of a frost-flake in it, and matched it against a pearl-grey denim button-down. He was dissociating himself from the day; his last patient had established a drink problem, an involuntary reliance on alcohol as a catalyst to character transformation. Withdrawn, cowed, complacent, the man rejected the routinal stolidity of his life as an accountant, and lived out the dichotomised split, customary with alcoholics, of developing a satellite character; a persona that threatened to possess him. In his hours away from the office he called himself Red; it was his drinking name, the wolfskin of his nocturnal bravado. It had all begun to go wrong the day he received a call at his office, and the female caller had come straight through on his extension and asked for Red. In his confusion he had cradled the receiver, but only after momentarily acknowledging that identity, with the blinding realisation that he must have affixed his professional number to a hastily written bar-slip. He had hurried out at closing time in the hope that the woman he had spent the evening masquerading to would establish future contact. Red? The name had stung him with the notion of something obscene; a blackmailer, a fraud, a person who didn't really exist.

Adjusting his collar and tie, Ernst Moravia reflected that he did not personally like the man. While it was his role to remain impartial, something about the man's demeanour disquieted. Perhaps it was his patient's exaggerated sense of an invincible mastery afforded by his switch of characters, or perhaps it was the ash-grey circle of rime around the cuffs of his otherwise meticulously laundered shirts that offended Moravia's taste? He had come to search for this tide-line of impurity. It was consistent with the man's dual personality. The grime was Red, it was the spotted skin of the plaice on the soft white flesh.

He poured himself a large Scotch, and watched the chestnut-fires of the spirit separate themselves on contact with the nuggets of ice. In an hour's time he would go across town to meet Claudette. He re-read her letter, astonished at the richness of her vocabulary, the literacy that he had never associated with someone whose life was so much the overpronouncement of her body. For the fourth time he found himself re-reading the text – he couldn't let go of it, it wound through him sinuously as a stream threading through stones. The letter was both a stimulus and a deterrent.

Dear Ernst,

My days lend themselves to reflection; a certain gold concentration in the late afternoon sunlight evokes the still-ness of a rock-pool into which I once stared, mesmerised, at the Ile de Houat. The gold sun-spot fitted into that pool like a contact-lens into an eye. Fire and water, their liquefaction. There was a time when my inner moods reflected the changes in the natural world, and I feel this correspondence returning, despite the fact that my location is a city. And you, do you have a garden, an area of green by which to monitor the seasons? Try as man will, he can never be free of nature's regeneration. 'Long live the weeds and the wilderness yet' as Gerald Manley Hopkins wrote.

You must be wondering how someone preoccupied with the physically unnatural can express so dominant a trust in nature, and the only answer I can find is childhood. We grow into and not out of things; what was once perhaps only half realised can without our properly knowing it become our motivating *raison d'être*. And another ten years? What will they bring, if we live to embody the fruit of their seed? We had a fig tree in the garden when I was a child. It largely went untended, and when the purple over-ripe skins split open, you'd find a constellation of yellowish-pink seeds. The potential of our lives, realised or unfulfilled, depends on our propagating the right seed. I had always crushed the black skin underfoot until one day a seed, in rubbing against the sole of my shoe, created what I can only describe as an internal friction. For an unquantifiable moment I was made aware of universal experi-ence, an illumination that has repeated itself in various degrees of intensity on three or four other occasions in the course of

61

my life. The last such experience occurred earlier this afternoon.

I was sitting here in my hotel suite, vaguely preoccupied with making notes for a novel, when I had the notion that I was watching myself participate in the action of being. It was not so much the feeling of duality, as an awareness that we can be both the perceiver and the instrument for recording the transmitted sensation of the thing perceived. Perhaps my illustration lacks clarity. Sometimes, when one establishes a familiar walk, and with it the anticipated perspective of a stand of silver birch seen always from the same line of vision, one is jolted back to reality by the knowledge of observing oneself and the path one is taking from the point of view of the trees. In that way one would see the thing near at hand that one always missed. Experience as we know it is like fording a stream. We're so preoccupied with locating the stepping stones, with finding a way round or through things, that we lose sight of the actual experience we are trying to negotiate.

Enough of this. I propose that we meet for a drink. My days are full to a point that I never expected. But it is your news I await; perhaps you'd care to meet between 8.30 to 9.00. How unexpectedly cold it is; an off-the-shoulder leaves me with goosepimples these days.

With best wishes,
Claudette

Uncertain how to construe the last phrase, other than in terms of sexual innuendo, Dr Ernst Moravia settled back into a fern-green armchair, and lit a White Owl cigar. The aromatic savour of the smoke helped to pacify his nerves. These were the blue smoke-rings Napoleon blew at St Cloud. Soirées and *la douceur de vivre*; how he envied the aristocratic line; the dignity of a man dispensing with one book from his rare library at ninety. The book, with its gold tooled Moroccan binding and its white silk book-mark, would in leaving its owner establish the beat of a wave on the shore – it wouldn't easily find a home or permanence; it would become a cherished item for successive generations. Its knowledge would be secreted and stored in the mind. Of such a book, Moravia reflected, one might say as Montaigne did of his *Philippe de Commines*: 'You will find the language smooth and agreeable, and of a natural simplicity. The narrative is clear, and the author's good faith shines plainly through it. He is free from vanity when speaking of himself, and from partiality and malice when speaking of others. His speeches and exhortations show honest zeal and regard for truth, rather than any rare talent; and he displays an authority and seriousness throughout which proclaim him a man of good birth, brought up amidst great affairs.'

If only life was a telescoping in on a shore reached, he reflected, and not this constant slipping back into mid-stream – the fatigue of the circumnavigator, every island a mirage, and the only identifiable landing-stage the one that projected from the banks of the Styx. The crossing undertaken in black mist, the boatman's pox-cratered face hidden, the imperious bark of his voice heard ringing between the near and farther shore. Moravia applied the finishing touches to his dress, atomised a copious spray of Vêtiver by Guerlain over his neck and wrists, and stepped out into the night in search of a taxi.

When he saw Claudette sitting outside the Coconut Grove in Barrett Street, he was struck by how perfectly she had come to assimilate the extravagance of her chosen identity. That old, untutored accentuation of femininity had been toned down in favour of an appearance that was unquestionably an identity and not an assumed affectation. She was smoking a mauve Sobranie cocktail cigarette; the Moët & Chandon was a green lighthouse packed in the ice of its bucket, his glass was waiting for him on the light as opposed to the shadow side of the table. Already she had assumed this advantage.

'You've just missed the 8.30; the next London train is the 9.15 to Liverpool Street,' a voice was telling David as he struggled to a halt with an intractably bulky suitcase. He was running away; he had no idea how or where, only that he must act on the irrepressible impulse, rather as he had made the figure of Branden assume superhuman proportions in its quest for human freedom. David couldn't free himself of his own invention; time and again the red fox-like figure of the bird-painter had come to invade his consciousness. Branden's voice had gone on speaking to him; it had burrowed into the fabric of his skull, it had found a fox-hole in which to go on living. What had begun as a figure modulated and identified by the imagination had grown into a

63

voice that he couldn't subdue. The previous afternoon, out in the barn, Branden's voice had become indomitable; it worked at a pitch higher than his own thoughts, its primal commentary threw his balance, he had rolled over and over in the meadow clutching his head, trying to drown the insane voice out. David had felt his face slapped, only from the inside, and the force of the blow had thrown him from one wall to another. Whenever he achieved a sustained degree of mental lucidity, the voice would break in obscenely or prophetically. It was like an air bubble trapped inside his skull; the bubble of an underground stream breaking through the rocks and carrying with it the demonic issue of the sibyl's voice. He had found himself in involuntary hysterics when his parents suggested he apply to a university as a means of protracting his education. His future had become their problem and not his. But he had seen fear register in his father's face at the abnormal velocity of his distemper. It wasn't so much a laugh as an obstruction forced upwards through his windpipe into his mouth, before his tongue rattled like a pebble clicking over stones in the wave's backwash. He began to feel that his thoughts were confiscated by an intrinsic parasite, and to outwit the inner demon had become his preoccupation.

As he hurried a few clothes and books into a suitcase, it was Branden's harsh indictments that he heard. When he looked into the mirror, it was the red stubble on the outlaw's cheeks that he expected to see. David would have to invent alternative narratives in order to free himself of this presence, but every plot he mentally conceived involved him inextricably in the life of this bird-voiced man from the woods. When your thoughts aren't your own, you're mad, he reasoned; he must get away from the countryside he knew well and, if he escaped, Branden might not come with him.

David sat on the train and stared out at fields of yellow rape. He was alone in his compartment, the twilight blued to black; stars were shivering in the immense void of the sky. He tried to read, but fear preoccupied his senses, something within him wouldn't be flushed out; he heard a muffled paw, the slow whine of a dog-fox at the entrance to a clearing. Sweat was standing out in droplets on his forehead; he lurched out into the narrow corridor and pressed his face against the glass. The attack was coming on, he could feel it build like the mauve eye of a thunderstorm; his chest was labouring to draw breath, each

64

inhalation was like dropping a bucket into a dark well, and pulling it up. When the bucket slipped a last time into the well's spiral shaft, it snagged, he couldn't free it for the unbearable weight; the train clattered into the pitch of a tunnel, and the scream came on. His body twitched convulsively, it was as though his throat had become a wind-tunnel; a fox had gone into him and was attempting to break out of its hole, he could feel the teeth savage his windpipe. When he came to, the ticket collector was standing over him, holding out a plastic cup of iced water. 'Do you have fits?' the man said. 'Are you epileptic, young man? You'd better take things quietly; we can get you off at Colchester, if you like, and arrange for an ambulance to stand by. Who's meeting you in London? Are your parents at the other end?' David blinked out of a red mist; he had been standing in a clearing watching a fox come out of the undergrowth, ears pointed, its nose inquisitively picking up on a scent. There was a causal relationship between himself and the animal; they were suddenly interchangeable – he could smell with the hot breath of a fox, and it in turn had tapped the leakage of his thoughts. It was when the fox had got into his head and leapt that he had screamed; thereafter he could remember nothing. His head ached as though he had lain in the sun all day in a field, and must now face the exploding petroleum canisters of sunstroke. Red and yellow flares were jumping like flak behind his eyes. 'Steady on, boy,' the man said, alarmed, 'drink some of this water, and try to tell me the name of your parents.'

David cradled his head against the seat, and said, 'Don't worry, I'm being met in London, I'll just try and sleep.'

'All right,' the man said, 'I'll look in again in ten minutes and, if you feel bad, I'll arrange things at Colchester; we're only twenty minutes away from there.' David could smell fox; the reek of the animal was exuding through the pores of his skin. A red brush smelling of rain and the scalding jet of chicken's blood. He wanted to burrow into the musty dark, go down a fox-hole and take comfort from the smell of his own skin, his own territorial privacy. He would lie in a dark sleep, and re-emerge at twilight.

By the time the train pulled into Colchester, David was sufficiently composed to convince an equivocatory guard that he was well enough to continue the journey to London. He sat quietly, looking up from his book, and answering the man's questions with the assured and lucid composure of one already dispassionately removed from the unrepeatable cause of his misfortune. 'I need your assurance,' the guard said, 'that your parents are meeting you at Liverpool Street.'

'They are,' David said, unflinchingly. The degree of concern in the man's voice allowed David some insight into the seriousness of his attack. For the first time in his life, he was evoking serious concern over the pattern of his behaviour. There were the night incidents that had precipitated his visiting a London psychiatrist, but no one had intimated he was ill; it was more that he wouldn't conform to certain behavioural patterns that society would demand of him when he left school. But it had to end in this, he thought, the scream had finally brought him to the attention of others; Branden's menacing possession had broken through the fabric of his consciousness.

The train was picking up speed again; in one hour's time he would be in London. And then? In his anxiety to outmanoeuvre Branden, David had lost all sense of the fear that London habitually induced in him. It was with a cold shiver that he envisaged arriving at Liverpool Street. He thought of the labyrinth of subway tunnels, and shivered at the impossible journey to the other end of the night. And if he got there, who would recognise or save him? He began to huddle into himself, then jerked back with a start. The deeper he went into himself, the closer he narrowed in on Branden. He physically winced; something like a pair of pliers was stretching the tendons in his neck – the muscles locked and he had to wrench to free himself. They were getting nearer to London; he could tell by the frequency of lights, the periscoping of office blocks into the night sky – that ochre smudge of deoxygenated vapour that oil-slicked above the city. He looked for stars, but couldn't find them. He tried to imagine that he was back in the countryside, out in the brake, concealed, chilled by the night dew, stomach pressed to the earth as he waited for a badger to emerge from a set, or a nervous deer to pick its way through the trees. That scutter in the crisp leaf-litter was a frightened vole. By morning, his parents would set up the alert; inured to his nocturnal absences, they would grow seriously worried when he failed to show at breakfast. He imagined his father discovering the pristine bed, the absence of human scent that would tell him that no one had been back. They would search the woods first, then the police

66

would highlight his disappearance as a cause for national concern. And where would he be? Adrift in London, or found savagely bitten to death – his throat a necklace of amethysts and rubies where the teeth had worked in? And after that, who would ever narrate the tale of Branden?

'It's been so long,' Dr Moravia was saying to Claudette, nervously averting his eyes, in the manner he would adopt to put a patient at ease. 'Is it ten years? Time plays tricks upon me that not even the most adept hypnotherapist could achieve.'

'It was 15th August a decade ago,' said Claudette, informing him by her incisiveness that she too allowed for no drift in the chronology of her past.

For a moment, the champagne nettled his throat, the fizz seethed, and made a sea-cave of his mouth. He looked up, expecting to perceive the changes in her, assembling her features from fragmentary glances, and trying to dissociate these from the superimposed memory of her that he retained. Faces defy a clear impartial assessment; they are forever in the act of instinctive self-defence, shifting their angle of alignment, adopting a profile, or using the eyes to deflect too concentrated a scrutiny of flaws. Everything about Claudette had become refined; she no longer wore the loud harlequin cosmetics of a decade ago, her face was no longer a palette of livid reds and purples and blacks. She had perfected the art of cosmetics. Her eyes were delicately coloured with pressed violets and bluebell shadows, the gold-lit blusher afforded subdued highlights to her cheeks, her lips were gingham red, and delineated perfectly by a lip pencil. She wore a simple black silk dress, her black leather heart-shaped earrings were offset by the violet frost-fires of a silk scarf worn at the neck. It wasn't that she had aged, Moravia reflected; it was more that she had worked upon herself like a sculptor chiselling marble to the contours of his vision. She had assimilated the change; he could feel how she resonated from the centre of herself, and not from a hysterical periphery. When he had known her, she used her body as an affront; it was a glaringly incomplete anatomy that she could disguise only by accentuating its inconsistencies. He could feel that she was forcing him to look at himself, to consider how a decade had altered him physically; his features had coarsened, but he'd retained his slim, youthful figure, the enquiring aliveness of his eye that trapped thoughts in the way that a spider's web becomes dotted with ladybirds, flying ants, the glinting of a green-bottle whose body tears the net. She had become adept at allowing silence to perfect its subtle alchemy; in that way she was spared the masculine pronouncement of her voice.

'You treat me as a patient,' she said finally, and took out a small package from her bag. 'I've got your tie,' she said, 'the bottle-green and pink one.'

He half took it from the container, unable to resist tracing his finger over the coolness of the silk. Yes, he remembered it now; it had been a gift from a grateful woman patient. Always flushed by the acquisition of a new tie, he had felt confident sporting it in Paris, conscious that its beauty would attract the discerning eye. 'I don't suppose I'll ever have occasion to wear this one again,' he said moodily, trying to force out of her the real reason why she had arranged this reunion. Their act of sex flashed through his mind again, only now it seemed something improbable; he couldn't any longer conceive of how their bodies had joined, a field had grown up between them, they were East and West, and a network of armed guards prevented the defection of one to the other. The tide-line of the champagne receded; but Moravia failed to experience the sensation of intoxicating clarity that usually accompanied the drinking of a good wine. The prospect of a second bottle left him feeling cheated of the excitement that the first had failed to induce. Already he was beginning to long for the solitude of a book, the sibilance of the plane trees outside his window, the divagation of night cloud across a sandy moon.

'When other people's secrets are your profession,' he found himself saying, 'one comes to serve as a reservoir for all the fish which are unable to make the journey to their natural spawning grounds. The cargo they are conveying to death is the contraband they are at liberty to unload and examine in my hearing. Festoons of fish-eggs, that's my profession. And I'm the self-appointed inspector of a pool that daily grows more turbid.'

'And I am the purveyor of a secret,' she said, 'that it's given to few to realise. I have already lived two lives; the implications of that are immense. I've turned myself out of one body into another, and perhaps in that way I can claim exemption from moral responsibility; who is to say if the cloudy lees are the male or the female's doing, or something unique for they belong to the issue of neither?'

68

Moravia lit a cigarette; the smoke turned lavender in the night air. 'But why did you wish to see me?' he asked bluntly. 'I don't understand. What happened between us is surely a matter of the past. Why dig up old bones, aren't they better left to whiten in the earth to which they belong?'

In the silence a buff-coloured moth flickered into view – an event of the natural world come to life in the city; it fluctuated over a lamp, its ivory spinnaker frantically twirling as it switched course, and went up high. Claudette took the weight of her head in her left hand, and focused both of her eyes to the right. 'I suppose you know David Thompson,' she said; 'I know from his father's letters to me that he's a patient of yours.'

'His father's letters to you?' said Moravia, the tone of his voice aggressively incredulous. 'And if, hypothetically, the boy was a patient of mine, what has this to do with anything?'

'Plenty,' answered Claudette, sensing her power was in the ascendant, and beginning to feel for the chinks in Moravia's insidious armour. He was like a crab, he carried an impregnable defence with him; she wanted to shell him and flip him over on his back so that his legs would revolve like the spinning pedals of an up-ended bicycle. 'Whether you admit it or not, I have it on the authority of a parent that he is consulting you about various aberrations of behaviour.'

For a moment Ernst Moravia's mind attempted to unlock a series of chinese-puzzles. His only communications with the boy's father had been concise and directly related to parental concern over a child. He tried to imagine how Claudette could be associated with the father, but the spontaneous image that sprang to mind was one that rebuffed him. He was back in Paris. He had an assignation with Claudette, but by some paralysis of memory he had forgotten his name and his intended destination. Each time he tried for the retrieval of his memory, someone laughed at him from behind his back. It was the low chuckle of an adversary, but he knew if he turned around there would be nobody there . . . The champagne bubbles danced on his tongue. He was beginning to come alight. He felt he could see with intense luminosity through a bubble ascending in the sparkling fizz. When it hit the surface of the glass with a sputter like the cancellation of a tricolour rocket, the situation exploded before him. The photograph that David so often recalled his father clandestinely returning to was of Claudette. She was the

69

girl in the black dress fluffed up above her shapely thighs. And hadn't there always been a hint of disquietude in David's voice when he recreated this image?

'I don't find myself disposed to discuss professional matters,' Moravia said quietly, allowing for no interval between his completed sentence and the inhalation of his cigarette.

Claudette was like a spider which has picked up the vibration of a trapped insect in its web. 'I could tell you much of the boy's father,' she said, 'but to what avail? There is a certain type of man who wears a mask so completely that you never come to question whether there's a face on the other side. You can prise a shell from a crab, but the mask goes with the human into death.'

Moravia could smell and taste rust; it was a sensation that he associated with moments of disquieting self-scrutiny. An ochre trickle was on his palate. He drained his glass, and said, 'Perhaps the boy's father's situation is no different to my own, but what of that? One doesn't spend a lifetime marking time like an ant in a globule of jam.'

'It's more serious than that,' Claudette reflected; 'the implications involve a network of people. They call him the Squire,' she said, 'the little red-haired man from the Rose and Crown who is most often away on business trips.

'The Squire,' she said mockingly. 'But you wouldn't know what goes on at Blue Rock,' she continued, 'I only had glimpses, but they were enough to send me packing from an outpost where I was putting myself back together, and to lose myself again in the indifference of a city.' *At the time I was sick, I had to disburden myself of all the grime that had found its way beneath my skin. My blood felt silted like the Styx. When I tried to sleep, an oil-refinery would blaze in my head. In my hallucination crowds circled round that fire and watched the gables and then the roof collapse. I used to hear the sweat crackle on their brows like hot fat. What I dreamt was terrible; people would jump with burning hair into the river and fatten a pack of alligators. I'd wake to find my blankets soaked, and my body feverish with icy sweat.*

That's when I was out at Blue Rock. I'd coaxed myself away from the cocaine habit I'd had for ten years, and the resulting paranoia had me startle at the intrusion of a shadow. I'd begun to think that there was no end to the mind's deluge of terror. I huddled into myself, trying to become invisible. And when the fire extinguished itself, the ice came. A blue cold crept over everything. I saw myself filleted on

blocks of ice by Eskimo seal hunters; the glare had my eyes ache as
though they were packed with fragments of a mirror. I grew so cold I
would light matches and work them into my skin. The blizzard was
constant; each night I would trek off into the white lunar face of the
frozen wastes. Once when I bent down and cleared the snow away
from a polished monocle of ice I could see my mind reflected in it like
the stained glass interior of a watch. And after the cold came the
vacuum, the weeks of readjustment, the implacable sea-glare, and the
wind slamming in with the big equinoctial seas at Blue Rock.

'These were my first months in England. I stayed alone in the
little granite cottage I'd rented at Zennor. It had once been the
local coastguard's. They wouldn't speak to me in the village;
they'd serve me and look away. At night in those dark lanes I
feared a lynching-party would come out for me. It happened
quite by accident. I was out walking one showery afternoon, and
a blue van sidled past me. It slowed at the end of the lane and
waited. When I came level with the driver's window, the glass
was wound down, and a man with red hair leaned out and said,
"I'll take you to the village if that's of any help." '

'And you mean to say that that was David Thompson's
father?' interjected Dr Moravia.

Their cigarette smoke mingled. Claudette clinked the now
empty bottle against the rim of her glass, retrained her eyes on
Moravia, and continued. 'Something had me pull up; it wasn't
only that the man's voice imposed a psychological barrier I
couldn't cross, it was also the fact that my curiosity was aroused
by the sight of the flour-faced teenage girl sitting beside him in
the cabin. The combination of the two had me lean into the
man's vision, and say, "Sure, take me to the top of the hill if you
like." I sat to the left of the man, with the girl in the centre.
"Blustery day," he said. "This is Jan; we're going out to the
millhouse if you want to come." It was his assumed air of
conspiracy that disturbed me; it was as if he'd already determined that I was a consenting party to his actions in life.'

'And what happens at the millhouse?' questioned Moravia,
attempting to slow the narrative down.

Claudette ignored his question; she was reliving the episode,
counting the trees along the country road, watching a ribbon of
light flash hail on to the van's bonnet.

'Oil,' she said, 'he smelt of oil; the neat suit under the
greatcoat, and the girl sitting there in red mittens, not saying

71

anything, just staring straight ahead as though there wasn't a left or right. "I'll drop you at your farm, Jan," he said, but the girl didn't speak, and that's when I jumped out and ran back down the road. When I stopped running, the van had gone on over the crown of the hill.'

'But I don't see the connection,' Dr Moravia was saying 'between . . . '

David startled. The metallic slamming of doors had him open his eyes. In his drowsiness he had imagined that two curtain-rods were frictionalising each other, only to find that it was the protracted squeal of the train's brakes as they slowed into a rusty siding at Liverpool Street. He could hear footsteps hurriedly reverberating across concrete. For a moment he didn't know who he was or where he was; panic stomped in his chest, before he righted himself and instinctively plunged out on to the lit platform. The cold station air sobered him. The cavernous alienation of the place had him struggle forward without any conscious knowledge of where he was going. The only route he knew was the Circle Line train to Great Portland Street, and from there the brisk walk to Dr Moravia's surgery. Instinct found him making for that familiar route; a new fear had taken over, and in place of Branden's carnivorous mask came the endless impress of nothingness – there wasn't a landmark he was familiar with, not a face he could summon to his assistance against the relentless exposure to a concrete void. He fumbled his coins into a ticket machine, and weaved a tortuous passage between the incoming and outgoing flux of passengers. Fear had brought him here to the centre of a city instead of the dark of a night wood; the fox that hunted him was temporarily held in abeyance by the night tunnel that threatened to swallow them both.

David got into the tube compartment and fixed his eyes on the map. He would count the stations off one by one, and then Dr Moravia's address was only a short walk; he had to convince himself he was going there, or else his mind, lacking a focal point, would have spun into a vertiginous orbit. Lacking central-ity, he felt like an expiring swimmer caught up in contradictory currents; he was being slowly stretched, now one way and now the other, towards the black rim of the horizon. An arm would go and then a leg, but he had to keep on swimming. If there was a way out of this it was through a shaft that Branden couldn't follow; his head on impact with the surface would detonate the red menace in his skull.

At King's Cross, faces swam against the opposing glass like moon-faced fish browsing against the walls of an aquarium. David braced himself to face the night crowd. He kept on thinking that there wasn't anyone sitting in his place, that he was the figment of a narrative that he and Bunny had contrived, and that he had only to expunge this alien self and he would be sitting with his back to the stone walls of the barn imbibing the deep indigo of the night sky. He fixed his eyes at an angle where they couldn't be used for contact, and tried to imagine that he was walling up a hole through which Branden was desperately trying to burrow. There was a girl sitting opposite him; the mauve of her skirt kept diffusing itself through his retinal filter. When he flicked his eyes at her she was staring back. At Euston Square the fox barked somewhere in the back of his mind; he had to hold on, one stop to go, and he could free himself from the crowd that would otherwise witness Branden's ferocious retribution.

He got out of the compression doors, and faced into the stairs. The fox had disappeared, but the girl was inching closer to him, looking to make contact, matching his pace with her own. He flashed a glance at her and felt the sympathetic radiation synchronise in her smile. 'You look like you've come back from a journey,' she said, 'somehow one always ends up back in the city.'

Her hair was cut short, black and spiky, the lids of her eyes were a deep violet; she wore a mauve skirt, a soft black leather jacket rolled at the sleeves, and jet earrings that looked like miniature totem poles. It was her smile that David warmed to; it seemed to register as the spontaneous expression of her inner thoughts.

His throat was parched, but he said, 'Yes, I'm down from the countryside, only I'm not sure yet whether I've got anywhere to stay tonight.'

'You look a bit frail to be out in the night,' she said. 'I'm Diane; there's a pub just round the corner if you'd care to have a drink.'

David vacillated for a moment; what if Branden's voice started to break through when he was speaking to the girl? But his fear of being adrift in the night was temporarily greater than his fear

73

of Branden, so he said, 'Yes, that's a good idea, why don't we go and talk?'

Rain was beginning to dust the air; not the twinkling crystalline raindrops that flashed on dock and ivy leaves, but a blotchy, unsoothing rain that tapped on the bonnets and hoods of stationary cars. Inside the bar David settled himself uneasily on the edge of a chair, his nerves disattuned by the bass throb of the music, his mind racing to fix itself on a subject that would provide a tenable focus. He thought of Stephen Hudson, and the novel he had begun to write and would continue once he had re-established the equilibrium necessary to concentrate. Diane returned with the drinks; two bottles of Pils lager with their lime-green foil tops looking like emerald rime on the bark of elms. 'I don't even know your name,' she remarked, 'you're so very quiet.'

'David,' he said. 'I live in Norfolk, I came down here on impulse tonight.'

'So, you've run away,' Diane said; 'but surely you know someone in London?'

'No one,' he replied, 'only my doctor.' He was beginning to feel dissociated; if he wasn't really here, where was he? And if he let go of his consciousness he would be possessed by another.

'Don't be too nervous,' Diane was saying, 'I can always put you up in my flat for a night or two. Or would you rather telephone your parents and make arrangements to go home tomorrow?'

'No, I'd rather stay,' he replied, profoundly grateful for her solicitude, but unable to find the right note of warmth to reciprocate an unspoken trust.

The alcohol served only to dislodge him further from the centre of his being. He was a spider afloat on two branching threads of gossamer – two thin blue strands insecurely tied between stones across a stream. When they got outside it was raining with increasing persistence. Jabs of late summer rain could be heard snicking the dusty plane trees. He followed Diane as though he was being controlled on an invisible thread. But, even if he survived tonight, what would he do tomorrow, and the day after that?

'This way,' Diane said, leading him down a flight of stone steps at the back of a building. For the first time, he became conscious of the swing of her hips, the good shape of her thighs.

74

'It's only small,' she said, her voice echoing as it searched out the room. When he got inside he was abruptly in her living room. The walls were painted white with a cobalt ceiling; the bulb suspended in a shade was a muted lilac. There was a wicker rocking chair, a table heaped with books and magazines, and two sack cushions on the floor, an ochre one, and a midnight-blue. There was a small adjoining bedroom and kitchen. David put his bulky black case down, and felt reassured as to her nature when his eyes picked out the two pink roses she had placed in a water-glass. Overblown, their pink cascading skirts were on the point of dissolution. Two or three scalloped petals had already fallen. She was busy in the kitchen making coffee.

He sat down. The smallness of the place already asphyxiated him; he had to push the walls back by imagining that behind them, and extending to either side, were black night woods, the tree-tops flying in the wind and sputtering rain. When she came back he could feel her sensitivity creating a spoor of light; the columbine and the foxglove on their respective mugs were an extension of her sensibility. 'I'm afraid you'll have to sleep in this room,' she said perfunctorily, a slight uneasiness clouding her luminosity.

'Thanks,' he said, hoping she'd retire soon, and leave him to continue his novel. The only way he could get out of here was to write himself into a landscape where he could be alone with the characters of his invention. For a brief moment he could hear an autumn stream in spate, the patter of acorn-cups raining on a woodland path.

'You look terribly overstrained,' Diane said, 'do try and relax a little, nothing can happen to you here. We'll talk about what moves you should make in the morning.' She owned a sleeping-bag, so this solved the question of David's quarters for the night.

'Go to the door,' a voice barked inside his head, after Diane had retired to her bedroom. He obeyed the dictate unquestioningly, and found himself face up against the white painted door, listening to the sounds she made as she undressed. He could hear her place her high-heeled black shoes on the floor, then the abrupt crackle as she unzipped her mauve skirt, and the panic of the springs as she shifted her weight on the counterpane. When he disengaged from the voice, he found himself, muscles locked, his body pressed flat against her door, his breathing suspended. It was as though he'd been stood vertically and not horizontally on the boards of a coffin. He backed off and sat stiffly on a cushion and stared.

When he resumed normal respiration, it felt like oxygen was returning to his bloodstream after a bout of diver's cramp. His circulation was coming back to him the way a sea maps out a familiar passage between rocks. The house was silent; the subdued roar of traffic could have been wind trapped in a stand of poplars. He took out his exercise book in the assurance that he could escape himself through fiction, and prepared to assume the role of Stephen Hudson in the increasing momentum of his novel's action.

Chapter 2

Ed slammed the weight of his body on the accelerator. By pushing the car in and out of a complex of side-streets, he'd managed to outmanoeuvre the police car. They could hear its klaxon mewling in the maze of alleys behind them.

'Calm down, and shut up,' Stephen was shouting to Cherry whose mouth was frozen in a rictus of preverbal terror.

Ed's face was strained into lit wires of concentration; the frantic messages typed out by his nerves were being transmitted into speed. 'We'll ditch the car,' he said; 'if we get out on to the coast we'll be the target for a police trap.' Ed's make-up was beginning to smudge; two distinct branching tributaries of eye-liner were charcoaling the textured foundation around his eyes. His lipstick was chapped and foxed. Stephen winced inwardly, for he knew how any blemish to his cosmetic veneer put Ed into a state of fidgety indisposition. They slewed into a yard, and Ed scraped the car into one of the two yawning garages that had been left open by their absent owners.

His retinal screen was a gnat-dance of images. For the last ten minutes he had seen nothing but diverging Cubist parallelograms, and oncoming lights powering into their windscreen, before the head-on blaze fractionally swivelled to left or right. That and the scream of the cornering tyres, the scutched rubber treads smoking over asphalt.

They got out and slammed the doors on the garage, and ran down a side-alley. There was no sound of any pursuer. They were somewhere behind the maze of dockland. They could smell the sea-air mingled with the scent of orange-peel and oil and flotsam.

The alley smelt of hemp rope beaded by sea-fog.

'Calm down, Cherry,' Ed was enforcing with austerity. 'Try and tell us rationally what you saw. Are you sure it was Ace?'

'It was his back,' said Cherry. 'It's a scarlet circle; somebody's killed him, Ed. I knew it before I saw him. The door to the flat was wide open; I could hear the clock-hands going tick-tock as though I was listening through a stethoscope. He must have fallen over the table, his back was arched and the blood had . . . I can't bear it, Ed, you've got to do something.'

Stephen kept muttering, 'I should have guessed it would end like this. It was trouble from the beginning. As soon as Ace started involving himself in those big deals, we should have known, and not gone back.'

They could hear a police siren intermittently bubbling on and off as it combed the labyrinth of the docks. A mist was feathering in; it put a blue peach down on the one lighted window facing out over the yard. They huddled there like conspirators in a gold light shed by El Greco. Cherry shivered through the white cotton of her blouse. 'We'd better remain inconspicuous,' Ed whispered, his eyes scanning a parked Ford. 'We'll get back later; it's likely that the police want us for breakneck driving, and not in connection with Ace.'

Stephen gagged for breath like a diver come up for air. Suddenly they could hear the metronomic beat of a footstep; someone was running through an adjoining street. 'Quick, get into the garage,' he whistled.

The footsteps were approaching louder and louder, and then David screamed as Branden's face asserted itself in the jaw-gaping, throat-hot terror of a fox's answer to the cry of a vixen. He must have rolled over and bitten his tongue, for he could feel fingers wedged into his mouth as his body shook in spasmic convulsions. When things came clear through a red mist, it was Diane he recognised, kneeling above him, forcing his lower jaw apart from the upper. He tried to make contact with a luminous ring of yellow light that dilated between his eyes, and lost consciousness in the dark of a primal forest as Branden sprang for his throat.

6

The sky was pea-green and, where a lavender streak braided out to the west, gulls hung in the transient dragonfly of a rainbow. The rain had dragged round the coast and gone out to sea. Medal-ribbons of rain were slanting over the tired crawl of a tanker on the horizon.

Jan had come back that afternoon from Pendeen lighthouse. From there she had watched the squall move in over Whitesand Bay and Cape Cornwall, rain that advanced vertically and in slow motion. It came on across the fields at a pace that had you believe you could outrun it. She'd walked the cliff-path from below Carnyorth to Pendeen, a tortuous rock-hewn trail that zig-zagged hundreds of feet above the blasting backwash of the Atlantic. The surf was a lather of post-hurricane pressure, smashing its green breakers against the jagged cliff-face and mounting up in a hanging wall of suspended spray. As each wave backed out it slapped into the white jaws of its climbing successor.

It was a kingfisher September day, and despite the apparent calm the sea was turbulent with groundswell. Surf roiled to the convolutions of a maelstrom, a huge dilating white rose that had swallowed ships, and regurgitated spars and timbers for centuries round the coast.

Jan stopped to pick the occasional blackberry, and let the sweet purple ooze stain her fingers and tongue. When she bit into the grainy juice-sharp berry she felt alive to the moment and independent of the boredom and fear that had come to constitute her life. Her red anorak was silvered with raindrops, little globules that pinked on to the bracken when she walked. In three days' time the man she knew as Spike would be returning. He disappeared and reappeared with a punctuality that frightened her. She thought of him now, his red hair parted on the side, his pebble-grey eyes moving like fish behind his glasses, the thin rufous line of his moustache, and his habit of periodically clapping his hands together as though he'd trapped a thought for ever in the hollow of his hands. He sniffed like a rat at a grain sack, snivelled inwardly as though he was trying to isolate a peculiar scent from the many that assailed his sense of smell.

When Spike was here, she had to go out to the old millhouse. Bats lodged in the roof, and wind stepped around the walls with monotonous regularity. Some days she felt as if her head was porous and the wind was trapped inside it. Its persistence made her senses swim. The wind out there was like a goldfish travelling round and round the circumference of a crystal bowl.

She walked aimlessly towards the road. She would hitch back; after Spike, what did it matter who she encountered on these quiet roads. The wind rested in the hollow of her back; it lay there like the pressure of a fist. If only she could leave this desolate place, she thought, but she could never be free anywhere, not now she had become a part of Spike's circle at the millhouse. She could smell the autumn; rooks lifted in a black storm from a field, and haggled raucously all the way to the crumbled ruins of the defunct tin mines, where they roosted. Not a car on the road, only a local saloon taxi making for one of the outlying farmhouses.

You could disappear out here, and never be found again, Jan thought. The mine-shafts or the white rabid mouth of the sea, both would ingest and spit you out when you were bones protruding through an old fish-skin. Mist was beginning to blow in from the sea; it came in like vapour smoke off a cauldron that stretched between here and the seaboard coast of New England.

She quickened her pace, jogging for intervals of twenty yards and then slowing again to a brisk walk. Everything was starkly silhouetted against the mist. A gull creaked over on rusty hinges, and she could hear the foghorn setting up its sick-cow wail around the coast. The monotonal punctuated voice of a banshee. She hurried on. What appeared at a distance to be a stationary figure in black waiting for her was no more than a raised post-box on a stick or a hump-backed gorse bush. She was soaked through, her damp hair smelt like a soggy dog's coat drying out by the fire. Even if she did encounter a car, the driver would never slow on a chalky fogged-out coast-road. A motorbike droned by with the irate buzz of a hornet. She heard it map out the bend of the road, its gold light diffused into a trickle by the settling mist.

Things were reaching blotting-paper visibility. What had begun as the blue smoke of a sea-mist had rapidly walled itself into the opacity of impenetrable fog. Left hand, right hand, she tested how far away her eyes could travel. Her clothes were getting heavier; runnels of droplets trickled from her hair to her cheeks. She found herself pulling up every twenty yards in anticipation of an imminent collision. It was like walking with your eyes shut, she thought, as she pulled up abruptly for the fifth time, only to discover that she had been walking on the crown of the road. It was the stillness which impressed itself on her; there was no sound except that of the mewling foghorn blindly spooking the channel. She was suddenly insulated from everything and everyone. Now that the immediate panic had left her, she felt comforted by the protection that the fog afforded. What had been familiar and contoured was a no man's land of dense vapour. For the first time she felt she knew what it was like to be invisible; the cold air she breathed scintillated with beads of the Atlantic. Her clothes were diamonded with blue water-jewels. She felt crazily happy. Perhaps the fog wouldn't lift for days; it would crown her with a tiara of rainbowed coruscations.

She tapped her watch. Someone was calling her; no, it was only a trick of the silence. What had seemed only minutes of fog-blindness was in fact hours; she had been walking for two hours into a white smoke-screen. She sat down on a stone gate-post, and cradled her head on her knees. That voice again; 'Jan . . . Jan . . . ' She began to think they were out searching for her on the headlands. Instinct told her she must rejoin the road and find a farm or inn. Surely windows would come at her out of the blur; gold rectangles behind which were faces on the other side of the fog.

Her feet dabbed over the grass of a ghost-planet. What little wind there had been had died down; the sky was one immense thistle-plume momentarily suspended before the wind would chase it away. When her hands touched something cold and tangible it was glass. She had come face to face with a telephone box. She stepped inside in order to place herself at a remove from the fog that had walled her up in this cocoon of eddying drift. If anything it was getting thicker; the white smoke spirals had changed to a pearl-grey tactile substance. Jan looked at the number on the dial, and was astonished to find that she was still in Pendeen. She must have walked round and round, or gone astray on the moor at Carnyorth. She knew there was a pub just up the road from the telephone box. If she could keep on the road, the pub's bearings would be to the right. She was suddenly tired, and, when she looked down at her sodden mud-stained shoes, she realised she must have been up on the moor where the cow-paths were ruddled with mud.

She sat down on the floor of the booth. The fog couldn't reach her here; it thumbed the panes of glass, a big blue moth whose wingspan shadowed a county. Now she could hear it again, the wail of the foghorn at Pendeen Watch. Its bull-snorted metallic note went out to sea and was swallowed by the fog. She imagined the brilliant white light of the lighthouse's beam invisible in the all-enveloping swirl of white vapour. When she slipped back on to the road, she felt as if she had abandoned the last habitable outpost before setting out across the Urals.

It can't be this one, she thought, as she found herself spidering the gable of a house, following the right-angle around until she met with a curtained window. She could just discern the glow of a light-bulb shut out by the heavy material of the curtains. A dog began barking somewhere inside the house. She froze, and felt the cold imprint of fog against her cheek. She had somehow to find her way back to the gate, and follow the bend of the road for a short distance.

She stepped off again into a myopic's blur of grey haze. It was like facing a white wall that would give only if you forced yourself through it, and all that was on the other side was another wall and another wall. This is what it must be like to go mad, she thought; the light in your consciousness keeps on shadow-boxing with obstructions. Just when you think you're through the opacity of one screen, another imposes. It couldn't be far though, her feet were on the asphalt line of the road; if a car came out of the wall with a diffused primrose of light, she'd be lifted through the windscreen, the driver anaesthetised by the numb whiteness, his nerves lighting up in confusion as the split tomato of a skull projected itself on to his lap.

She drifted sideways again, caught off balance like a magpie blown into a rapid flurry by a cross-wind. She scraped against a jagged granite wall, and knew from memory that it was the car-park wall leading to the Smugglers' Arms. She jutted her elbow against it, smarting from the abrasion, and followed it as a guideline, a series of handholds she wouldn't remit, even though her fingernails tore out moss embedded in fissures. Now that she had become aware of time she repeatedly consulted her watch. It was 7.30; she estimated that the fog must have descended at 5.00. If she could get to the inn, she could at least secure warmth against the cold that was chilling her. They'd probably have a hearth fire, and the prospect of gorse-yellow flames leaping against a sooty chimney infused her with anticipated warmth.

She was almost there; her right shin jarred against the fender of a car she would have walked into. She rubbed up against its convex enamel, the front of it, and encountered another car. People must have been trapped here by the sudden mushrooming of sea-fog. An atmospheric rip-cord had released a parachute of dilating saturnine-rings. Now she had it; she could hear a concordance of voices behind the glass that divided her from the clear-sighted, those who had no reason to walk with their hands outstretched and their eyes hooded like a falcon's.

She found herself up against the door, face to it, her lips snail-tracking over the asperity of grain. When she located the other side, she was stunned by the clarity of vision that was suddenly hers. Curious eyes swivelled to meet the moon-faced bedraggled intruder from the outside world. She was exhausted; kind hands came to her rescue and sat her down in the firm support of a wooden chair. The lining of her mouth caught fire under the resonant amber ignition of brandy. She could feel its inflammatory vapour run to a blue flame over the scorched tissue of her throat. She was inhaling liquid fire, the pressure in the base of her skull dispersed, her eye-pupils ceased to be droplets of molten lead solidifying. Everything cleared and shone out. The curtains were drawn against the night, the voices heatedly discussed the possibility of ships going down, the cancellation of a snooker match, the unprecedented opacity of the coastal fog. 'This one will be called the big fog,' the barman arbitrated to a communal chorus of assent.

Jan looked at the concurring faces, then retracted like a snail recoiling into its shell. Right over in the far left corner of the bar, squinting from beneath a hound's-tooth cloth cap, was Spike. She could see the familiar red hair escaping over the tops of his ears, the eyes fidgeting near-sightedly behind his glasses. He was morosely staring into a head of Guinness; the beige froth standing above the dark liquid gave the glass the appearance of a painted bollard. He must have seen her, but he portrayed no sign of recognition. With his right hand he tapped a ballpoint pen on a red and white Marlboro packet, while his left was cradled in the pocket of a tweed hacking jacket. He could never get his clothes right, Jan thought; they were always too loose and seemed dissociated from the line of his body. Her loathing for this man would have had her back out into the fog again, but the brandy she had drunk had created a euphoria, a resinous hazel ring of well-being that expanded from the pit of her stomach to the dull throb in the back of her head.

She slipped up to the bar to buy a drink this time, and watched as the amber measure was decanted into her warm glass. No one questioned her age; they were too busy exchanging fishing anecdotes, and remembering former friends who had been lost at sea when a blanketing fog had come bubbling off the face of the deep. Jim Grebe was the most recent, only last summer his lobster-boat had broken up in mist, and they'd fished his botched body out of a cove weeks later. 'It was like a squid,' said a little white-haired man with a whippet, *it was marbled red and mauve with welts*, 'the face was a gaping wound. They had a job to identify him but it was Jim Grebe all right.' His widow still kept on the cottage at Cape Cornwall; someone had been out to see her that weekend.

Jan froze; she could feel Spike's furtive eyes searching her out, travelling over her body like an intangible light-ray. She didn't look up; she stared fixedly at the dart-board and then at the Breda beer-mats on her table. He must have been travelling out to the millhouse and stopped off here when the fog came up. The van would be out in the car-park. His lack of sociable manner meant he had no friends locally. He sat like someone both used to and perturbed by his own company. If he had suddenly to divulge his thoughts he would be anywhere, but not here. He lit another cigarette, prolonging the action, grateful for the distraction it caused.

When he did come over it was with his usual insidious movements, so that suddenly he was sitting in the chair beside her, when it had looked like he was taking a circuitous route to the conveniences. She heard the weigght of his glass resonate on the table, and smarted under the double blue column of smoke that issued from his nostrils. 'Didn't expect to find you here,' he said perfunctorily. 'Playing truant from the village, are you?' Jan didn't answer. In a crowd her oppressor appeared diminutive;

the big waters of his private pool left him stranded in the company of others. He resembled a dogfish thrown up by the tide. Jan was determined to ignore him; she would rebuff him with a wall of implacable silence. 'I'm down for a few days,' he said, 'I was going to send you a message tomorrow. This damned fog has anchored me here for hours. You got caught out in it, did you?' She thought of her pet jackdaw called Silver. She could see the brightness of his eye coruscating like a raindrop. *The sooty blue of his plumage, the damaged wing which he trailed that had never properly repaired, the grey ear coverts and the bluish irises.* He was more distinct in the clarity of her mind's eye than in reality. Spike was still talking. 'I'd like you to come out to the millhouse tomorrow, Jan,' he said, but she heard him from a long way away as though he was speaking long-distance on a line that was badly connected. She knew that for once she held the ascendant; he couldn't create a scene in front of the locals and, if he did, she would expose him. The insulation and calm that the fog afforded had opened up a lucidity of perception that had been previously closed to her. The process of blurring had sharpened her senses in retrospect.

'So you're ignoring me, are you?' he said. 'Do you want another drink?' She stared off stonily, resentful that even here his red shadow would fall on her. He was a weasel or stoat, a little man slinking through the grasses to prey on those who lacked proper defences.

He went up to the bar and got himself another drink. It was his insignificance that surprised her; she had always seen him too close and so not seen him at all. Today she could perceive the slight stoop in his shoulders, the isolation apparent in his demeanour, the chubby nicotined fingers that raked in his bar change. She noticed too, for the first time, the slight defect in his posture, how his head and body leaned fractionally towards the left. The barman was slow to serve him; no one seemed to want to acknowledge his presence.

He didn't attempt to rejoin Jan; he went back and sat on his stool, and pretended to absorb himself in a local newspaper. Jan knew he wasn't reading it; his eyes were watching everything to left and right, his glasses were a screen for his innate furtiveness.

The second brandy was sending up detonating satellites behind her eyes; everything it pained her to remember was flooding her consciousness with needle-fine precision. It was two years ago; she was walking back from school to the village through autumn lanes yellowed with crisp drifts of chestnut leaves. The hedges were scarlet with hawthorn; the sky was a windy azure with amethyst rain clouds bowling across it. The car was on her before she was aware of its existence; he must have rolled it down the hill with the engine shut off and the window turned down, for when she responded to his voice, it was as though he was walking level with her, only lower down, working his voice up to her height. 'I'm on the road to Zennor,' he said, 'why don't you jump in, you can show me the way.' She stood there mesmerised, frightened at first, and then curious, and he got out and went round to the other side of the car and opened the door for her. 'I don't want to get lost,' he said. 'I'm heading for the old millhouse, I've taken a lease on it. Why don't you come out and see it?' he added. 'It still needs substantial renovation, but come and look around, and then I'll drive you home.' She neither consented nor refused; she felt powerless before his effortless decisions on her behalf and the soporific blow-back of the car heater.

'It's just off the road to the right,' he said, after what seemed like a series of endlessly circuitous detours. There was a wind blowing, and a moor stepped off on to the horizon, clouds building to a bank of heather – mauve and flinty blue. The house was sparsely furnished downstairs; a maroon rug, a table and chairs, things left or grouped together without purpose. 'Now I'll show you the upstairs,' he said, and she followed, not really knowing why, only that she had to, and he pushed a door ajar into a room in which there was no light, only a chink like an elongated silver hairpin dancing into the volume of black. 'This is my room,' he said, wading into the airless void, so that she could only hear and not see him. He sounded a long way off, as though he was speaking into the base of a bottle through the neck. It was a dead sound, an indistinct Tannoy's metallic haze. 'Where are you?' he called out, when it should have been she who was enquiring of his whereabouts. 'I'm over in the far corner,' he squeaked, imitating a bat's flight. She stayed put in the doorway, the steep flight of steps dead-dropping behind her. 'Come and find me,' he persisted, and she froze. She knew what was going to happen; she imagined the balls of his fingers finding her out, the gradual increase of pressure as he tightened his grip. She couldn't believe that she was still free to act, that a hoop of air surrounded her waist. He's mad, she thought, but his ventriloquial acts were terrifying; he assumed the whinny of a horse, the hoot of an owl, the hiss of a cat. She could make him out in a fold of the curtains, doubled into himself, expelling his voice through the constricted passage of his throat. Then he came at her in a circle, a wide sweep that emphasised his control over the room, and then narrowing in with each successive run. His eyes weren't even on her; they were focused on the ritual he was performing inside his head, the weird dilation and contraction of a frenzied ring. She stood there mesmerised, her muscles not even responding as he worked in closer, low down, dropping almost on all fours, rounding her up as he spun like a top slowing its orbit to a still centre. She kept waiting for his rough hands to find her out but, when the mad frenzy of his delirium had slowed, he dropped down at her feet. He had removed his glasses, so that she didn't fully recognise his face; the areas of exposed skin around his eyes looked like the bald patches on red-necked fledglings. In the silence she could hear a tap dripping; it was the leak of his nose, a red bubble followed by another red bubble was escaping from his nostrils to the carpet. The silence was terrible. The throb of her own heart was that of a muffled hammer hitting a wall in the adjacent field. Each diastolic beat swung back and hit her.

The displacement of air told her that she was walking backwards, one step, two steps, three, and he was following her on his hands and knees, only it wasn't her that he was looking at; it was her scent that he was following, like a dog blinded by the stag that still hangs on in the pitch of its momentum. Her stiff legs were too upright; somehow they wouldn't bend to take the pressure of her weight, and then she was falling. It was the whirr of the ceiling that was incongruously travelling with her, and she went backwards down the stairs, her back punched hard by a stone ridge, her legs suddenly remotivated as they kicked out without any surface to hold on to, and Spike's face was left behind as though she'd been looking at him through the close-up of binoculars, and was now looking at him through the blinding lights of her eyes.

When she came to, he was sitting smoking in the kitchen. The light hurt her head; she seemed to have no layer of protection against it – it was like having one's unlidded eyes pressed into a mirror. He looked at her as though he wasn't sure whether she'd remember the scene prior to her falling downstairs. 'I'd better take you home, soon,' he said; 'here, have a sip of brandy and water, you'll feel better after that.' She obeyed mechanically, and gagged as the liquor set her throat ablaze. Things were coming back to her; she remembered his ventriloquial squeals, the delirious rhythm of his mimetic spasm. Then the telescopic overshoot into unconsciousness, the light of her consciousness going out like a white hare into the dark of a hole. He was sucking tobacco grains off his lip, saying, *sometimes one has to go to the edge, but you know I was acting, don't you? I do these things occasionally, and out here there's no one to see.* She was too shocked to hate him; she could see the intermittent wander of his left eye, as though it didn't quite fit beneath the lid and wanted to come free. 'I'll take you home soon,' he kept saying to himself, 'then you can come out here another day and just look around on your own. The house is quiet; if you want to use it as a den, instead of going to school, you're very welcome.'

She didn't say anything; the pain in the back of her head was turned on like a white floodlight. She couldn't locate how she had got here instead of there – the road home had been a simple one; there were sloe-berries and hawthorn, and red and white posters advertising a forthcoming paperchase. Out here there was wind, the big spaces in a lonely man's head; he had viewed her as someone to take inside his mental zoo.

'I'd like to go back,' she said, 'I'm expected home before six.'

'You will come again, though,' he mused, and she realised that if he apologised he would be putting himself in the wrong; he still couldn't determine how much of the jigsaw puzzle had broken up when she fell.

She hadn't hated him then as she did now; his chemistry had asserted a fascination that compelled her in the way that birds fly into lighthouse cupolas on stormy nights. On the drive back she had mentioned nothing. He was going to Paris on business, and she was occupied with studying for A levels. He had dropped her off in the lane before her house. She, rather than he, had said, 'I'll see you the next time you come to the millhouse.' When she got into the lane, the sky had turned a patchy black ultramarine, rain clouds were bull-charging across the sky. He had waited with his headlights turned on; he was still there when she looked back before opening the gate and hurrying up the path.

He was watching her again from his corner of the bar.

87

Suddenly he had sidled over to the window, drawn the curtain back, and returned to his seat. The big fog was still occluding the sky; it was the colour of a moonstone, it was wall-eyed and impenetrable.

The brandy was putting a firelit lining in her head. A third glass had been placed beside her second; he must have put it there without her seeing. This was his art, and the art of the kleptomaniac; his eyes asserted such a powerful magnetism that, drawn towards them, you never got to see the actions of his hands.

A second time, a third time, a fourth, she found her footsteps directed towards the millhouse; she didn't know why she went there. She was alternately attracted and repelled, and one day she found herself simulating a voyeur; she crept round the house, looking in through every pane, and found him in the kitchen. He was sitting contemplating his features in a portable shaving-mirror. He stayed there a long time, holding the pose, pressing his nether lip down with a finger, trying the angles of his cheeks; she was fascinated by his narcissistic experiments. Was he looking for the right face, the one he recognised as his own, but which was rarely seen, the mask kept hidden within, the mental image of the self that no one else ever knows or sees? Eventually he got up and lit a cigarette. He placed his two hands behind his head and stood contemplating a stone wall. It was like a film, she thought; when people are alone they act out the inner dialogue they never dare reveal to others. When he left the room abruptly, she waited, then went round to the front of the house and knocked. She didn't know what compelled her to act in this way, or why she was seeking out the company of a man who had terrified her with his ventriloquial chortles, the bat or owl mask of the theriomorphic god.

She stayed at the millhouse overnight, telephoning her parents from a call-box with the fiction of her collaborating on a study project with a school-friend. When she woke up in the light of the early morning she felt she was overexposed, that she was so naked that no envelope of skin could ever conceal her inner life. She burrowed like a mole into the dark huddle of blankets and cried. She had lost her imperviousness; henceforth strangers would look right through, her skin had assumed the transpicuous texture of glass.

He spoke to her, in his less guarded moments, of David, his

son, who was a few years older than she, and of the grist of his broken marriage. Periodically he would visit Paris; he had told her that his income came from an area in life that she wouldn't understand. He called it his unresolved conflict. At other times he would denounce everything he had told her, and the pattern of confusion was terrifying; she felt he comprised too many selves for her ever to find a single focus into his person. There was already talk in the village of his intermittent comings and goings, before she had learnt to hate him. That hate had grown up overnight, over one particular night in which she vowed to put a spade through his heart when he was buried.

She put her glass down, and the headlights of the van were again acidly powering into her face.

It was a cold day in March. Garrulous rooks had begun nest-building in the elms. He had come down after an absence of two months and taken her to St Ives. The day was luminously blustery – lilac clouds scudded across a sky that alternated between grey and blue. They drove back through quiet roads; he had a fixation about the van not being seen too often passing through villages. They pulled into the overhang of a copse, and she said she didn't want to see him again. She thought he was settling the shock within himself; his calm was disquieting, he checked his identity and let it stabilise in the rear-view mirror. 'People are talking,' she said, and he didn't reply. He resembled someone in the interval between swallowing a sleeping tablet and its becoming absorbed into the bloodstream. She could hear the clamour of rooks through the partially open van window. He didn't say anything, he went on looking at that nothing which is something, jumped out of the van, and opened the rear doors. She was too numb to predict his movements, the ruckling grind and anvil-like percussion, as he began to smash in the front bonnet with an iron bar. She stared out disbelievingly as he wielded the instrument, his face knotted into a white fury, the headlights splintering in frosted shards over the grass. She was so frightened that she couldn't hear him, she could see only the fish-mouthed 'O's of his imprecations, and instinct had her throw herself to the left and out of the door, as the windscreen shattered into a spray of polished fragments. It looked like ice, except that each splinter was a jagged vicious barb.

She didn't wait this time. She ran, and in the panic of her flight, she overtook herself. There were two Jans; one that ran

89

like a hare beside her in the grass, and the other labouring under the gulping intake of air that scorched her lungs. How many roads were there to her village? They seemed to have sprung up as she ran, multiplying themselves into a maze. Nothing was familiar; she was running towards a landscape that invented itself as she ran. When she got home, her teeth still shook; she told her parents that she had caught cold in the wind, and went straight up to her room. Had it really happened? The diamond studs of glass on the backs of her hands were a confirmation that it had.

For days afterwards she lived in a state of delayed shock. There was a division between what she saw and felt, what was spoken and what she heard. She was late on the uptake; someone told her she was sleepwalking. For nights she dreamed that she was in a labyrinth, and each turning led to another and another impasse. The blood on the wall of the slain monster's den was brushed into the word Spike.

She jerked back and forth between the past and present. She had still to return through miles of fog, and the red-eyebrowed weasel had her scent. She tried to convince herself that she was safe; she had only to make a telephone call to her parents, a friend's house and, when the fog lifted, she could be collected. She didn't want to look at him; his magnetic field might reassert its centre of gravity in the electric mains of her nerves. He had a way of looking down at his glass like a rook in the act of jabbing the earth with its beak. He seemed forever to be concentrating on some invisible light globe that was discernible to him alone, a particle sensitised by his retina on to a light-plate. When that globe expanded his mind blew up in proportion to it; he entered on a theriomorphic dance of self-destruction.

Out of one ear she could connect with a fisherman's yarn; someone was talking about a forty- or fifty-pound conger that had been lined in at the back end of January. Its open jaws had dog-barked on coming to the surface, its lip a museum of rusty fish-hooks. Its powerful girth had lashed the boatboards; Robert Hawker had lost his index finger before they had squared up with it. And the night afterwards, again bottom-fishing in the graveyard of the deeps, they'd fouled with an eel that dragged the boat round in a circle. Its head was as thick as a bulldog's; they'd seen its massive trunk of a body in the boat-light before it had cut free and dived for the bottom. And the night after that at the ebb . . .

90

Spike was a long way from their world. This man of adopted masks, morosely drinking, while the alcohol puddled in the cave of his stomach. She looked at her watch. It was 9.00. If the fog was still down at closing time she'd face Spike and a white wall. Her panic was irrational; no one would be evicted on a night like this, but the proximity to danger was too close – she was already beginning to feel like a fly that had jerked free of its brushing contact with a spider's web, but at the cost of a leg or wing.

The fog wouldn't lift; the landlord telephoned the local meteorological station to be told that there would be no improvement until noon the next day. The fog had earthed itself and come to stay; the lighthouse was an abominable snowman wailing from the edge of the world to the white spaces.

Jan was intent on devising an escape, so she surrounded herself with a calm that would deflect from her intentions. Spike had taken it for granted that she wouldn't go back to the fog, and for the first time she noticed he was reading a local paper, and not simply scanning it as a means of deflecting attention away from his scrutiny of the room. Very quietly, she put her glass down, and walked unobtrusively towards the ladies'. He must have watched her go, but her movements could arouse no suspicion. She went on through the outer door into the inner cubicle. It was cold in there due to the damp, and an open window looked out over the fogbound car-park. *What if she got free only to fall over a cliff; wouldn't it be better to stay put under lights that afforded protection against the blue smoke-hole of the Atlantic?* She clambered up and stared out. There was nothing to see. A ground-floor window that she had only to squeeze out of to reach the tarmac of the car-park below. It was too easy, and while she was thinking that, she felt the palms of her hands pressing against the gritty surface of stone. Her hands took the weight of her body and caterpillared her out into the night. She stood up; she had only to move ten paces forward and the inn lights were obscured – she could neither see nor hear anything. She swung her arms round like a windmill but the fog wouldn't disperse. She was stone-cold and shivering, and broke into a hesitant run in order to restore warmth to her body. She veered left, establishing that she was wide of the inn, and by lowering herself on to the crown of the road she made out the fluorescent white traffic line. She must learn to feel with her feet, to keep on the road; anything to right or left could lead to danger.

91

She started out at a quick pace, her hair was matted again from moisture; the cold air formed pockets in her stomach. She knew she'd done the wrong thing, but she couldn't repair it; the fog broke up around her movements like segments of a thistle's pappus and then regrouped again. She must have run steadily for fifteen minutes; her footsteps were like a heartbeat in the insulating fog. Suddenly someone was calling her name; she could hear the syllables pitched into the fog, and the echo return to the ovally strained mouth of her pursuer. She stopped and put her hands to her head. How could anyone have followed her zig-zag line through the opacity of a fog that walled her in like a gravestone? She'd come off the road; her baseball boots felt the springy marram grass beneath her feet. She guessed she must be on the headland, and all the time the voice was growing louder: 'Jan, J-a-a-n, J-A-A-N. Where are you?'

The timbre of the voice was Spike's but she couldn't under-stand how he could be pursuing her. No one could follow you through that smoke-drift unless you were luminous. She found herself on her wet knees in the grass, then she raised her voice and shouted her own name. 'J-A-A-A-A-N.' It was a howl of dementia. She listened to the echo; the other voice didn't reply. She must have been running and shouting out her name to the blank moon-face of the sky. The damp was inside her skin; she could feel the unwelcome osmosis threaten to fill her body like a water balloon. She would have to begin the search for bearings again, find a call-box when she got back on to the road, and assess her direction. The soggy bulk of her clothes weighed like a diver's suit; she headed off in the opposite direction, feeling with her feet and hands, expecting at any moment to locate the hard surface of the road. She had to invest the balls of her feet with the sensitivity of her finger-tips, and as she walked she developed a pathological fear of glass, of quarry pits that yawned with a rusty-eye of water at their base. She could smell her own fear – it had the scent of cold stone, of moss packed between mortared crevices in a wall.

When the road came up to meet her feet she burst into a fit of spontaneous and uncontrolled laughter. What she had always taken for granted had now become the guideline by which she would balance her life against the suffocating opalescence of the fog. She broke into a run again; her lungs sawed at the damp air. Her wet feet squeaked with every stride. Getting there was everything – if she could ever locate a place at which to arrive. Memories from her childhood began to stream into her head. There was the first of the wrecks she could remember. A trawler had gone down in heavy seas with all hands lost, she had never forgotten the angry green of that sea, a glowering stormy grape-green, and for days people from the village combed the shingle cove, raking up driftwood, looking out for the lacerated bodies that had fallen a prey to the sea's undertow. After that, the loss of fishermen had become a way of life for her, those who lived on the ocean eventually became fouled on its reefs. Some never came ashore, others were smashed to a string of gristle on bone and were lodged by the wave on the foreshore. Mauve and blue and red, their bodies were scarcely identifiable.

The faces of the drowned streamed through her consciousness. She had met with them again in the frozen contorted mouths and eyes of fish laid out on the marble of fishmongers' slabs. The blood trace still apparent on the mullet's lip; the crescent moon of the skate's mouth; the oval rictus of the bass frozen in the instant of death, its mouth proclaiming an unspoken agony. How many miles to go? And if the fog never lifted she would be a figure running towards the edge of the world; she would disappear like the drowned into the sea's mouth.

'How much further?' she kept reiterating. The words had shaped themselves to conform to the pattern of her breathing. She kept firmly to the surface of the road, following its bends, lining her strength up with each new prospect of the straight, labouring a hill and falling flat on her face with exhaustion at the top.

She could get there now. Archways were beginning to appear in the fog wall, spirals and whorls, an architecture of shapes that allowed her to see chinks in the distance. She was obsessed with the fear that Spike might somehow get through – what if he was waiting for her at the other end? She looked at her watch. It was fractionally after midnight; her parents would be up and awake worrying about her, anxiously telephoning her friends only to find that no one knew of her whereabouts. She had constantly to ward off the desire to sleep which overcame her; sleep was the inner mist which threatened to erase her consciousness. She fought against an inner and outer smoke-screen.

When she came to she checked her watch. She had slept for fifteen minutes face down in the middle of the road. A dog was barking somewhere, and she seemed to be looking through a series of arched bridges, each finely delineated by charcoal lines of smoke. The fog was shifting; it was wreathing itself into patchy curlicues. She couldn't understand the sudden infusion of light. She looked at her watch a second time; it was 7.00. She must have slept for hours. She could just discern the gable of a house, and somewhere the tangerine of the sunrise was watering through. There was a primrose glow behind the fog; light was returning to the world.

She dragged herself towards the silhouette of the house. As she did so, the dog's alarm increased. It must be outside the house, she thought, its voice challenged her every footstep. When the animal growled and she spoke to it, pacifying its territorial vigilance, she realised that there was light enough to see its eyes. She was looking at the chocolate-coloured eyes of a nondescript black mongrel as though it was an act of visual retrieval, as though she was seeing clearly for the first time. The dog warmed to her; its tongue found her hand as she pressed the yellow cat's-eye of a doorbell. She didn't see who hauled her in out of the damp, but was aware only that the voice was beginning again inside her – 'J-A-A-N, J-A-A-N'. It followed her all the way into unconsciousness.

7

Diane looked at the note David had left behind; a sensitive calligraphic hand, the blue ink running to occasional rose-thorns on the scrap of paper he had salvaged from her desk.

Dear Diane,
    I know you will be surprised at my electing to take off into the unknown, but my nervous condition is such that I feel a burden in company, and a stranger to myself when alone.
    I may stay in London for a short time, although I begin to think that I should go home. At least there, I'm on familiar territory.
    Your kindness has meant a great deal to me, and rest assured that if I can't find a way through I'll return. No matter what, I hope we can meet again under less strained circumstances. I'll send you an address, once I am a little more settled.

With thanks,
David

She sat down and tried to envisage his movements in the city. She hoped he had taken the underground back to Liverpool Street, and was now sitting in a carriage making the slow painful journey home. He would recognise nothing, she thought; things looked so different on the return journey. The way forward was never the way back; things hardly seen in the rush of anticipation gave way to preconception, the expectation of familiar things informing you that nothing had changed. When she thought of the possibility of his being adrift in the city, she grew alarmed at the sound of sirens – the urgent ululation of a police car snaking through jammed lanes of traffic, or the sibilant tonnage of a fire-engine powering its way towards a burning office-block. She thought of his mind pulsing like a bell inside the fragile dome of its skull – the transmission of its alarm-signals an endless telex semaphored in red ink.

David slid the window up and stared into an empty room that bore the psychic signature of its owner. The air was redolent with cigar smoke, that masculine scent of decaying rose petals with which he was familiar on Dr Moravia's person. Before travelling to London, he'd stolen one of Dr Moravia's letters to his father, the one on which he'd used the heading of his home address, and not that of his Harley Street practice.

He'd reconnoitred the empty street, and got into the back garden by an off-the-latch door. Face up to the back of the house he couldn't be seen, pear trees screened the one wall which was overlooked, together with a green welter of ivy and straggled honeysuckle. Gold chrysanthemums bushed the garden, and hectic spiky dahlias, scarlet and maroon and pink, fringed like stars, a galaxy of starched pleats in the late September sunlight.

The back door was locked, but a push-up window had been left partially open. Certain that by this hour Dr Moravia would be at his practice, David manoeuvred himself head-first through the window, got inside, opened the back door, and took his suitcase out of view. His obsession with the doctor, that had led him to wear a purple satin tie, had brought him to search out the man's residence. In an oblique way David held him responsible for Branden's existence; Dr Moravia had stirred up the sediment-whirlpool of a subconscious that was better left with the flat sea-surface of a serene high tide. His probing had unleashed Branden's fox-eared persona, that wiry red bolt which had sprung through the bracken into the tunnel of his skull.

The downstairs room was green and mauve; scattered periodicals and books lay on a glass-topped table, there was an inlaid writing-desk with a shaded lamp and two silver candlesticks. David realised that it must be his sitting-room, there was a record-player and miscellaneous album sleeves, Mahler, Delius, Mozart, Monteverdi. Bottles were grouped on a small drinks-table; David uncapped a bottle of whisky and took copious gulps.

It was the upstairs that attracted him; he wanted to root into the most intimate secrets of his psychiatrist's life. The house was spacious and built on three floors; he went from room to room, a book-lined study, a guest-room, a bathroom with gilt taps in the shape of dolphins' heads, a rose-pink room which looked as though it might have suited a maid, and then another flight of stairs leading up to an attic bedroom.

David pushed the door to and found himself breathless with anticipation. It was a weird symbiosis, this desire to conjoin himself with a stranger's life through his personal effects. The bedroom had a feminine smell, an amalgam of perfumes and colognes commingled in a static heady dust. A satinwood commode stood by the bed, and on it were figurines, a Sèvres vase supported by gilt dolphins; on one wall there was a round fan painting of a bush clover in Rimpa style, the eighteenth-century Chinese wallpapers depicting coloured birds and insects poised on branches had a backdrop of brilliant green. A Fabergé gold-mounted strut clock stood on a black laquered table beside the bed. There were mirrors let into the ceiling above the bed; a black silk counterpane translated the light into a night sea. David looked at these things in awe; he felt he had trespassed on the inner sanctuary, the aesthetic sensibility of the man was copied out in the things he had gathered around him.

Tentatively, but irrepressibly, David began his search. The commode and desk drawers were locked, but when he swung open one of the wide mirrored wardrobe panels, the face that sensuously laughed out at him was that of the blonde woman he had discovered in his father's wallet. Only she was bigger here; the photograph was blown up to poster size. The cosmetic lines were overaccentuated; they were designed to conceal the face; and the lips, framing the voluptuousness of a lipsticked pout, were heavily sensuous; they reminded David of a vermilion rose which is beginning to collapse around its centre. In this panel of the wardrobe were a dozen suits, wool and linen for winter and summer, and above these on a shelf were hundreds of yellow Kodak photograph folders. He resisted the temptation to begin riffling through these, and instead swung open the other panel to be met by a multicoloured rainbow of silk ties. Five or six deep, each meticulously hung on its tie-holder; the colour spectrum was dazzling. Each was a miniature rainbow; the stripes flickered like the iridescent bands of a waterfall. David found himself filling his pockets with the most extravagantly eye-catching, surprised by his compunctious avarice. Mauve and red and green silks spilled from his pockets; it was as though by identifying with these possessions he was taking on the powers of the man himself.

He strung a pink and silver tie around his dingily creased Viyella shirt, and stared at the poster-sized photograph which complemented the first. This one was taken from the torso down, and exemplified the long shapely legs sheathed in black nylon that had been so much the prominent feature of his father's wallet-sized photograph. The stiletto heels supporting elegant black pointed suede shoes must have been seven or eight inches in height. The wardrobe was stacked with cologne bottles; Vêtiver by Guerlain, Jules by Dior, an unopened flask-shaped bottle of First de Van Cleef & Arpels; felt hats from Tommy Nutter of Savile Row, and silk handkerchiefs grouped like a bed of pansies, dark bordeaux reds, ivy-green, blue with a red polka-dot, flamingo and turquoise jockey-silks. David put a holly-red handkerchief into his top pocket; he was becoming part of Dr Moravia's identity. He lay back on the bed unable to repress the acute sexual desire that the black silk counterpane induced in him. Light filtered into the room through Venetian blinds; the muted, sumptuous quality of everything had David languorously stretch out like a cat and savour the exhaustion of the last days. He had to fight against the sleep which would have overwhelmed him had he submitted; he had to keep on exploring, he told himself – the more he identified with Moravia, the more he would hold Branden at bay. Instead of Branden entering his head, he would enter Dr Moravia's.

Supine, spreadeagled on the bed, the light played over his body in a dusting of gold. Branden was temporarily held in abeyance; David felt his nerves pull tight and revelled in their synchronicity – he must learn to close the gaps in the circuit and keep the fox out. He must have slept, for he awoke with the sudden lightning bolt of a fish breaking the surface of the water, the sulphurous zig-zag spiralled into his consciousness, his heart beat out the drum-rhythm of a tribe in the hills. He remembered the photographs, the tiered stacks of yellow folders, and jumped up from the bed, his hands unloading the visual inventory of Dr Moravia's private life.

He opened the first folder and, as he had envisaged, the wallet was packed tight with photographs of the blonde woman who stared out at him from the wardrobe poster. The photographs were obsessive in their detailed fetishism; the first showed a series of thirty shots of her lips, each fibre visible through the film of lipstick, the tongue protruding or withdrawn, the expressive stylisation always erotic, always provoking a loaded sensory response. Moravia had marked the wallet 'Autumn – Dior Holly Red'. The folders were clearly categorised anatomical studies; David spent a long time poring over the wallets marked 'Legs', the seamed black stockings, the nib-thin stiletto heels. The wardrobe was a photographic vault; he began scooping out armfuls of yellow folders, they splashed over the carpet like an autumn fall of leaves. The whisky that he had gulped was taking effect; it had mounted from his stomach to his head, he could feel his thoughts rotating with the slightly warped revolutions of a record on the turntable of a record-player. A gold sunburst of light was flaring up inside his head, the dust-motes dazzled like moths, he could feel the energy-charge shoot like starlight through his veins.

In a spontaneous blaze of energy he stripped his clothes off, and pulled down a green mohair suit from the wardrobe-rail. He fished a pastel-pink shirt out of a linen drawer, and shivered as the cool lawn material moulded itself incongruously to his body. It fitted his shoulders, but was too loose at the waist. He slipped into the suit trousers, packing the shirt in where the waist-band didn't meet. When he caught sight of his eyes in the mirror they were black dilated marbles; they were so fixed that he wondered how they co-ordinated with the fish-jumpy fluidity of his nerves. He was preparing himself for the sensual ritual of fastening the tie he had already selected. He knotted it slowly, working the knot upwards; when he pulled it tight into position he wanted to assume his doctor's identity. The jacket was sufficiently tapered to become him; the pink rose-bud of the tie-knot intermeshed him with the other man's psychophysical presence. He found himself measuring out Dr Moravia's considered sentences: *but, David, could this be due to a disharmony between your mind and body? Don't you think that if you normalised your hours of sleeping you'd be better equipped to meet with the demands of the day? The need to retire from the company of others may suggest your inability to make a friend of yourself.* Whole sentences formed and re-formed in his mind, the energy-blaze he had experienced was having him turn the room inside out and upside down. It was only after his hands had raided a drawer that his mind connected. The carpet was littered with shirts and photograph wallets, aluminium cigar-tubes, books, a miscellany of keys and pens. It was then he began to grow frightened; the cold reality intruded on him that he was in a stranger's house, at any moment he could be apprehended. The reversion of his stimulus was a chilling sobriety; he wanted to disown his actions, to walk off and claim that another had done this, and that he, David, was the horrified witness of an act of reckless vandalism.

Once or twice he startled, but it was only the wind riffling through the Venetian blinds. It was 11.30. He stood at the window overlooking the street, uncertain as to whether he was a participant in the action of the moment, or had performed this all in the mimetic dance of a dream. There was blood on one of his fingers; he must have scratched the nail-crescent on a coat-hanger, three red ladybirds had flecked the white of a dress-shirt. It's like a robin in snow, he thought, as he ran to the adjoining bathroom and watched red whorls of blood caught up in the whirlpool of spinning water. He found a plaster in an onyx-handled cabinet, and staunched the blood-flow. It hadn't occurred to him what he would do if someone came back to the house. How could he be sure that Dr Moravia lived alone, and what if a housekeeper or friend disturbed him trampling on the trophies of his morning's pillage?

The air in his lungs was becoming oppressively heavy. The flow of oxygen was gritty like sawdust; he could feel the pressure building up in him like the static heat preceding a thunder-storm. He ran downstairs and nearly choked on a copious drag of whisky; the flame candled inside him and burnt with a steady blue light. Upstairs again, he went into the spare-room; it was all rose and pink pastels with a Victorian dressing-screen of filigree roses embossed on flamingo silk. There was a sepia photographic portrait beside the bed; it was a head and shoulders of a woman, her deep-centred almond-shaped eyes appeared to be looking at something the photographer could never have divined. Her intense light of inner focus was concentrated to intersect with the shutter's click. She had high cheek-bones and clustered ringlets, a single emerald or sapphire star stood out in the hollow of her throat. David opened the wardrobe and found it stacked with books, more photograph wallets, and a blue velvet-lined jewel-box in which there were a gold heart-shaped locket, a sapphire and diamond engagement ring, the sapphire star pendant at her throat, miscellaneous drop-earrings that scintillated with the crystalline light of snow, the thin gold band of a wedding ring on which baroque cupids had been traced, and a small notebook in which she had written out poems by Hölderlin, Valéry, de Nerval, Shelley, and lyrics by Herrick and Lovelace. David scrutinised each detail, he copied everything out in his nerves; he needed to in order to enforce the fiction of his new identity.

When his watch registered noon, he estimated that he should stay no more than another hour. It was possible that Dr Moravia would be without afternoon appointments; he felt an uneasy presentiment run like an insect up the length of his spine. When he tried to establish order in the looted debris of the bedroom, the whisky had his nerves misfire. In his efforts to rehouse the photograph wallets he succeeded in creating a landslide of folders. Things were moving too fast, he told himself, a rift was opening that threatened to swallow him into the vicious turbulence of a maelstrom. For the first time since he had left Diane's flat he felt acute pangs of hunger; he hurried downstairs again and raided the refrigerator, ladling paté and rounds of cucumber between wedges of bread, and cramming his mouth with the snaffling ferocity of a starved dog. Food had the effect of slowing down the orbit of his mind. He was learning to focus again without disjuncts in time, and to associate himself with the reality of his actions. He was suddenly frightened; it was he, David, and not a fictitious persona, who was responsible for the mosaic of disorder in the upstairs bedrooms. But frightened as he was he couldn't extract himself from the house; he was compelled as if by a magnet to retrace his steps back to the attic bedroom.

The stillness of the room reassured him; he could almost make believe that he was lying in the old barn relating his mental journeys to Bunny. The sunlight had formed a solid gold bar on the counterpane. He lay back with the light crossing his body, drowsy again, but cat-alert to the least sound. He envisaged Moravia returning to the house, his shocked consternation on finding an intruder in his sanctuary. David tried to imagine the cinematics of the man's reactions – his slow-motion or speeded-up responses – his controlled or hysterical voice.

Fascinated by the aluminium tubes containing cigars, he uncapped one, and inhaled its resonance of balsa-wood before proceeding to light it and savour the blue smoke which tasted of rose-petal tea, of a slightly musty wine fermented in scented casks. His absorption of the man's idiosyncrasies was complete. He stood in front of the mirror in the tailored mohair suit and created a mist of cigar smoke. He began to question his motives in Moravia's voice, studiously focusing his averted eyes on an imperceptible dust-mote in space. The floor was solid beneath his feet; if he kept on acting like this he could hold Branden at bay.

It was the inroad of air setting the dust-motes dancing like gnats over a pond that told him that someone had entered by the back of the house even before he heard the door open and as suddenly close. Someone was dragging a box over the floor; he could hear the tinkle of glass as the angular walls of the bottles jingled. The box was sandpapered into the kitchen, and he could hear the bottles being unloaded, the slight stomp of those placed on a flat wooden surface, others were being secured in a rack of the refrigerator. The air-spiralling flip-flop of a cap told him that someone was pouring out a lager. The image of a white head on the blond liquid rose to his mind; his mouth was furred with a parched thirst after the dehydrating process of the whisky.

He stood stock-still for what seemed an indefinite period, extinguished the volcano-tip of his cigar, and picked one thought out of the teeming fry of messages that jammed his head. He had to get down to the next floor, slip into the pink bedroom, and make a hurried exit as Moravia climbed to his attic bedroom. He figured out that he could escape in the moments when Moravia's shocked surprise held him transfixed to the disorder on the carpet. David's movements were cat-light, he couldn't remember how he came to be free of his shoes, only that he was. He was about to exit from the room when he remembered his case. He'd lugged it upstairs with him. A spotlight came on in his memory and played over the contents, the things he had taken with him in the event of his never returning to Norfolk. A few clothes, a few books, his notebooks; he had travelled light, but the weight had increased with his own fatigue.

Whoever had entered the house was pacing around below; David sensed it was someone who had detected the scent of an intruder – he could hear things being picked up and put down. He tried to remember whether he had replaced the whisky cap; to a man as meticulously ordered as Dr Moravia the slightest displacement of an object would signal the introduction of a foreign hand. And crumbs on the floor, traces of food; fortunately in his hunger he hadn't used a knife and plate, but he had eaten rapaciously, negligent of the scraps he dropped. It was as though he could follow the man's movements through a glass lens inserted into the eye of a whirlpool. The accelerating pulse, the slight churn of the stomach, the realisation that someone's eye film had tracked over possessions known only to him. He must have been seeing things as his eye had never seen them before; surfaces had a new clarity, and depth a more lucid opacity. His movements were quicker now; he was clearly establishing a mental inventory of what had been misplaced rather than removed, running his finger over the lines of books, opening and shutting drawers, mapping out the shape of a porcelain vase. In a split-second it would occur to him that if someone had been downstairs they may also have been else-where. David heard the door of the sitting-room open, and a voice calling up the stairs, 'Is there anyone there, is it you Claudette, who's there?' The echo returned each time at a slower speed than the voice had travelled. David shrank so deep into himself he thought he'd stopped breathing. But even in the grip of paralysis he was still conscious of his own big-eyed image staring at him out of the frosty blue oval of the mirror. Poised for flight or for self-defence, he was aware of the division in himself that couldn't reconcile his actions with reality. The voice shouted up the stairs again: 'Is anyone there, come on out will you!' The timbre of the voice denoted fear, it quavered rather than challenged, it was not a prelude to physical assertion but rather a tasting of self-confidence.

David felt trapped. Moravia's feet could be heard tentatively mounting a second and third stair, his caution was evident in the ponderous carriage of his step. He started up the stairs like a man who hoped he would never have to reach the top. David was ready, he couldn't get down to the lower flight without being seen or heard. He had either to hide or confront the man who had grown into a fixed, mental obsession. A fourth step and a fifth, it occurred to David that he could hear the other man's breathing, the loud stony tock-tock of his heart amplified inside his diaphragm. A sixth step and a seventh, the voice resumed again, calling out once and importunately. He must have feared with every step the prospect of someone materialising on the stairs. Eight, nine, ten, he would be reaching the first landing with another two flights to go. David was effectively cut off from escape and through the humming of his nerves he felt the inevitability that they should meet. Moravia didn't check any of the rooms on the first floor, rather he began to climb the second flight of stairs. Eleven, twelve, thirteen; he had ten to go before aligning with the attic flight that separated him from David. The latter made no attempt to conceal himself; he stood fractionally behind the half-opened door with his suitcase within reach of his hand. Fourteen, fifteen, a protracted pause, and then sixteen, seventeen, eighteen; fear rather than confidence was pressing him forward. David's throat was parched again; an almost imperceptible bark in the back of his mind told him that Branden would be on the prowl again after dark, his instinctive ferocity unleashed, his teeth raised to a livid moon. Nineteen, twenty, twenty-one, twenty-two, then a pause before mounting the threshold of the second-floor landing.

He must have left the door to the pink bedroom ajar, for he heard Moravia open it out with the slow forbidding creak of an elm branch punished by storm. If David had taken advantage of the moment he might have crept downstairs as Moravia busied himself with opening the wardrobe. He could hear his shocked exclamation on discovering the photograph wallets, his terrible realisation that someone else had become a party to his private sexual propensities.

David bundled into his case the old clothes he had been wearing, the jacket and trouser pockets crammed with silk ties and letters and photographs. There was no way out of this but to confront the owner of the house. He could sense from Moravia's violent slamming of the wardrobe doors that timidity had given way to anger. A seething indignation had awoken in him; David heard the crack of the ice and trembled. His mind wouldn't steady sufficiently to allow him to know what he was doing here, but the reddish dust-storm in the back of his mind told him that he was about to face the dual arrowhead of Branden and Moravia.

Moravia started up the attic stairs to his bedroom. He was shouting now, 'What bastard has done this? If I lay my hands on him . . . Who in hell's name . . . ' David sat on the bed; he was going to meet the man's eyes full on. After all, it was he who was Dr Moravia, and not this indignant stranger. He'd managed to stow most of the photograph wallets under the bed, and had hurriedly forced clothes back into the wardrobe.

He was looking square at Moravia as the latter's eyes met him, the pupils dilated with fear, the grey irises having receded like a

104

tide from the beach. An artery had pronounced itself in his forehead, and two nettled red patches had sprung up on either side of his nose. For a moment he didn't speak; shock swallowed his words before he could articulate them. He was leaning slightly to the left, one hand outstretched against the wall, his eyes slightly bleary as though he had been drinking in the lunch-hour.

'What in God's name are you doing here?' he shouted at David. 'What right have you to be going through my belongings? Do you want me to call the police?'

'How can they be your belongings?' David replied. 'I am you, it's you who should get out of my bedroom.' He soothed his fingers on his pink silk tie in imitation of Dr Moravia's most dominant characteristic. 'Don't you think you're mistaking a latent desire for a consummate action?' David went on, carefully measuring the cadence of his voice. The tension simmered; it was like the suspended pause between the crack of a whip and the welt it would inflict.

'If you don't offer an adequate explanation, I'll call the police,' Moravia said. The distance between them didn't narrow; it was as though each was stationed on an ice-floe with a rip-current dividing them.

'I don't think that would be wise,' David said. 'One's private life isn't a subject for police scrutiny; it's more likely to be material for an analyst.'

'Are you trying to infer that you have some hold over me?' Moravia's voice denoted the desperation of a man who has been found out. He would have liked to erase the scene from David's memory. The secrecy in which he had enveloped himself for half a century had been infractioned by a disturbed country youth, who stood there, inviolably precocious, sure as an admiral of his prerogative to walk the bridge.

'I see that you and my father share the same exquisite tastes,' David said, allowing the acid coat of his irony to eat into the plate. 'He too is obsessed by the woman in the photograph.'

Moravia's stare was a fixed gorgonic one; a knot of venom was tightening in his throat, he could feel the little snake-tails entwining themselves into an indigestible ball. He felt physically sick; his past had become an excrescence, an ugly blotch of fungus heads that rooted on the counterpane. 'My private world is in my head, and not in this room,' he said carefully. 'We

105

manifest only what we care to externalise; our material possessions are keys to quite other things,' he added, feeling with confidence that he'd locked the one door of access that David had thrown open.

David could sense that he'd de-fused Moravia's initial offensive; the stridency in the latter's voice had graduated to a defensive hesitancy. 'Why don't you try and talk about these things?' David said. 'I see no adequate reason for your dissociation from certain areas of private experience.' The more he talked, the more confident he grew that he could act out a role for sufficient time seriously to dent Moravia's morale.

'I can have you ejected by the police at any moment,' Moravia tried, conscious that the situation could at any moment resolve itself in an act of physical violence. His anger rose as he realised for the first time that David had raided his wardrobe and was wearing one of his suits. He didn't know what to do; whether he remained or was arrested, the boy still possessed the same dangerous knowledge.

'I've already told you of my strictures against the police,' David said firmly; 'it's for those reasons that I haven't called them to have you removed.'

The statement goaded Moravia like a wasp's sting. He could hear the tiny hiss of punctured skin and the poison fanning itself out around the surface of the wound. Moravia advanced a step and stopped. He would have liked to grab the boy and push him out of the window, only there would be questions; all of his life there were questions. He felt tired; anger had given way to a paralysed sense of shock. He wanted to turn around and find that David was gone, that this had never happened, and the boy who had missed his morning appointment was in fact ill at home in Norfolk.

David could sense the chinks in the other's armour. If he acted on the ascendant he could force his way out of here, and leave Moravia with the horrifying prospect of being unable to call in the law as a vehicle of redress. David held him in the most subtle pincers of blackmail; when he chose to apply the heat Moravia would scream like a man in irons.

'You're allowing the fear syndrome of your ego to interfere with the assemblage point of your consciousness,' David ventured. The voice in the back of his mind had remembered all this; it was shutting Branden out. Somehow he wanted to fix the

106

red dye of Branden's seed in Moravia's subconscious – a transference of possession that would bring the doctor face to face with the bloody mask of the fox.

'I think you'd better come downstairs and explain your actions,' Dr Moravia said, regaining his professional composure. 'We'll have a drink; I see you've already raided my whisky. And anyhow, I'd like to speak to you about a letter I've received from your father . . .'

'Why would my father write to you?' David retorted. 'He's permanently unobtainable. What good would it do anyway? He's dead, he died yesterday, although they haven't found him yet.'

'How do you come to this conclusion?' Dr Moravia said, allowing his words to develop an alderman's stroll. He was disquieted; either the boy wished to erase the memory of his father, or he was lying. But the latter seemed motiveless, it served only to eliminate a bargaining point – the boy's suspicion that the two men were conspiratorially implicated in the life of Claudette.

'As the paranormal is, in your terms, simply a refutation of science,' said David, 'I won't elucidate the certain knowledge I have acquired.

'I see we have only ten minutes left,' David mimicked, and he was going to make Moravia sweat through each one of them.

'And what are you doing wearing one of my suits?' said Moravia. 'How dare you lay claim to my personal wardrobe? Get changed, and come downstairs,' he said imperiously.

'Nine minutes to go, Dr Moravia,' David said.

'I beg your pardon,' Moravia said. 'Are you intending to hold me to ransom in my own house?'

'My house,' David replied, his eyes scanning the red second-hand on the lunar face of his watch. 'Eight minutes, Dr Moravia.'

David watched the dust-motes dazzle in the light again. 'Seven minutes, Dr Moravia,' he said.

'Listen here, I won't tolerate threats from you or anyone,' Moravia said, raising his voice; 'if a distressed patient finds his way into his doctor's private residence it's a matter for the law.'

'Six minutes to be precise,' David said. 'Soon it will be five.'

'Yes, it's a matter of minutes before I call the police,' Moravia rejoined, his voice quivering with impotent rage.

'Five minutes, Dr Moravia,' David said, his voice cooling to the dispassionate dictates with which Branden commanded his own obedience. It was Branden's voice which was coming to predominate; its articulation was as clear as the periodic shriek of an owl in a frozen night wood. David could see the clarity of snow powdering elm branches, the moon flooding through a haystack of cloud, its light throwing everything into a world of silhouettes. A black calligraphy of bare branches writing on snow.

'Four minutes, Dr Moravia,' he said.

In a series of kinetic nerve-flashes, Moravia feared for his life. The flashbacks were disconcertingly those which related to childhood in this very house. He could see himself rolling marbles across the parquet floor, his embarrassment when his mother found out he was filching the liqueur chocolates from her box – something for which she'd blamed the maid – his first coloured drawings of boats and a desert island with gold sand and mop-haired trees, his first conscious realisation of savouring the pleasure of being all alone, and how his mother took off her high heels and ran all the way up the stairs on her return, just to see if her son was safe. She'd always found him reading, comfortably propped up on cushions, and not at all disquieted by being alone. It was she who had sought comfort, while he had remained characteristically drawn into himself.

'Three minutes, Dr Moravia,' David said.

'You are not going to dictate to me in my own house,' Moravia replied. 'Kindly come downstairs and we'll discuss this whole distasteful incident.' The flashbacks were streaming through now; there were the afternoons when he slipped on his mother's rings, her sapphire and diamond engagement ring, a blue star clustered by scintillating planets, her emerald, diamond and turquoise dress-rings, the thin gold bands of bracelets, and a heart-shaped locket in which there was a pastel miniature of her at seventeen. All black ringlets and flamingo-rouged cheeks. Then there was a first visit to the countryside, intermixed with his ruminations while driving to work this morning.

'Two minutes, Dr Moravia,' David said with a note of disarming sadism.

'Two minutes to what?' Moravia shouted, as a series of images formed a tableau representing the occasion of his first visit to the countryside. They'd stayed for a week in a converted farmhouse close to Withermarsh Green on the Essex/Suffolk border. It was

108

high summer; jays screamed in the beech woods, red- and black-spotted burnet moths swarmed on the mauve thistle flowers, the cornfields were greenish blond – in a month the corn-ears would be gold. There were owls at night and foxes. He was suddenly overwhelmed by the image of a fox. He'd woken in the night, his heart pounding with the rhythm of a tribal drum. The scream that he had heard was something so high-pitched and blood-curdling that it seemed trapped inside his head. When his mother had come into his room and, anticipating his fear, had placed a night-light beside his bed, she had told him that the noise was only the cry of a fox in the wood.

'One minute, Dr Moravia,' David slowly articulated. He was not allowing the doctor the slightest intimation as to what he would do with him. He felt detached, switched off from whatever act of physical violence he might perpetrate. His eyes met Moravia's full on. For a second they were like two men involved in an imminent collision, the cars seeming to hang back in a fractional second of suspended mobility.

David watched Moravia open his mouth as though to speak, but what issued was the demented fox-shriek of Branden's voice. Moravia felt something fasten within, his head was throbbing with a blood-sack, the pointed nose and sharp ears of a fox asserted itself in his consciousness, the pressure in his head expanded; propulsed forward by the motion, he was projected on to the bed, his mouth a lather of spittle, his eyes gone wide as though he was trying to find an exit through his pupils.

David didn't wait to see the attack reach its culminating frenzy; he grabbed his case and hurried down the stairs in a state of disbelief. Over and over he kept thinking that he was trapped in a time-rift, and that if only he could see to left or right of the obstruction he would find himself back home in Norfolk, lazily stretched out in the old barn, relating the narrative that he was enacting to Bunny and Louise and Rachel. He steadied himself by the back-door; his head was clearer, his nasal passages no longer smelt of fox. He felt disburdened of the mental foetus he had been carrying; he couldn't believe that the intensity of his thought projection had transferred the possession to Moravia. He was exhausted. He got out into the street, wishing that there was a field or wood in which he could take refuge, and not this monotony of concrete, the exposure to eyes, the remorseless vapour-leaking hubbub of traffic. A builder's lorry was unloading sand in a nearby garden, a cement-mixer gaped with a cyclopean eye; there were still blue battered crowns of agapanthi in a neighbouring garden, and red hollyhocks contesting with sunflowers.

David was too tired to walk far. As soon as he was out of the street, he hailed a taxi. He was confronted with the choice either of returning home via Liverpool Street or going back to Diane's flat. He chose the latter. If she permitted him to stay the night it would be a tentative threshold from which to devise a plan for the immediate future. Shut off behind the glass of the taxi, David felt more composed than he had been since the arrival of Branden.

He was anxious to read the cache of letters he had looted from Dr Moravia's bedroom, and particularly the ones in which he had recognised his father's spidery handwriting. He found himself unconsciously remasting his tie, searching for the coolness of the pink silk between his thumb and forefinger. The city rushed past; for David it was like watching the isolated jumps in a film. Windows caught the bronze glitter of the late afternoon sunlight, a woman in a cerise suit stepping out of a chauffeur-driven Rolls was backlogged in a retinal instant to be replaced by a jogger coasting towards the traffic-lights in a red singlet and yellow shorts.

'Which side of the crescent do you want, mate?' the cabby interjected, pulling David abruptly out of his contemplative state.

'Just drop me next to the station,' he said, bewildered by the anticipation of finding coherent landmarks in the labyrinthine maze of streets. He disembarked with his case, overcome suddenly by a profound sense of *déjà vu* and, unable to decide whether it was a former experience of his or Dr Moravia's, he busied himself in looking for the small mews lane leading to Diane's flat. 'It could be here and yet it's over there,' he muttered to himself. His relief at being free of Branden was incalculable; he could feel his nerves go limp after weeks of overstrain, of being jumped at from the back of his head and thrown to the ground in delirium.

He found the mews entrance to Diane's building and prepared himself for what he anticipated would be an indifferent reception. The back of the three-storey building was run down and in need of paint, pigeons were periscoping their necks on the topmost ledge, a coruscation of violet and green oil chased into the pebble-grey of their bodies. The fire-stairs shared by the adjoining property were rusty and unusable. Moss sponged in emerald tuftings between cracked paving stones; the downpipe leaked a dank ooze of impure water.

He calculated that Diane should be home by now; he could see a light on inside her flat. He knocked on the green painted door and waited. After a time someone came to the door and fumbled the latch. He thought he could hear voices whispering. When the door was partially opened, a young man squeezed his head into an expression that was slightly more than a profile and waited for David to speak. 'Is Diane in?' he said. He was conscious of the unresponsive hollow into which his words dropped. He could hear the amplified ticking of a clock in the room before the young man said, 'I'm afraid she's not here, she's gone away for a week,' and slammed the door.

David heard the bolt drawn on the other side. How quickly a sanctuary can turn into the lair of an indifferent enemy, he thought, as he retraced his steps up the lane, and walked out into the street. The light was marigold in the chestnut trees; he was alone in the city at the time of the evening rush-hour. He would sit down in the park and determine what to do. Already the first premature leaves were falling; two donkey-eared yellow chestnut leaves fell at his feet. He picked them up and walked on.

8

It must have been evening. For a split second on awakening Jan
flinched with a reflex of terror. Her circuitous itinerary through
the sea-fog had brought her to the millhouse. Plaid blankets had
been heaped over her; red and blue, and green and grey woollen
rectangles. She was naked beneath the covers; someone must
have removed her sodden clothes, and she had slept through the
day, comatose, lost to a dreamless blank screen over which
occasional monsters of the deep lumbered – the lantern-fish, the
whale-fish, the giant eel. Everything moved slowly through the
dark deoxygenated cold.

Her watch had been placed by the bed together with a note
that read, 'Don't worry, Spike's not here, it's Pauline. I'm
downstairs when you want me.' Jan looked at the big childish
writing; the pink felt-tip magnified the simplicity of the hand –
the vowels were moon-shaped, and the verticals went up like an
aerial projecting from the bonnet of a car.

Jan could feel the heaviness of her body; her muscles ached,
each movement was the equivalent of acting for two people. She
thumped on the floor to attract attention, and could hear a radio
suddenly extinguished before Pauline ran up the stairs two at a
time and came into the room, her sea-green eyes lighting up
beneath an auburn fringe, the twinkling playfulness of her
character highlighted in the angles of her cheeks. 'Let me make
you a cup of tea, Jan,' she said, 'then I've got something to tell
you.'

Jan listened to Pauline hastily busying herself downstairs in
the kitchen. She had come here for a summer vacation job, and
Spike had asserted his pressure to make her stay. Pauline was
hedonistic and lacking in self-discipline; when she stayed at the
millhouse she would sit up all night drinking, then sleep through
the day. She was child-like but unshockable, a perennial visitor
who never left and always required money. Her untidiness led to

a paperchain of clothes festooning the floor of her room. Her irregular hours meant that she lived an unsociable life, but she was of an uncomplaining disposition, always alive to the moment, felicitously vital to those with whom she felt a bond of trust or sympathy.

She came back into the room carrying two cups of tea on a black lacquered tray depicting a Yangtze fisherman serenely contemplating nenuphar on a stream. It was the one possession she valued; it served as a foundation for all of the little keepsakes and trinkets she had acquired in the course of her peripatetic life.

She placed a cup of tea beside Jan, and faced the window. 'He's dead, you know,' she said, looking out at the skyline. 'They picked him up off the rocks today. He must have gone over the cliff in the fog.'

'Whom are you talking about?' said Jan incredulously, a goosepimple spreading over her forearms like a sudden shower of rain.

'Spike,' said Pauline. 'It's in the evening paper. Fishermen discovered him this morning in the cove at Blue Rock. He'd fallen four hundred feet to his death. Jim Hale, who stopped by in the village this afternoon, said his skull had caved in like the split toecap of a boot. They found the head ten feet away from the body; they'll stitch it on before he's buried, or at least that's what Jim said. Do you realise we're free?' Pauline said disbelievingly. 'Free, Jan . . . '

'God, he must have followed me through the fog, Pauline,' Jan said, looking into that mist again and recollecting the smoke-wall of guttering blankness that had poured in from the Atlantic. 'When it overtook me at Pendeen, when I was tapping like a mole through the luminous whorls of vapour, I got to the Smugglers' Arms. Spike was in there.' *The red ferret wouldn't let go of my scent once he had discovered me; I climbed out of a window and went back to the fog rather than face the red hairs on his wrist, the slight beer-line that curded above his lip.* 'I thought he was going to become violent in the bar.' *He was having to restrain one of those ventriloquial outbursts, you could feel the pressure fanning out from his body. I must have drunk three or four brandies before I dodged him, I could feel a blue fire coursing through my blood.* Jan stopped speaking and imagined Spike's desperate lunge into the fog, his running everywhere until eventually he didn't know that he was running, only that he had to keep on in order to find the object of his search. She envisaged him gasping for air, his body doubled up, his voice shouting her name through the fog, his willing himself on until he was still running, only there wasn't a surface beneath his feet; he must have realised it for the first few accelerative seconds, the hurtling flail of his arms, the plummeting weight as he spun over and over, every nerve in his body alert for the face of the earth to rush up and meet his fall.

'I'm scared, Jan,' Pauline said. 'They say he had a knife in his jacket pocket; the police are going to open an enquiry into the circumstances of his death.'

Jan could feel her heart beginning to race again. That voice which she had heard coming at her out of the white wall had been Spike's, and not simply the audio-hallucinations of fatigue that she had rationalised as the cause of her terror. She could hear it again, a voice out of nowhere shouting her name to the horizons. 'J–A–A–N . . . WHERE ARE Y–O–O–O–U . . . J–A–A–N . . . J–A–A–N . . .'

'He was after me, Pauline,' she said nervously; 'I kept hearing someone calling out my name, and then I turned in the opposite direction as I was on the grass of the headland. I had this horror of going over the edge.'

'I always knew something like this would happen,' Pauline said. 'Only don't upset yourself, it's over now. Don't look, but your legs are blue with bruises; you must have hit every obstacle in your path. They say it's the worst fog in living memory; three or four boats are reported missing along the coast. They'll be combing the shore for bodies once the wind gets up.'

Jan was still too shocked to assimilate everything that Pauline was saying. Fixed in her mind was the image of Spike plummeting into the vertiginous spiral of his death-drop. The two incompatibles flesh and stone marrying to the accompaniment of impacted splintering bone.

'I'm going back home,' Pauline said emphatically; 'I don't want to be around when the police start making enquiries. You knew about the room, presumably; the one that we assumed was a scullery, and which he was forever checking to see if it was locked? Well, I got in there today; it's full of photographs and children's toys, rocking chairs, teddy bears and clowns' masks, but it was terrible somehow . . .'

Jan sank back into the pillows; the room had turned an inky blue, she could only just discern Pauline standing by the window. She could hear a rook straggling back to roost. Then silence; the dilation of the mind as it relived events that seemed no longer to co-ordinate, Spike's reddish face in close-up, the green eye of the well at Oak Farm, the sadness in her mother's voice as she reviewed the years of frugality, the cold kitchen with its cottage-loaf and perennially steaming kettle.

'Show me the room, Pauline,' she said. 'I want to know what he kept in there before the police take things away.'

Pauline didn't answer, she shrugged her shoulders apprehensively and continued to stare out at the inky twilight. 'All right,' she said, 'but put on a dressing-gown or you'll catch cold. Are you really sure you want to see it? It's dark and it's behind the cupboard in his bedroom.'

When they opened the door, Jan half-expected to see Spike brooding over the blue column of his cigarette smoke. He would sit like that for hours, scheming; you could see his mind hunting in corners, ferreting out the one grain of wheat left on the flagstones of the barn floor. The room was unaired; it was at the back of the house and looked out over moorland; the wind ran in the grasses with the motion of eddies in a stream – it set up a perpetual hissing current. There was almost nothing in the room; a narrow unmade bed, a few maps and magazines on a rickety table, an open wardrobe with empty hangers. The air was killed by a hangover of musty smoke.

'It's in there,' Pauline said, switching on a light inside the wardrobe, and opening a door that was cleverly cut into the wardrobe's interior. 'It must have been a dressing-room,' she said, as she made way for Jan to manoeuvre herself into the narrow opening. The cold air layered itself on her skin as she focused into the muted pink light of a slightly dank brick-walled anteroom.

The room looked like a child's nursery – pink and blue elephants shared a corner with glass-button-eyed teddybears, some with an eye or nose missing, grizzly, rufous, patched. There were Chinese silk kites draped like exotic stingrays against one wall, and, on another, clown masks with scarlet lips and white papier mâché faces were interspersed with pierrots – single black tears escaping from their eyes, lips framed in *fin de siècle* pouts. There were leather masks, one in the form of a turquoise fish, and an elaborate Victorian dolls' house with a miniature crystal chandelier in the drawing-room. The one disquieting reminder of Spike's adulthood was a studded leather coat hanging up on a hook in the door. It looked like a fall-out of nails embedded in an oilslick. Jan could feel Pauline's breath on her shoulder. 'Let's go back into the other room,' Pauline said, 'it's too cold in here. Sometimes the draught in this house reminds me of the chill of an underground stream.'

Jan allowed herself to be guided back to the bedroom. She found herself wondering what happened to such desires at death; was the end of the body a cancellation of the involutedly complex fetishes devised by the mind? Was Spike now free of those obsessions or did something of them persist in the man after death? She was baffled by Spike's unlocatability; thinking of someone's location in death was like trying to think yourself into the mind of another, or a bird or a fish – one was deflected by the elusive individuation of what made things separate and alone. When you faced someone eye to eye you were no nearer their person than the entranced movements of a fish observed beneath ice. Human life is without union; even in its apparent movements of deepest fusion it is still a shadow-dance, a meeting of ice and fire except that the ice could never melt and the fire never burn.

Jan tented herself in tartan blankets. 'We'll leave first thing tomorrow morning,' she said. 'As you've told my parents that I'm with you, there's nothing to worry about. The police won't come out here tonight.' She could see the consternation in Pauline's mind; the image of Spike was everywhere, his movements tracked their each evasion. He had grown into the red embers of a fire one couldn't bank.

'There are letters too,' said Pauline, 'I've scanned them briefly and read all that I need to know. Take a look at this.' Pauline handed Jan a letter. The pronounced black majuscules and embroidered seriphs were embossed on a pale-green handmade paper. She took the letter out of a vaguely scented envelope and read:

Dear Spike,
Your letter surprised me. The Ernst Moravia whom you mention is without doubt a doctor with whom I had a casual relationship in the summer of 1960 (I have a masterful recollection of dates) and who subsequently managed to

116

acquire a vast collection of photographs of me that had been in the hands of a private collector.

I see from your letter that he is still in pursuit of his bizarre quarry; that club you mention called the Blue Rabbit is notorious everywhere for its clientele, I'm surprised that a man of his apparent circumspection risks it.

But more serious and to the point is how he managed to come by the huge collection of photographs that, as far as I know, my American benefactor requested to be burnt shortly before his death. I ask your assistance in this matter; you say that your son is attending Moravia for professional advice, so perhaps you will find that you have a leverage here.

Paris isn't a good place to be at present, and although I'm no longer a part of that scene, I've decided to come and live in England for an indefinite period.

Do keep me informed; I'll send you a forwarding address when I have one.

Claudette

'Claudette's the blonde in the photographs,' Pauline said, 'her signature is on the reverse of them.'

From her familiarity with Spike's secret room, and in her relating what she had found, Jan surmised that Pauline was intimate with Spike's obsessions. People are so secretive, she thought; they carry their lives within them rather as an oyster compounds nacreous grit into a pearl. That's what secrets are, a necklace on which we string black pearls.

Jan wanted to be left alone to rest; her nerves were still overstrung from the terror of the fog. But, try as she did, she couldn't erase Spike's image; his face swam up to meet her like a lantern-fish patrolling the deeps, or the red eye of a hare on the poulterer's tray that insisted on catching one's own in passing. The window presented a cobalt screen of space, the only light on the horizon was from a farm way off on the moor.

She was tired; she felt as though she was lying beneath a great weight of sand, and that her bones had solidified to lead bars. Sleep interrupted her in mid-sentence; she was about to say, 'Ernst Moravia, what a strange . . .'

When he came to it was dark. He was lying face down on the black silk counterpane, fully dressed, unable to determine how long he had been there, or what had happened. His open mouth

117

had formed a silver crust of spittle; he experienced that peculiar sense of disorientation that one feels on waking for the first time in an unfamiliar room. For a protracted moment one is caught up in the panic of not knowing who one is or where one is – it is an intimation of the faceless amnesia we take with us into death.

He got up shakily; some radical mutation that he couldn't locate had taken place within himself. At first he feared that he had undergone a stroke; he recollected a blinding red flash that had carried with it the force and weight of an animal's spring. Why was it that he recollected the bared teeth of a fox? And the terrible scream of something drawing blood in a night wood. And then there was the business of David – he looked at the debris on the floor, the corrugated creases in his suits and shirts, the landslide of photograph wallets littering the floor. As far as he could see, nothing had been stolen, none of the valuables had been touched, but however would he account for his uncatalogued pyramid of photographs? Many of the shots were in duplicate or triplicate, and in some instances that had peculiarly excited the original collector, there were upwards of twenty prints of a particular angle of provocation. If the boy had wished he could have gone off with a selection of the most uninhibited photographs.

Above all, Moravia feared that a scandal would ensue. The profession in which he had come to be so highly regarded and the personal life that he had been at such pains to conduct with boundless discretion had within the course of a single afternoon become subjects under threat of public scrutiny.

He went downstairs and poured himself a large undiluted Scotch. Sitting in an armchair facing the subdued green light of his desk-lamp, his confidence began to reassert itself. He felt islanded from the world, no one could encroach on this territory that his mother had built into a sanctuary for him. With the euphoric mushrooming of spirits into his bloodstream, he was able to convince himself that David wouldn't have taken any of the photographs; his purpose had been to vandalise and menace. He would write to the boy's parents suggesting that David's problems were outside his field of speciality, and personally recommend a colleague whom he thought more suited to assist.

But within seconds he realised the inadvisability of such a line of action. Confronted with the loss of his object of fixation the boy would be more likely to impart his findings, and to fabricate

118

a network of stories as to why Dr Moravia wished to discontinue advising him. Increasingly he was faced with the insoluble dilemma that knowledge derived could not be extinguished. Wherever David went he would carry in his mind the indelible watermark of his discovery. It had become a sunken water-lily; at any given moment David could have that flower dilate on the still surface of a pond.

Running parallel with his fear of exposure was the disquieting realisation that he had been subject to a fit. He felt a heaviness, a sense of intrusion from within, as though he was being stalked and watched by eyes that would suddenly light up in the darkness. His pulse was regular but a reddish mist behind his eyes hung motionless like a dust-storm drawn up into the folds of the wind. He lit a cigar and contemplated things through the tableau of blue smoke. He drew on the moment; they haven't got me yet, he kept telling himself, and with each inhalation of the cigar he savoured the smoke more sweetly. He took down a volume of his favourite Burton's *Anatomy of Melancholy*, but found that he couldn't read. The chaos of his own thoughts made it impossible to concentrate. He was like a man who has been shot but still gets up in the belief that he can walk it off, and that the wound will disappear if he discounts its reality. But deep down he couldn't disguise the knowledge that something was very wrong. He had been dislodged from his centre, thrown out into an orbit that he couldn't properly control.

He got up and walked back and forth across the room, but none of his familiar panaceas served to pacify his distraught nerves. He appeared to be doubling on himself; each time he turned round from one window and walked towards the far one, he thought he passed the simulacrum of himself walking in the opposite direction. Shoulder to shoulder they brushed in an incongruous meeting. At each successive intersection the double integrated through his left shoulder and disappeared.

He sat down. His pulse was picking up speed with uncomfortable acceleration; it resembled footsteps running down a stone corridor, louder and louder, then fading away, only to return again. Advancing and receding, an influx and reflux. He was startled from his inner fears by the sound of the telephone ringing. He quickly poured himself another drink and uncradled the receiver. He knew from the tumbling dice of the coin that the caller was in a telephone box.

119

'246 8020,' he said.

There was a pause before he found himself involuntarily saying, 'Moravia here, who's that?'

'It's you,' the voice said.

'Who are you?' he asseverated sternly.

'Ernst Moravia,' the voice said, 'don't you recollect, I'm your doctor. I'm sorry to trouble you at home, but I wanted to remind you of our appointment on Wednesday next. It's my fault for not having finalised this at the conclusion of our last appointment.'

'Where are you phoning from?' Moravia enquired.

'If it's any business of yours I'm standing in my own living-room,' the voice went on, 'a cigar in my left hand, and a tumbler of whisky just out of reach of my right hand. And if you're that inquisitive, I've just taken down the second volume of Burton's *Anatomy of Melancholy*, so there's a slight gap in the arrangement of my quarto books on the oak-wood shelf.'

'You'd have to be in the room to know that,' Moravia replied.

'But I am,' the voice said. 'Why do you continue to question my identity?'

'Because I'm me,' Moravia replied indignantly, 'and you are you.' He was beginning to panic; he realised that if he put the telephone down the voice would continue inside his head. He found himself questioning whether he was listening to a pre-recorded tape or a dichotomised inner dialogue.

'It's no good turning round,' the voice continued; 'your reflection wouldn't show in the unpolished glass of that oval mirror. Eighteenth-century with a baroque ormolu inlay.'

Moravia felt as though an ice-cold wire had been inserted into his spine. He sensed that if he turned round he might meet with a face in the mirror that he didn't recognise.

He was about to terminate the conversation abruptly by placing the receiver down, when the line went dead on him. His caller had anticipated his action. He listened to the fuzz inside the ear-piece; it sounded like the purring fizz of bubbles that attends the uncorking of a champagne bottle. Now it was a sea-shell that he was holding to his ear, now a wave expiring on shingle. He placed the telephone back in its cradle, aware of the magnified self-consciousness of his each movement; it seemed as though everything in the room had conspired to watch his movements. He swung slowly round, relieved that he telescoped into an empty room, and slumped into his armchair; the one with the silk cushions monogrammed by his mother. He would never be the same person again, he mused; the events of the day had severed his lifeline with the past. Rather as a person who has undergone radical surgery knows that they will never again inhabit the body that they have recognised since birth, so he sensed that something alien had come to establish a disharmony in the exquisite balance of his mind. Inured as he was to rationalising extreme and disturbed mental states, he could find no satisfactory elucidation of his own degree of confusion. His assumption was the irrational one that it was something externally imposed on him and not engendered from within. He couldn't remember whether the large Scotch he was sipping was his third or fourth, for the effect was neither tonic nor stimulating. Bit by bit he attempted to make a jigsaw puzzle from what he remembered of the afternoon's events. The shock of finding David impersonating him and laying claim to his rights of ownership, but the voice at the other end of the telephone was not David's; it was a voice so unmistakably like his own that he could attribute it to no one of his acquaintance.

He began to drowse; in his state of half-consciousness he drifted into a blizzard out of which faces showed through: the hypnagogic nebulae that stormed the nether regions of his consciousness, snouted antediluvian reptiles that swarmed across a marsh, a pterodactyl feeding on the gut-split membrane of a smaller lizard. He was watching black spearmen running through waist-high grass towards an amber sunset when he was forced out of his primal landscape by the ringing of the telephone. He was reluctant at first to answer it, he thought he would let it go; but compulsion and curiosity got the better of him, and he blundered across the room to answer the importunate ringing.

This time he recognised the voice instantly; it was Claudette's.

'Ernst, darling,' she said studiedly, 'I hope I'm not disturbing you from your bookish reveries. I thought I'd take advantage of a brief respite from working on my novel to call you. How are you?'

'Very well,' he replied; 'rather tired from an exhausting day, but my life's often like that . . . And you, are you well?'

'Yes, I'm fine, I've never been so attuned to my psycho-physical body. But what I was really calling about, Ernst, is David Thompson's father. He's dead.'

121

'Dead? But why should you call to tell me that,' Moravia questioned. 'Why do you assume that I am intimate with a patient's family, and a patient of recent standing, I hasten to add?' A lucid channel was clearing in his mind; he knew he was telescoping with his customary clarity.

'I knew the father, and thought perhaps that you did,' Claudette continued. 'He was interested in a facet of my early life – photographic modelling. The blue sleeze of the pornocratic underworld; I had to pass through that hoop of fire in order to instate an identity on my rebirth. It must have been around that time that we first met.'

'I don't see the connection,' Moravia said, abruptly. For the second time, he sniffed an intimation of blackmail; he could feel a trickle beginning in his throat, and simultaneously he was aware of the smell of fresh ink drying on a lined page in the wooden classroom of his first private school.

'I won't keep you,' Claudette replied. 'It's just that he went over the edge of a cliff in Cornwall, and fell four hundred feet to his death. The police have put out a message that they want to contact his son; I just wondered if you . . . '

'If I what?' Moravia questioned. 'I don't wish any part in this affair, and frankly it doesn't concern me.'

'I'm sorry to have disturbed you,' Claudette ventured unrepentantly, 'it's just that I thought we might both have a common interest in his death.' In the protracted silence that ensued she could hear Moravia thinking.

'We'll speak another time,' he said, 'I have a guest,' and hurriedly but courteously disengaged himself from the conversation.

Claudette put the receiver down and settled back into the chair in her bedroom suite. She had frightened Moravia; she knew she had injected a luminous dye into his nerves that would flicker on and off all night like the red flasher on a marker buoy. Having made it known to Moravia that she knew of a link between him and Spike, she would use it to her advantage to devise a means of laying claim to the photographic collection that she suspected was in Moravia's possession.

She reassessed the surf of papers that lay on the counterpane. Wherever she was she spread her materials out like this; they were an archipelago of fragments that one day would be stitched up into a whole. The inconsistency of paper and inks attested to

122

the novel's sporadic making. *Gold on Black*; she had been writing it a lifetime in her head and now the mosaic of her accumulative experience was beginning to materialise in actual words. In this way she could create handholds in the landslide of the past. Her life had been lived at an accelerative pace; it was only now that things had slowed sufficiently to allow her to focus inwards, and she found herself walking backwards, clearing a path through a fallow field that had been overrun by weeds for a decade. Thistles, tares, goutweed, a proliferation of angry nettles. She had to proceed with caution; too violent a sweep at the aberrant flower might result in the irreparable loss of a key memory. Years of maximising on her inner strength had taught her how to isolate her inner world from the external predators who would maim it. She severed the mental image of Moravia with the ruthless efficiency of a knife cutting through a diver's lead. She watched his phosphorescent shape sink back into the darkness, and continued structuring the second chapter from a motley of notes.

Chapter 2

It was raining over the maritime yards. A fine rain that flickered from a pearl-blue sky had set in at twilight, and now gave a fish-sheen to the pavements and the slate roofs of the houses that looked out over the bay.

In the room above his chemist's shop, Martin sat browsing through his thoughts as a philatelist might turn the tissue covers protecting a page of mounted penny-blacks. The red, green and amber dispensing bottles that he displayed in his shop window were an endless source of fascination to passers-by. Their colours winked like traffic-lights on the wet pavement. Andy should have arrived an hour ago; it was inconceivable to think that someone so infallibly punctilious should have been delayed on the roads. Ever since his initiation into the sect, Martin had become conscious of the dichotomy between an inner state of timelessness, and the demands made on him by the temporal imposition of his job. It was not that he regretted his pharmacological training, it was more that he had come to feel increasingly dissociated from the routinal demands made on a chemist; he needed time to read and prepare himself for future meetings of the sect.

He took up his book and read: 'It was not only the Pythagoreans and Plato, then, that concealed many things; but the Epicureans too say that they have things that may not be uttered, and do not allow all to pursue these writings . . . Further, those who instituted the mysteries, being philosophers, buried their doctrines in myths, so as not to be obvious to all. Did they then, by veiling human opinions, prevent the ignorant from handling them; and was it not more beneficial for the holy and blessed contemplation of realities to be concealed? But it was not only the tenets of the Barbarian philosophy, or the Pythagorean myths, but even these myths in Plato . . . '

He was startled out of the drift of the text by the urgency of the door-bell. He expected to find Andy standing there in his casual jeans and soft black leather jacket rolled up at the sleeves, and a black scarf escaping from his shirt. Martin knew by heart the lilac shadow that stubbled the outline of Andy's jaw, the hollow cheek-bones acquired from long nights of study and the copious inhalation of hashish.

When he unlocked the door it took him some considerable time to realise that the figure standing before him was Andy. At first his rational faculty rejected it; he stood there in silence scrutinising the figure on the pavement, looking for those familiar marks by which we recognise a friend, marks which are not physical features so much as an interplay of emotion and expression which accord that person their particular individuality.

'It's you, Andy?' Martin said somewhat hesitantly. The man standing before him was radically changed. His hairline had receded, his eyes had turned inwards; they were like grey sunken lakes that appeared to be watching an inner event, and to be unconcerned with outward things. The lips were thinner, the body emaciated, but most striking of all was the mutation of the voice. Andy's always quiet, carefully articulated placement of syllables had turned into a stammering whisper. His voice had acquired the urgently thrown sibilance of a vagrant in the subway who keeps his importunate request mute for fear of being repulsed by violence.

'I'm sorry I'm late,' Andy whispered; 'the motorway was an unchanging snail-crawl of cars all the way from outer London.'

Martin sensed the lie in Andy's voice; a miscoordination of inner balance that he could only attribute to shock played too near the surface of Andy's mind for it to be concealed.

They went upstairs, Martin leading and doing his best to instil

124

a little *joie de vivre* in his friend; he could hear Andy's tired step trailing behind. He had lit a friendly lamp in the room, and now motioned Andy to one of the two easychairs, and poured him out a sherry. By the gold light of the lamp, Martin could discern the pinched greyness of Andy's cheek-bones. His features had turned inwards on themselves as though his body had decided to contract about an invisible centre.

'I've been reading Mead's *Orpheus*,' Martin said, by way of an opening gambit. 'I'm preparing a paper on Orphic Theogony to be circulated to each member of our sect.'

Andy appeared not to have heard. Martin could see him searching within himself for a lead to confession. He inserted the fingers of one hand into the gaps of the other, a characteristic of his, and looked at Martin with eyes that broke down all physical defences, before saying, 'What I have to tell you is a matter of the utmost gravity; it is an experience that does not easily lend itself to words.

'Briefly, I've returned from the experience of death. Three weeks ago I was sitting on my bed, projecting out of my body, and conscious that I was living as an independent astral entity, a thinking satellite, when a man broke into my room and fired a shot through me that punched the back out of the window. What happened within the violent turbulence of those thirty seconds is unrecordable. I can only compare it to the detonating rush of someone hurtled through a windscreen, who survives the ordeal unscathed, but within those seconds has made a journey through time that has aged him visibly and irreparably.' *The young blond-haired man, who only seconds ago was sitting serenely behind the wheel, is scooped up by the stretcher-bearers as an etiolated grey-haired man heavily disfigured by the apparent stress of his life.* 'The invincible magnitude of my psychic body must have reconnected with the physical and repelled the shot. I remember being conscious of a sharply defined spider's web that scintillated like filigree. It was the vibrating fibre, the resonance of each strand, that protected me and allowed me to survive the ordeal. Last week the man who shot me, but who in my case committed murder without a body, was apprehended on the fire-stairs of a building at Marble Arch. He'd locked his victim inside a wardrobe and set fire to it with petrol.

'There's no visible scar on my body.' *The explosion took place inside; I felt as though I was being sucked into a vortex, forced so far*

125

back into myself that I was a tiny figure motioning to a low-flying aircraft. At first I thought no one would ever see me; I was at the walled-up end of a tunnel looking into a luminous circle of light, and then hands were kneading the substance of my flesh, forcing me to sit down on the bed, and I was hurrying to be on time to intersect with their voices, to convince them that I was here and alive. 'You can see for yourself how I've aged.' *I've become like a colour at the edge of the spectrum – invisible because it's out of retinal focus. My skin no longer picks up ultraviolet photons; it's dusted the colour of smudged lead. I've become like a fish that loses its sheen on extraction from the water.* 'The doctor that examined me diagnosed severe shock, or what I would call a dislodgement from the centre of being. Cancer tests have proved negative; there's no biochemical foundation for my radical physiological change.'

Andy stopped speaking and looked out of the window at the lights coming on in houses. The sky was airforce-blue; the hiss of tyres on the wet road told him that it was still raining. He couldn't let Martin know how fatiguing the ordeal of driving down here had proved. There was too great a gap between himself and the windscreen; he had felt as though he was sitting in the driving-seat of the twentieth car behind him and looking through his own windscreen. He'd never properly come back from the experience of being blown apart; he was still the semaphoring figure in a field watching the black shadow of the aircraft form a cross on the dehydrated grass.

Claudette re-read what she had written. Perhaps it was the experience of seeing the transformation of her own features in the well, all those summers ago, that had germinated the seed for Andy's narrative. Writing a novel was such a long journey; you had to go from A to B via every letter in the alphabet and yet appear to have made the move effortlessly. She wondered how she would ever form a coherent narrative of her mosaic of coloured inks. She would need trust, that and the ability to learn from the spider how to anchor a bridge-thread before beginning the work of constructing a web.

She got up from the chair and went to the window. The old feeling of excitement at the prospect of making a solitary raid on the night city had kindled a glow in the pit of her stomach. She would risk it; she'd take a taxi to the Blue Rabbit or After Hours and re-acquaint herself with the lifestyle she had abandoned. She needed to do this, to convince herself that she could re-enter the lair of the wolf and come away unscarred. Leather and silk, these were her weapons; she re-acquired that sensuous second skin, and went out into the night. A taxi with its amber light pulled over to the kerb for her. As she climbed in she could feel her adrenalin spiralling to a white glow. Neon rouged the pavements; all the way to the Blue Rabbit she found herself singing Billie Holiday's 'I Cover the Waterfront' – she had it word by word. She would go back to hell for one night; the explosion of silver and red lights in the club's entrance hall told her she'd arrived. Now she would burn.

9

When Dr Moravia woke up the light behind his eyes had the packed glitter of frost. For a moment he stayed there in no man's land, before consciousness startled him into an awareness of events that he had hoped sleep would expunge from his memory.

He had a full day of appointments ahead of him; six hours of demanding analysis on less than four hours' sleep. The rusty blood-spot in the back of his mind was still visible like a moon that lingers on into the day hours in opposition to the scarlet sun of a winter's dawn. He found himself looking for a change that hadn't occurred; there were no outward physical manifestations to concur with the state of inner estrangement that had him walk downstairs with the uncertain step of someone negotiating the roll of duckboards. He consoled himself with the ritual of dressing, draping a bold red and silver striped tie against a double-breasted blazer with gold nautical buttons. Likewise he complemented his charcoal cashmere trousers with black and white correspondent shoes that were polished to the consistency of a mirror. A splash of cologne revitalised his senses as he poured a tomato juice into a glass of ice shards. It was inconceivable, he told himself, that there was anything wrong. There had been the shock of finding David in his bedroom, but the irrational symptoms that he detected in himself subsequent to that disturbance were things he could attribute to no other cause than nervous anxiety.

He went through his papers meticulously. The volume of Burton's *Anatomy of Melancholy* was still open on the table beside his armchair; the faded purple ribbon that served as a bookmark reminded him of the silk dress that his mother wore on the afternoon that they had discovered the little secondhand bookshop in which they had procured the volumes. It had become an inveterate fixture in his life, that red-painted bookshop with its discreet pipe-smoking owner browsing over recent purchases at a rickety desk. It was from that shop that he began initially to assemble the vast collection of books that lined his house. One discovery led to another. His passion for Baudelaire had led him to Huysmans, and from the former's imaginary voyages he had taken up with the reality of Conrad's sea passages, while his love of Burton's *Anatomy of Melancholy* had found its modern extension in Djuna Barnes's *Nightwood*. His library attested to the development of his own literary and aesthetic tastes, and from his shelves he could select a book for any mood or season.

Once he was dressed and prepared for the day, the irrational in his mind receded. He found himself mentally anticipating his first client, a girl whose morbid fear of illness had resulted in her gradual withdrawal from life. Her aversion to sexuality was a part of her obsession with contamination. She had stopped menstruating, refused to eat solid foods, and lived a solitary anxiety-ridden life in the basement flat of a great-aunt's house. It was the shy alertness of a tiny wren observed outside the window that had instigated this train of thought. Patricia reminded him of a frightened bird; her beady eyes were the sparklingly expressive highpoints of her otherwise emaciated features.

It had become a custom with him to sit in an easychair and look out through the window at the garden for thirty minutes before setting off for his rooms in Harley Street. He luxuriated in the beneficence of those stolen minutes; it was the quiet hour, the time in which he settled into the centre of his being before facing the demanding exactions of his profession. Outside the window he could see red and pink hollyhocks, and a late flowering double hibiscus, a maroon badge inlaid into each blue flower. Against the wall yellow chrysanthemums were pompom-tight in the crisp early morning air. He savoured each minute of this respite and health came flooding back to him with an urgency that took him by surprise. The sun had come clear of the low-lying mist, and its amber rays polished the window. This was the essence of life, he assured himself, the inner and outer worlds conjoined with the unnoticeable pressure of rose petals all grouped weightlessly around a common centre of red fragrance.

He gathered papers and a few books together and placed them inside a snakeskin case, checked his appearance in the hall mirror, and took the scarlet Jowett Bradford out into the slowly building traffic. It was going to be a good day; he could feel it in the hum of his nerves and the equally fast pick-up of the motor that responded to his foot pressure. He motored towards the outer circle of Regent's Park; the chestnuts had begun to turn auburn and here and there scarlet at their crowns, the poplars were split into goldleaf by the dazzle of sunlight. A good day; twice he overtook cars before tailing an indomitable taxi that rode squat on the crest of the road. He could glimpse the passenger inside turning over the pink pages of a *Financial Times*. Twice he was about to risk an unnecessary acceleration, and twice his intuitive faculty warned him of the imprudence of such a move. His misjudgment would have involved him in a collision with an oncoming cement truck, the big painted letters BLUE CIRCLE standing out on its tank.

As was his custom, he arrived ten minutes before Miss Vince, and anticipated her work by assembling Patricia Riley's file on his desk. He found himself impatient to meet the day, and was conscious of a gap existing between his sudden energies and the tasks at hand that he had to complete. When Miss Vince arrived he found himself in the odd position of watching her movements in the outer office through the crack of his partially opened door. He could see her reshaping her lipstick line, quizzing over minute points of misdefinition before she plugged her typewriter in, and checked the appointment book off against the filing index.

He went into the outer office and greeted her cordially; he had picked her a yellow rose from the garden, and she was admiring this as he entered, tracing out the red spiral in a yellow petal with the delicacy of one who has an eye attuned to detail. He caught himself furtively assessing his own profile in the mirror as he spoke to her, and for a moment imagined that he glimpsed the profile of a fox, russet-haired, ears pointed, nose twitching for the scent. A slight flicker of disconcertment in Sandra Vince's eyes informed him that something he couldn't adduce was disquietingly wrong.

He requested his usual glass of mineral water, and returned to his office. He liked to sit and reflect over the purity of that frosted tumbler of water. The bubbles rose laconically and expelled themselves on contact with the surface. Sandra Vince came back into the room with an assortment of mail which he decided to ignore until the interval between his first and second appointments. A discreet purr on his internal line told him that Patricia Riley had arrived.

130

Patricia greeted him shyly and sat down. She always dressed tastefully and unprovocatively. She wore a black woollen cardigan with a simple white cotton skirt and, despite the unchallenging simplicity of her appearance, it had been put together with considerable care. The morbid aversion she expressed for her body also took on an obsessive fascination with its proportions, and she would confess to sitting naked in front of the mirror for hours, narcissistically attracted to what in turn she repelled. She invariably carried a book with her, and this morning she had a Penguin copy of Nabokov's *Lolita* under one arm.

'How have things been since we last met?' he began, smiling to put this brittle girl at ease. 'Have the tablets I prescribed been of any help in terms of appetite?'

She had the habit of rapidly blinking her eyes when she was perplexed, rather like a bird fanning its wings before flight, and he had anticipated the idiosyncrasy before looking up to discover it in motion.

'I'd rather not answer that,' she said. 'My weight is something of the mind, I don't think of it in physical terms.'

'You mean there's a radical dichotomy between how you conceive of yourself mentally, and how you present that image of yourself in physical terms,' he instructed, conscious as he spoke of a disquieting pressure in the region of his nape. 'Isn't the trouble partly that we expect others to accept us on terms known only to ourselves?'

'I think so,' Patricia replied thoughtfully, 'but I've reached a stage of exclusion whereby I can act out the parts which would otherwise be taken by others.'

'Then why do you need me?' he questioned. 'Don't I represent a thinking body external to yours, or am I just a projection of your own consciousness?'

'My answer to that would be ambivalent,' she replied. 'I imagine my inner world as comprising a protean clay from which I create a tableau of others. It's a diseased clay, full of poison . . .'

'The deistic form that you own to seems to admit to a deep flaw in its nature,' he said. 'Not that it's inconsistent that creation shouldn't be infractioned, but it does imply an inversion to convert dark into dark. What sort of contact are you maintaining with your aunt?'

'We meet once a day,' Patricia said, 'but we don't really share

131

any common plane of communication. As I told you last time, my aunt has her own friends, her own rather mundane interests; we neither of us fit into each other's lives. If I wanted to know her I would recreate her through my own perception. She'd wear scarlet hats and zany dresses and recite Stevie Smith to her friends over gunpowder tea.'

'And would you be a part of the gathering?' he said, intrigued by her notion of the exotic, her reductionism of all things to accommodate a particular facet of her character.

'I wish to enact my own psychodrama,' she replied. 'I want to withdraw to an invisible entity, to retain consciousness, but to be dead to the world; in that way I can create without being challenged.'

'But isn't this the ultimate narcissism?' he found himself saying. 'To create without the knowledge of others, and in a state of wilful concealment, implies an aspiration towards an unreal perfectionism.'

The vehemence of her response startled him; she raised herself from her chair, and spat the words 'lying bastard' into his face. She'd kicked off her shoes and was threatening him from the side of the desk nearest to his telephone. Years of practice had taught him to maintain an implacable detachment; he busied himself with riffling through the notes in her file, until eventually she calmed down and resumed her seat.

'I didn't wish to provoke anger,' he said, somewhat diffidently; 'my concern was to have you disburden yourself of some of the tension that has been building up in you for a long time.' He knew that the session would deteriorate; it always did after he'd forced her like a spider out of her lair. She would sit frozen on the edge of her chair and refuse to respond, and days later he'd receive a letter of contrite apology, a girlish letter in which the sentiments expressed were contrary to the emotions felt.

When Patricia left, he rooted himself in mental space. He felt himself to be on the edge of a discovery similar to the pupation of the caterpillar into a moth. Something was happening internally which was going to manifest itself in external terms. He could feel the blaze in his nerves, an acute restlessness which was directed towards an end which he couldn't determine or control. He had the uncanny feeling that he was reading a book without having to look at the pages, but more distressing was the faint animal odour that he detected on his skin. His wrists and hands smelt as if he'd been stroking a dog that had come in out of the rain, only the odour was doubly pungent. Twice already he had slipped into the bathroom and lingered over the comfort of moulding a tablet of soap between his hands. The effect was always a quieting one; ever since childhood the immersion of his hands beneath a jet of water had brought about a relief from tension. It was his most simple distraction but, lather his hands as he did, he couldn't erase the distinct smell of something canine. It was a scent that David had left behind the afternoon he had found him tyrannising the exquisite order of his bedroom. Somewhat unsettled, he returned to his consulting room and flipped through the autumn fashions in *Vogue*, his eye alighting on a green Jacquard woollen sweater, and a black full-length coat by Gianfranco Ferré, both of which would complement his intended winter visit to the resort of Le Caribou. He also singled out a paisley wool scarf in aquamarine and russets by Claude Montana; this would add a little discreet panache to his autumn tweeds in London.

After this necessary and pleasing interlude, he returned to the subject of his next patient. He looked at the file – Robert Blakestone M A. His patient still subscribed to the old-fashioned manner of appending his masters to his name. A private tutor in his early fifties, he appeared to have entered the grey waters of a middle-aged climacteric. His fear was impotence, an obsession which had dogged him sporadically throughout his life, and kept him from entering into any form of sexual relationship. A tall, thin, bird-like man, over-fastidious, excruciatingly polite, punctilious to the second, painstakingly exact, he had made an unsuccessful and largely half-hearted attempt on his life last winter, during those iron-skyed remorselessly black days that precede the winter solstice. Short days in which one walks between dark and dark in a state of primeval drowsiness, and when only the robin's song brings a brief note of triumph to the dying year. The old gods are in hibernation then; they invite us to follow them into the dark of the bat's, the weasel's, the squirrel's sleep.

Dr Moravia prepared for his patient. The restlessness he felt inside showed no signs of abatement. He compared it to the apprehension a bird must feel in the days prior to migration – the sonar crackling in the tiny skull, the body fuelled by its additional weight, its eyes beadily focusing into the sun

133

from the tightrope of a telegraph-wire.

'Good morning, doctor, and an exceedingly pleasant one too,' said Robert Blakestone, as he carefully arranged himself in the chair opposite Dr Moravia. He crossed his legs, freed his jacket from the possibility of its becoming trapped behind him, and lowered his head in sign of concentration. Moravia couldn't help thinking that the man resembled a blackbird, stock-still, ruminative, listening in the quiet for the tunnelling of a worm.

'Would you mind awfully if I smoke,' he apologised. It was a phrase he repeated at each appointment, before carefully opening a silver monogrammed case and tapping the ball of a cigarette on its sounding-board. This was evidently a great part of his pleasure – using the cigarette as a delicate drum-stick before finally committing that carefully manicured head to flame. He directed his smoke away from Dr Moravia, and closed his eyes in readiness for the not always easy questions that would touch upon the most sensitive area of his being.

'Well, Mr Blakestone,' Moravia began, 'has there been an intensification or decrease in anxiety symptoms since we last met? I'm hoping that the Ativan I prescribed will have helped to modify specific anxiety crises. Have you been able to fulfil your work schedule?'

'Yes, the tablets have been a considerable help, doctor,' Blakestone replied. 'I've largely been on an even keel although I have one incident to report if you'll bear with me. It's altogether rather beastly.'

'To you or to someone else?' Moravia prompted, doing his best to facilitate this shy man's need to confess.

'To two parties, doctor,' Blakestone admitted reticently. 'If I'm to relate the crisis I'll have to tell you everything. Well, after all these years I finally made a pass and it proved negative.'

'How did you enter the relationship?' Moravia enquired, playing his fish downstream for fear it might snap the line and run. An experience that had happened to him far too often, and literally, in his angling days, fly-fishing the liquid sinew of a stream, floating an iridescent kingfisher fly into the mirror glare, then feeling the strain as the fish pumped hard and ran muscularly with the current, unwinding his reel with a screech of rainbow catgut, the rod springing back into a vacuous arc as the fish broke free with the trophy of the hook embedded in its lip.

'The traumatic incident involved a pupil,' Blakestone admitted timorously. 'Let me tell you of it in the most compressed synthesis that I can construct. For several years now I've been seeing on and off on an obligatory social basis a student of mine whose mother committed suicide; vulnerability and acute loneliness on both parts allowed the habit to form, and it developed into routinal custom. Margaret, or rather Miss Adams, expressed a profound love for the Romantic poets – Keats, Shelley, and Coleridge in particular; it became a part of our shared language, "Adonais" and "Endymion", Coleridge's great "Ode to Dejection". Well, things developed, and rather precipitately, and without having made any overt advances I found myself in the assumed position of being her fiancé. Nothing was expected of me until two weeks ago, when what I had feared came true, and my inadequacy was put to the test.'

'And is Margaret physically attractive to you?' Dr Moravia enquired.

'It's hard to decide in the affirmative or negative,' Blakestone said authoritatively, as though he was assessing an enigmatic metaphor in a line of poetry that wouldn't lend itself to interpretation. 'She's five years my junior, her figure is, for a woman of her age, not unattractive.'

'How could it be made more attractive?' Dr Moravia interpolated. 'You speak as though you were desirous of attributes that Margaret lacks.'

Blakestone pondered the question, although it had become apparent to him that he couldn't altogether avoid an element of salaciousness. 'I like longer legs,' he said, 'or should I say that aesthetically I incline towards longer legs.'

'And do these play a part in your sexual fantasies?' Dr Moravia enquired.

'I rather suppose they do,' Blakestone assented, beginning again the ritual of drum-tapping the base of his cigarette. 'I know we've discussed the question of masturbation before; confidence is mine when the mental image is illusory, it's the act which so disturbs me.'

'You mean your fantasies only involve women?' Moravia queried. 'I would have thought that you were also preoccupied with the image of the male body; could it not be that your physical retraction when faced with the female body implies a latent gravitation towards members of your own sex?'

Blakestone remained surprisingly unperturbed. 'Before I tell

135

you about the disastrous incident with Margaret,' he said, 'I thought . . . ' and then he broke down.

'You thought,' Moravia said, 'that you have an admission to make to me that you have previously kept concealed, and which is vital to our case. I know it's painful, but you must externalise it.'

There was a pause of minutes before Blakestone said, 'All right, it only happened once, and I was coerced into it. It happened quite unaccountably; it was the year after I had graduated. I had come down from Oxford with a first in English Lit., and was doing a few private tutorials before I assessed my future prospects. I had this pupil called Dover, Dover Racanthorpe, who'd been sent down from Eton for obvious reasons. It just happened one day. We were reading Marlowe at the time, with a view to Dover eventually finding a place at Oxford, when I felt his hand resting on my thigh. I had been fantasising during the tutorial and was already erect. When he touched me I didn't go limp as might have been expected, but on the contrary my erection responded to the nimbleness of his fingers. Although I kept imagining they were a girl's fingers, I followed along until desire blinded me . . . After the act I kept telling myself that it had only occurred because I was aroused prior to the stimulation.'

'And did Margaret offer such foreplay?' Moravia enquired.

Blakestone drew heavily on the red bulb of his cigarette. 'No, I felt it incumbent on me to make the initial advances, but having aroused her, I was incapable despite my desire of fulfilling her.'

'Did you end up in bed,' Moravia asked, 'or did things fall short of that?'

'We were on the sofa,' Blakestone said, with evident disfavour. 'I couldn't get my nerves alight, no matter what fantasy I conjured as a surrogate to Margaret. Awful business, I haven't dared to contact her again.'

'But what exactly does she expect of you?' Moravia enquired. 'You assume that she wishes intercourse, but what if she already guessed that you lacked positive desire for her? Wouldn't this establish a tributary through which you could escape? But does the trout that has come free of the hook ever escape, and if so, where?'

'Into a stagnant pool, I assume,' Blakestone deliberated. 'But why is it that some men are born with a pistol they can't fire?' he said sadly.

'Because it's a weapon they direct either against themselves, or towards their own species,' Moravia replied. 'Homosexuality is the gun that's loaded with blanks; its discharge is unregenerative, every ejaculation ends in a literal death. For you, it's a matter of establishing a balance; fear prevents you from loading the cartridge because you're uncertain of your aim. But that's something I'd like to talk about in greater depth when we meet in two weeks' time; up until then, continue with the Ativan. They're not going to solve your dilemma, but they can be used as an intervention to disperse panic-thresholds.'

'I feel we've made progress today, painful as it has been,' Blakestone affirmed. 'One last question, however. Should I continue to avoid Margaret?'

'Not at all,' Moravia said. 'I would suggest you refacilitate the social side of things, and take it from there.'

He could hear Blakestone studiously double-checking the date of his next appointment, and Miss Vince's unlimited courtesy willingly prescribing to the former's archaicisms. Once again he was glad of the respite when he heard the outer door shut. He shifted at once to reverie, for of late he had come to find pleasure in his childhood memories only. In the ten minutes allowed to him he could surmount the hurdle of four decades, and place himself inside a cultural enclave in the way that a beautiful shell is preserved in a glass case. Was he ten or twelve when it happened? It was the day when he had turned down his mother's suitor. He had been aware by the increase in the number of times she went out each week, and by her new wardrobe and the little flask-shaped bottle of scent, that she was seeing someone without his knowledge. Possessiveness and an inextinguishable current of jealousy had forced him to instigate a show-down. Young as he was, he had argued like a husband wronged by his wife's infidelity; he was simply not going to tolerate a third party detracting from the exclusive cynosure he had become to his mother.

He could see her still, little seed-pearls of tears flecked the perfumed face powder she had applied with such care. She was dressed in a short cocktail dress with a draped ostrich boa, and the sheer black silk stockings she had bought to complement the costume were intended to invite admiration. He wondered now

137

at the fact that he could have acted so tyrannically; there were scenes, he locked himself in his room, he threatened to starve himself to death unless his mother remained with him tonight, he wanted to read Hugo's *Toilers of the Sea* to her, he wanted to visit the bookshop before it closed at 8.00.

There were tears on both sides, but at last his mother had gone to the telephone, and when she returned she was smiling, she called him her only one, and together they went to the bookshop and purchased a vellum edition of the poems of Christina Rossetti, bound in a fuchsia coloured suede. Then there were Lindt chocolates to buy, and a new bottle of violet ink. It was only when he woke up before dawn and heard his mother crying in the room next to his that he realised what he had done. But he had remained unrepentant; his own very special life demanded the undivided attention of his mother, he told himself, and he was frightened of losing the self-indulgent privileges that had been granted him, for what might prove the questionable love of a step-father. His mother had never reproached him; it was only after her death that he read the inconsolable love letters that she had written and never sent. She must have continued to write one every day of her life, she confided everything in Joe; and it was with a bitter shock that he had been forced to admit that it was not he in whom his mother had confided the profounder realisations of her life, but in unmailed letters to her unrequited love. It brought home the unwelcome truth, too, that he had never loved another with this self-effacing intensity. His unnaturally close relationship with his mother had been one in which all things are unconditionally tolerated, but not necessarily understood or approved. Their wrong directions were right ones according to their own code of behaviour, but both had become fogged, mistracked, willing to have their own thicket catch fire rather than search out a clearing. The thread had ramified over the years and become inextricably convoluted in each. But neither their outbreaks of temper nor the chimerical persona that each adopted could finally sever a union in which compromise had become the forcing-house to survival. He remembered his concession. Rather in the manner that Dante Gabriel Rossetti had ordered his wife's grave to be opened in order to retrieve poems that he had buried with her, so he had ordered his mother's coffin to be opened two weeks after her burial, in order to consign to it the large packets of love letters that had so

138

obviously formed an integral part of her emotional life. That done, he had walked away from the grave with some small feeling of solace.

He was immersed in his reverie when Miss Vince buzzed him to alert him that his next patient was in the adjoining waiting-room. In his confusion he neglected to ask who it was, and had barely time enough to read the name Miss Claudette . . . when the door to the room opened, and he was confronted with Claudette's unmistakably tall presence, made additionally so by the scarlet stiletto heels on which she pivoted. She was dressed in black; a skirt that moulded itself to her with parasitical ferocity, and a black top that pronounced her overdeveloped figure. In the seconds before speech Moravia glimpsed the strain in Claudette's features; it must have been terrible, the inner agony, the misdefinition of gender, and the loneliness that was married to the decision to transpeciate. It was a gestation period far more harrowing and prolonged than any pregnancy, for it involved the ultimate misconception – the adoption of a new gender. No matter her willingness to change; at some moment Claudette must have retracted in terror, the genitalia to which she had become accustomed at birth were no longer hers – they were now in the surgeon's ice-box.

Moravia felt his nerves charged to a needlehead, and some-where in the back of his mind the pacing began again, died down, and devolved into a dog's yawn. The sleepy but alert characteristics of a creature that lies low by day in a tunnel of earth had exhaled at him a dog's bare-teethed exposure of the instruments of its nocturnal hunger. The precisional rapacity that bites the head off a rabbit or chicken.

'I might have guessed,' he began, 'that you'd even search me out here. Let us get to the point without malice or equivocation; what exactly is it that you wish from me?'

'It's not quite that simple, Ernst,' Claudette replied, exagger-atedly pouting her scarlet lips. 'It involves several things, some of which may imply a little guesswork on your part. I suppose you've realised by now that it's not by accident that I sought you out in London. I may have done so in hell, if it was necessary to enter the inferno to find you.'

'I repeat my question,' he said, with glacial reserve. 'How can I help you? You are taking up the valuable time of people who need my professional advice.'

139

'Ince Martin Jnr,' she drawled, imitating a Midwestern accent. 'Does that name mean something to you, or did you deal through one of the ectoparasites that grew on him like coral? They all come to a bad end, Ernst,' she admonished, 'including Spike Thompson who went headfirst over a Cornish cliff.'

Moravia winced. Having spent a lifetime circumventing physical violence, he now found himself confronted with a psychological threat tantamount to the blows he had often imagined but never received. It stung his cheeks like wet leather, a sensation he associated with the taste of blood drying in the throat.

'Let me be frank,' he said. 'If your purpose is to try and coerce me into conceding to blackmail, then you've chosen the wrong person.'

'I don't think blackmail's the appropriate term,' Claudette said. 'Isn't it more a case of a mutual understanding between turncoat generals. I mean we've both deserted our fields and opted for a deserter's spoils rather than the gold-ribboned medal.'

'I don't altogether follow you,' he said grimly, 'and furthermore, how did you manage to arrange an appointment here without a prior recommendation and my own consent? I don't feel like protracting this conversation; I have an exacting day ahead of me.'

'Appointment or not,' she said, 'it's not your occasional flings with me in the past that brings me here.' *I have no intention of dangling you by a rat's tail above the yellow pond. Mutual aberrations are easily consigned to dust if one has the consent of both parties. One can travel to hell on a laden or unladen cart; I'd prefer to unload some of the prosecution's files before crossing the river on a raft of files each tagged Pending.*

'Can't we meet tonight to discuss this in greater privacy?' he said with some urgency.

'But what greater privacy can one have than a psychiatrist's rooms? Isn't this the confessional where you hear out your patients' most intimate and excruciating traumas?'

He realised he was trapped, in the way that David had cornered him, jinxed his mind with the adoption of his own personal characteristics. He wanted to disappear, to shrink himself into a poppy-seed, or project himself into landscapes that he knew: the Côte d'Azure, Venice, the arid mid-summer scrub

140

of the Aegean Islands in the dog-days, a lavender symphony of bluebells from Monet stumbled upon in a beech wood in Essex. He kept glancing at his watch but the small-hand remained immobile. A russet blaze crackled in his head, then settled down again. He began to loathe this misconceived woman, this hybrid anomaly who dogged him like a setter which won't give up once it has established a scent. He was known to her, and to be 'known' to someone is to concede the most terrifying power of all. He remained cogitatively silent, before she resumed speaking.

'I want two things,' she said with absolute precision. 'The photographs you have of me from my Paris days, and the whereabouts of David Thompson.'

Moravia felt his heart jog with an irregular jumpy beat which brought two cold beads of perspiration to his hairline. Instinctively his fingers sought out the cool silk of his tie, that inveterate and unfailing palliative that had pursued him from childhood.

'A photograph,' he said, 'particularly if it entails a negative, is a duplicative thing. It can no more be erased than the photographic cell of memory which retains the incident in the mind. What if I returned the photographs to you? What assurance would you have that I or someone else, the previous owner, had not disseminated copies to others? This is surely the incriminating and unreliable facet of photography – if there's a negative, there may be a hundred copies of its exposure.'

'You don't have to circumvent the issue,' Claudette said; 'it's the bulk I want – the whole celluloid tableau of erotica that Ince Martin contrived. I want those morbid archives, and I'd also like you to tell me where David is.

'Furthermore,' Claudette ventured, like a spider releasing its poison glands once it has impaled its victim from behind, 'there are photographs of you, dear Ernst.'

'Of me?' he whined incredulously, for a moment lapsing from the dignified professional hauteur that he was determined to maintain.

'You drinking Bollinger out of a Louis-Quinze chamberpot, my black lace suspender belt hooked around your waist. You playing chess with dildos on my apartment floor, or posing in a green evening dress; don't you remember your temporary flirtations with drag on your summer vacations in Paris? I could go on; the photographs may not be great in number, but it is their

141

variety and explicitness which makes them of interest, and don't forget, Ernst, it was I who took them.'

He averted his eyes and looked towards the window. It seemed to him as though one's actions were recorded, a cine-film, and each was inerasable, so that at any moment someone somewhere could buttonhole you in a bar and say, 'Remember Berlin 1936; you were with Franz, and we went back to . . . It was the padded shoulders of your chalk-striped suit I recollect.' Or it was the raincoated figure standing by a kiosk in the Rue Madeleine who said to you out of the fog, 'I know who you are, you once knew me, but have forgotten,' and the fog came down again. Does anyone ever forget if they have known you?

'All right,' he said, conceiving a scheme whereby he could renege, 'I'll give you access to the photographs, if you'll grant me the return of mine.' His words sounded hollow, for already he knew that the photographs were a pretext for something else. His mind was throwing up satellites from its deepest vaults in an effort to anticipate the insidious tack of Claudette's reasoning. He watched them explode like a bouquet of fireworks across a black night sky, but was unable to isolate the incandescent flower that Claudette in her own mind was preparing to release.

'And David,' she began, 'what of poor David Thompson? The victim of a corrupt father and equally corrupt doctor, am I not right, Ernst?'

'I don't follow your implications,' he replied. 'The boy in question is a patient of mine. I know what you're trying to suggest, but any intimation of misconduct on my part is out of the question. I have a patient waiting,' he said with genuine alarm, 'can't we meet one evening and discuss these disquieting private affairs?'

'Where is David? You knew what went on at Blue Rock, and you can't pretend otherwise. Spike's dealings with young children – you were surely a party to these things.'

'What are you trying to tell me?' Moravia said austerely. 'Are you trying to imply that I advocate the appropriation of children? I don't intend to continue this discussion further,' he said; 'I suggest, however, that we meet for a drink on neutral territory at 8.00.' His emotions froze; he felt as though he was immured in a deep-freeze, or that he was a cod nosing down from Iceland to the North Sea. *A green unfathomable depth of cold, and if a man hit those night waters he died instantly, the shock of the cold put out his*

142

heart. He used to undergo a similar state of paralysis when summoned by a master at school. For the entire five years of his senior schooling, he somehow always felt culpable, as though he was being called to apologise for his existence, rather than to receive the approbation of a glowing teacher who wished to commend him on another profound Shakespearian appreciation, a depth of analysis that gave him an indisputable first in the class and school. But this time he faced a death-trap, the condition of a man who is confronted with a terminal illness and knows that he will never again find respite from the consciousness of that little crystal of death circulating in his bloodstream.

He barely heard Claudette depart; rather he sat contemplating an impasse, a walled corridor on which his name was written in blood. He recapped his aquamarine pen, the one with the cobalt and yellow marbling; it looked like a sea-bed, the floor of the Adriatic seen on a day of prismatic sunlight.

The imminence of Miss Knight's appointment saved him from breaking down. He buzzed Miss Vince to say that he was running late, and would she ask Miss Knight to be so good as to wait a further ten minutes. Miss Knight was one of his most exacting patients – a menopausal depression complicated by thrombosis. The latter had developed into a barely containable obsession. It had resulted too in chronic agoraphobia, a fear of being away from the immediacy of a telephone in the event of suffering an accident. Her one concession was her fortnightly appointment, when her desperation was overcome by the still greater need to seek analytical help.

In the urgency of his thoughts, his mind exploded into the glare of mirror shards. What he imagined was a desert at noon; tanks were swarming across it, and in a burst of red fire an aircraft came down in a mushrooming billow of smoke. But with Claudette his engagement would be on a level of astute chess strategy. How often in talking to her he had frozen a word in mid-speech, contracted on its suspension, and watched her own thought deftly manoeuvre to avoid taking up the issue she had intuitively anticipated.

He asked for Miss Knight to be shown in. It was his last appointment of the morning, and if things ran according to schedule he could be back home by 4.30. This would allow him sufficient time in which to devise a strategy to save his future.

Miss Knight was less troublesome than he had anticipated.

She was fractionally less centred round her obsessive fear of injury, and the coagulative bleeding that the latter threatened to entail. She even admitted to having gone out by taxi to visit a friend. It was a monumental step forward, and one which afforded him a degree of private satisfaction. The retrieval of a person from the insidious current of a neurosis that would in time carry them out to the deeps and drown them. This was what his life's work comprised, the reactivation of things swallowed up by the black ebb tide. It took a long time for the deep to return the bodies, but the flood tide brought its surprises, jettison that could be reassembled. 'Severely damaged but still functioning' John Berryman had written of himself towards the end of his life, and it was the criterion by which most of Dr Moravia's patients managed their lives.

When he drove home early that afternoon, he had the impression that he had aged twenty years. Impatient to find security in the quiet of his sitting-room, he was unfortunate enough to encounter a hearse and its attendant cortège of black limousines. When the funeral car turned off by Chester Gate he caught a glimpse of the massed blue irises, white lilies and vermilion carnations that wreathed the coffin. He had three hours between himself and the improbable fires of the pit he had always dreaded. Exposure is like fire; it incinerates the former person and leaves a simulacrum dusted by the ash of his own cremation. He slammed his foot down hard on the accelerator and drove into the orange glare of October sunlight – a clear afternoon on the roads; he would be home in ten minutes.

10

Once inside Moravia felt better assured about the prospect of meeting Claudette at 8.00. He looked at the clock on the marble mantelpiece. The time was 4.25. It was too early, but he would risk a drink, and took an ice-packed Martini with him to his favourite chair. He had no sooner sat down and drawn up the foot-rest than he was overcome by a deep-rooted fear that David might be upstairs again. He felt like a burglar in his own house, cat-footing across the carpet to the door, inhaling shallowly so as not to describe his presence. Involuntarily he felt compelled to search the house, and began the ascent slowly, stair by stair, climbing with the sensitive palps of a spider's legs. Light from a window in the first-floor corridor cast a transverse beam of goldleaf across the floor.

He recollected that there were no visible signs of an intruder having entered downstairs. But one couldn't be sure; Moravia could smell the presence of someone – it was an indefinable warning scent that came to him in moments of crisis. He went on up to the second floor, calling out as he had done before, his mind periodically hallucinating so that he half-expected to find the materialisation of his fear in the form of a psychopath waiting to confront him on the topmost stair. He went into the little pink room as he had done last time, and found it undisturbed. He promised himself that if he lived he would make spiritual reparations. When he climbed the stairs, one by one, like a man mounting the scaffold, he could hear the organism of his body in revolt as though he had an ear attuned to the seismic upheaval of his abdomen.

His nerve had broken. 'It's only me,' he said; 'tell me what you want and you can have it. Are you there, David? There's no need to act in this way; I've come to offer you help. If I forced you into something, I'll make amends, you wait and see.' It startled him to realise that he was using the wheedling tone of importunacy or apology that he had used in childhood in order to prevent his mother from snatching those few brief hours with her undeclared lover.

Even before he pushed the door gently to, it leapt out at him. The mahogany wardrobe doors were open, so that his dark jacketed image swung to meet him with a fish ripple. He confronted his triple image, a Bacon triptych, as a means of counteracting shock. The wardrobes had been emptied of their photographic wallets. When things that have long been in store disappear, the wardrobe breathes again. He could smell its own peculiar mustiness, its aroma of a cigar-box in which stamps have been kept to take out on rainy autumn nights. A bright red line ran through the reflection of his torso – the word PERVERT was monogrammed across his navy-blue reflected blazer.

He must have stood there a long time steadying himself, finding a central pivot from which to prepare for the shock, letting the mirror absorb his image like a dye, before he broke the spell by opening drawers and cabinets. Whoever had come here knew precisely what they wanted; not only his personal archives of photographs had disappeared, but also folders of private correspondence – the private record one keeps for a lifetime on the assumption that one will burn it before one's death. Burn it like the marigold blaze of autumn leaves that expire in a thin blue smoke, and like the body he had imagined inside the coffin at Chester Gate; it would be ash now, a grey smudge of dust dispersing over London.

He went back downstairs, holding tightly on to the invisible lifeline that the self becomes in times of acute crises. Even in the state of potential ruin with which he was faced, he still found consolation in that inner sense of conviction which had remained with him a lifetime. No matter how far he fell, he could escape into his inner sanctuary. No one could gain access there. The light was on all night and all day; and the ejector-seat in the white cell released one into death. At certain moments in life one entered that cell; it was a means of reconciling oneself to the eventual mystery of death.

He settled into his evening chair, a deep-seated sea-green armchair with a glass-topped table beside it for books and cigars. The chestnut leaves turned blue in the late afternoon cross-light. He reached for a cigar and toyed with it. Comforted by his familiar surroundings, he applied himself to an analysis of

Claudette's strategy. It didn't seem plausible that she would involve herself in so crude a theft, only a matter of hours before their intended meeting. The act lacked logic. And if the photographs had been stolen by an accomplice of Claudette's, then he was safe, he reasoned, for she required the photographs for the erasure of her past life, and not as a leverage to bring about his own ruin. But there was a missing thread and, no matter how he argued himself out of danger, he relapsed into the very plausible suspicion that he was trapped. Something within him was already owning up to this; there'd been an inroad into his freedom, an abrupt severance of what he had come to consider as the continuity of his private life. He was now in the position of someone who has been found out but obstinately clings to the belief that his innermost truth could only be interpreted as a lie.

Since his mother's death he had formed the habit of conferring with no one, even colleagues, over a diagnosis that might have been elucidated by a second opinion. His friends were few, and he fashioned his life so that it gravitated towards solitude on one plane, and on the other, a sexual web of anonymous acquaintances. To fraternise in either sphere would have been to place a strain on the slender thread that held his duality in check. He left his social acceptances unreciprocated, and his professional colleagues had come to accept out of custom the impractical bachelor life that prevented their being invited by way of return. Instead he had cultivated the art of the tasteful present – Swiss chocolates, champagne, a flask of Guerlain for a colleague's wife, a box of cigars; these had come to serve as an unspoken trust that the dinner was appreciated but would not be returned.

Other men faced with his position of not wishing to report the theft would have telephoned their most loyal and sympathetic friend. For a moment he thought of summoning someone, but there were no illuminated faces on the screen, just cold, mineral nebulae receding into the galaxy. Dr John Taylor was the only person he could remotely construe as a friend, but his humourless circumspection struck Moravia as a character truth and not a professional manner that could be divested over a large Scotch. And anyhow, what could be considered a friendship was founded on a mutual love of book collecting; neither of them had probed the vein of the other's life, and it was better, he reflected, to leave things like that.

Yes, he would break all rituals today; the precedent set by his mid-afternoon drink led to him breaking the taboo of lighting his after-dinner cigar. His rituals were disciplined and inflexible, but today his nerves clamoured for assuagement. The blue resinous smoke spiralled into gunpowder clouds; they went on up, ring after ring symbolising the process of his thoughts. It was nearly 5.00, and he found comfort in periodically watching the clock-hand make the dilatory passage between one minute and the next, which was his childhood method of slowing time. Once you ceased to look at a clock it raced; if you met it eye to eye it showed all the fear of a bird stilled by a cat's eye in the grass.

He got up and paced back and forth across the room as he had done on the night of that insolubly disturbing telephone call. He ascribed the wrongness in his nerves to overwork, for he could rationalise that and, as he returned in thought to Claudette's visit earlier in the day, he found himself physically twisted round by the scream of a dog. It was twilight; a blueness filled the garden, tree-shapes had grown indistinct or had merged into the gathering dusk. He knew there were foxes in London that scavenged at night on the outskirts for garbage, but the scream was so loud, so intrinsically near that it could only have come from within. As always in time of severe shock, he went straight to the mirror. His eyes had reddened; he could clearly define russet lines around the abnormally dilated and bright pupils. He could rationalise the disrhythmia behind audio-hallucinations, but the distinct physical symptoms that he was beginning to manifest, an accelerated heart-beat and periodic constriction of the chest, were visible orders of distress about which he should seek consultation. He would settle matters with Claudette, seek Taylor's advice, and go away to the sun for three weeks. It was true, he told himself, that he was psychophysically exhausted; he gave his patients too much of himself, and the constant need to analyse disorders, aberrations of nervous behaviour, and to retain his own equilibrium, was taking an exacting toll on his health. He had no wish to enlist amongst those of his colleagues who were regularly carried from the field – the maimed alcoholic psychiatrists, those who jumped into the sea, and those whose defences broke down so that they came to identify with their patients, and were subsequently traumatised by the neuroses they had sought to elucidate.

The one way to steady his nerves was to get dressed for his meeting with Claudette. He took down from its hanger a

148

pistachio shirt with ice-white collar and cuffs, and matched it with a graphite cashmere suit. The pairing of this outfit with a silk tie in understated arabesques of pink and green with cross-hatchings of red filigree was his personal form of ikebana.

He dressed slowly, conscious of the red dilation of his eyes, the hirsute bristling of his skin. He had the remission of an hour before him, a period he would divide into five-minute intervals, in the hope that by focusing his eye on the movement of the clock-hands he could delay their inexorable progression. Conscious that a climax was imminent, the coolness of his reflected image soothed him; it was like fishing, watching a trout or mullet poker the calm surface into ringed labials. He would fish for his own reflection, a red fish that seemed increasingly to be supplanting his former self. He felt as someone does on the edge of an illness; the symptoms were inherent within, but they had still to realise themselves in a way that made it possible to diagnose them. This was the experience of childhood, in which all the terror was in the not knowing, the fever and the dizziness before the metamorphosis occurred, and the combination of a doctor and thermometer gave a specific name to what before had been an inner state of revolt. Anabasis – the march of fear, bacterial armies swarming the blood cells.

What he couldn't erase was the red blood disk that had become a permanent feature of his mental landscape. He was waiting for something and something was waiting for him with still greater patience. The hunt would begin when one of the two showed the greater weakness – a chink in the armoured carapace, and the adversary would force a way through.

The crispness of his green shirt cooled the fever of his skin; he could feel the creases work in like corrugations of cold. But the pungency of animal scent was still there; it had come to pervade the house. Everything was impregnated with the reek of animal; it was as though a dog had rolled over and over on his carpets, its coat soured by the dankness of a marsh. He found himself gathering the necessary items – car-keys, money, pills to counteract tension; he was like someone preparing for a transatlantic airflight, edgy before lift-off, convinced that the aircraft would blow into a pyrotechnic flash of lit petroleum. A red and yellow blast that would take the back out of the sky.

He went down one flight to the pink room which had formerly been his mother's bedroom. He had kept it unaltered with an

149

almost Proustian reverence. The rose silk counterpane had a single crease in it in the shape of a circle; it was like a full moon risen in a sky of flamingo silk. When he checked the calendar he saw it was the 28th, the night of the full moon, which would be bloody as it so often was in October. 'Twenty and eight are the phases of the moon' came to his mind, as he looked behind him to see a copper ray of moonlight catching on the bedroom window.

It was already 6.45; he had left time to itself and it had slipped by unawares. He was in the process of being overtaken. He slipped on his mother's sapphire and diamond engagement ring, the one that fitted his little finger, and which he had tried on so often. Tonight he could wear it as a talisman. He went through his mother's possessions, her photograph albums, her rings, her lace and silk scarves, the little vellum-covered books of poetry that she had kept locked up in a rosewood cabinet. Things that were imbued with her presence. He took the dresses out of the wardrobe, and tried on a champagne silk evening gown, draping it over his suit, and for an instant was metamorphosed into his mother as she had been forty years ago.

He was searching for something; a clue, an identity that by its very distraction would allow his mind to find the connective that he sought. Associations came to light like that, the intuitive flash came out of the obscuring dross of ephemera. He unhoused old carnation soaps that retained a slight fragrance, coins salvaged from journeys abroad, invitation cards with their ornate italics, an emerald necklace, each stone of which shone like a viridian grassblade seen through a prismatic globule of early-morning dew. Touching these symbols, and assigning to them the properties accorded by him and his mother, was to be re-endowed with the magic and strength of childhood. He systematically set about refinding the sequence of associations whereby he could establish an intimate psychic union with his mother.

He glanced at his watch again; he was obsessed with time. It was 7.15. Things were narrowing in, but he had made his peace with all that was important to him. All that remained was to fasten his tie, an act that he reserved until last in order to have the pleasure of slowly fashioning a knot in silk, and drive to their rendezvous in a wine-bar in Charlotte Street. The moon was now gladiolus red; it flooded the house from a cloudless sky granulated with lucent stars. A low yelp startled him as he went upstairs to his room, a sound that he could only attribute to a dog in a neighbouring garden. But again, as with the ferocious scream that had occurred earlier in the afternoon, the red mist behind his eyes quaked like the unsettling of a quicksand. Particles decomposed and regrouped rather like iron filings returning to the central field of gravity established by a magnet. He ruled out the likelihood of a stroke; a recent check-up had verified what he already knew – that he was in good physical health.

He delayed the fastening of his tie, meticulously forming the bulb so that it fitted perfectly into the V of the collar. Search as he did, he could find no signs of a forced entry into the house; only the fractional gap in an unlocked downstairs window gave any intimation as to how the intruder could have entered. The other possibility that sprang to mind was that David had found a key in one of the bedroom drawers, and had thus been able to let himself into the house without any visible evidence of having done so. He threw the houselights on upstairs, but not without flinching at the prospect that the intruder might still be inside waiting for him to go out. Things had doubled in his life, the *doppelgänger* that stalked him within had assumed an external counterpart. He looked for a gap in the circuit, a break in the pattern of recent events through which he could retrieve his former self.

He purposely avoided the hall mirror, finger-tapped the barometer, and let himself into the garage. Once again he found his olfactory senses overstimulated; the black dribble of accumulated oil that had puddled on the concrete floor over years of garage use invited the nostalgic recollection of his first car, a green Triumph Spitfire that his mother had given him for his twenty-first. He could remember still the excitement occasioned by inhaling the smell of the leather upholstery, and the oil-leak that he had come to associate with cars. Standing in the muted light of the garage he felt sheltered, as though he was taking refuge from a rainstorm beneath the protective canopy of a chestnut tree.

He would take the Bradford; its varnished wooden dashboard lit up with greenly illuminated planets. Its controls responded to his touch with the intimacy of sensitive typing-keys. He put on the octagonal-lensed glasses he wore for night-driving, and eased the car into the heavy filter of evening traffic. He cruised into a

151

congealed artery of build-up immobilised by the scarlet glare of a traffic-light. Sachets of neon split across the hard dazzle of the night road. He could feel the redness beginning to disperse again in the back of his mind; it was opening into a tunnel of earth. He appeared to be looking into a fox-hole, into the black eye of it, through which he could discern the gape of teeth, the glint of jet eyes. The reek was terrible; a taxi was sounding its horn in his rear, a belligerent klaxon of impatience, as he realised that he was stalling the traffic building up to his rear. By the time he got away the lights had returned to red. In his rear-view mirror he could see the irate expression of the cabby behind him, the man's face awash in gold light from the on-off flash of a neon sign advertising a restaurant. The delay in his reactions unnerved him; for an experienced driver he felt unaccountably uncomfortable boxed in by parallel lanes of metal. The circuit was closing; he thought of turning round and motoring the short distance home, but he had slipped into the on-going lane and had to comply with the signal to go forward. Images from Dante's *Inferno* sprung to mind as the cars herded forward; he was caught up in an irreversible procession. There was only a way forward now, as he moved into a dilatory second, flanked on either side by faces rigid with concentration. Everyone was locked into the containment of their own world, walled in by glass like fish in an aquarium. It was an underwater light he peered into, flickerings of red and green weed patrolled by armour-flanked monsters from the deep. He intensified his concentration; the rust-coloured snout of a fox was looking him full in the face, he could see the quiver of moisture on its nostrils, the rapacity of its eyeballs. Its breathing too was audible now; the hot air exhaled by a dog-fox was working into the stream of his own breath. When he exhaled he was conscious of the alien heat, his breath was doubled, he was breathing for two, and his lungs laboured at the expenditure of effort. He looked to right and left as the traffic stalled in an interminable queue. To his right the driver of a blue Ford van was lighting up a cigarette, cupping the lighter flame in his hands, and to the left the driver of a maroon Jaguar was nervously tapping the fingers of his right hand on the steering-wheel. Anonymous identities that the green light would disperse into divergent arrows. He could feel the car palpitating beneath his touch, the engine was throbbing to open up on a clear road. He felt constrained; the fox-head leering from the telescopic lens

152

of his subconscious had him trapped. If he was savaged to death, sitting in the maelstromic eye of London traffic, no one would know of the ferocious inner paroxysm that had left his shirt front a wash of red. He worked the manual stick up to second again, as they crawled out from the lights into the cross-town blitz of traffic. He was jumpy now, his eye searching for danger in the most improbable situations. Twice he was the subject of vehement horn interchanges as he allowed traffic through with too liberal a margin of foresight. He was like a horse that wouldn't run caught up in a stampeding circle; his cautious movements signalled danger to the metallic steeds that closed in on him. His mind was beginning to explode with shooting-lights, but there was no way out now unless he abandoned the car in the ruck of milling traffic and calmly walked away with the keys.

He nosed forward, the streamlined polished bonnet suddenly lighting up blue from the urgent gyrations of a police siren. He had time in which to think as the traffic awkwardly massed itself to the kerb in order to allow the manoeuvring police car through. Dinosauric lorries trundled to bottom gear in a hiss of expiring brakes before the lanes regrouped and lumbered forward with an elephant's gait. He tried once to roll the window down, but the volume of toxic fumes was stifling. Once again he found himself trapped and regretting the assignment he had so impatiently arranged with Claudette. His acute physical discomfort was starting to show in his clothes. The inside of his collar was clammy with sweat – he imagined the discoloration spreading like lichen spores.

He decided to make for the outer circle of the park, assessing that the traffic would be less concentrated there. Judging by the incessant blare of ambulances and police cars to the rear of the traffic block, there must have been an accident somewhere, and this accounted for the congealed trickle of progress that has motorists caught up in that wasteland of ennui they encounter when they are denied movement. Trapped in that insulating capsule there is the diversion of a radio and nothing else.

Everything had slowed to a ponderous halt. Moravia fumbled with a cassette of Debussy's 'La Mer', hoping to enlist the calm of the sea and its graduated moods as a diversion to his state of inner panic. Once, catching sight of himself in the rear-view mirror, he didn't recognise himself; he swung away from the haggard face like a boxer drifting wide of a forearm swing. He could have sworn that the line of his chin showed a gingerish stubble, a red line that was the colour of bracken turning in autumn. If he had embodied in his life a belief in the mythic nature of metamorphoses, then he had done so on a plane that understood myth as a state of inner consciousness. Now challenged by its reality, he felt like someone unable to disengage from a dream of fire which was in fact the fat-crackling roar of autocombustion.

Very slowly the traffic queues began to filter forward; the motor-arena where battle was done was lit with exhaust fumes – motorway veterans with clipped wings and doors badgered forward, new saloons still glossy with garage wax slipped into lanes alongside the indomitable tank bodies of taxis. This time he wasn't going to miss his cue; he eased forward with precision, the clock-hand showing a sedate 30, the engine simmering in low key, waiting for the responsive foot to open out its power. He caught a momentary glance of the copper moon high in the cloudless black sky, and then the bullet punch of a fox's head asserted itself clearly in his mind. He gagged on the fetor of a fox smell, and fought the window down in the hope of being able to breathe. All his life he had imagined his death as an especially individual one – he would die asserting power over his own death; he had imagined it as a light growing radiant, he would be looking into this light until he wasn't seeing at all because he would have become that light. No effort, no pain, just this transference of the light of consciousness into something that was both abstract and individual, the seed become a blue flower cupping the white light. He had held on to that; it had become his own death in the way that he lived his own special life. It was the single blue cornflower awaiting him in a crystal glass at the top of a rock stair, the thunder of surf down below, a landscape of caves and goats, harsh cliff grass dotted with yellow poppies and sea-pinks; this was his prelude to the transformation he imagined occurred at death.

His mouth was locked into a dry rictus; he could feel the muscles clamped tight all along his jaw, once and then twice a whine forced itself out of his throat. He was panting, his breath scorched in the passage out of his nostrils and mouth, his saliva tasted of caries, he was dog-faced, red-eyed, blind to everything but the mesmeric focus inside his mind.

He pushed his foot down squarely on the sensitive accelerator-pad and swung into the outer circle. The needle raced like his heart – 60 to 70 to 80 as he jack-knifed between a sand truck and the Volvo which was beginning to pull away into an overtaking position. As he coaxed the car to 90, the flashbacks of his life unreeled with a corresponding speed. He was like someone watching a cine-film played at the wrong speed, yet able to isolate and identify each caption. Thousands of stamp-sized windows singed his retinal nerves; faster and faster the light scorched through him, and this too was a traffic, only it was flooding in a direction contrary to the arc of his trajectory.

95 – he was going to do it; everything that approached him appeared to be standing still, he wondered why the traffic was suddenly immobile, and then a scream broke out of his mouth, the cry of a fox answering a vixen. The needle went over 100, wavered there at a green apex then continued to climb fractionally. 105 – he had it in his sights; a white oncoming Jaguar wouldn't move, it hung there, so that he thought the car must have been abandoned in the middle of the road, must have been driverless, and the ignition of adrenalin in his nerves told him he could go clean through it, he could power himself through a wall and go on unscathed, the car intact, his windscreen unfractured by even a rose-thorn of glass.

He cramped his foot down and caught the image of a man throwing up his arms to his face as he desperately tried to slew wide of the head-on sports car. Those arms thrown up in frantic supplication shielded the face, so that he was conscious only of an immovable obstacle, an impediment that he couldn't break through as glass exploded with tempestuous ferocity across his face and lap. It was a detonative hail-storm, followed by a cyclone of red flames; he again believed in his invincibility as he was thrown forward, hitched into the air like a high-jumper suspended in the act of lifting to fall. He was going higher and higher, bulleting forwards and upwards, every nerve in his body livid with pain, he was broken over glass, thrown clear and up, then his skull drove into metal, went into it like a drill boring a rock surface, the skin was being drawn back over his head like a squid turned inside out, he was a mollusc without a shell being cut into by a cleaver. Before his consciousness fulminated and went out, he was aware only of incongruities; the fragility of the walls of his skull forcing themselves against the angular cutting surface of metal.

155

11

A tap was dripping – a metronomic tick-tock, tick-tock of silver droplets descanting to the white porcelain of a basin. Claudette's dress looked out of place in the small badly lit basement flat in which Pauline and Jan sat drinking acrid wine out of water tumblers. Claudette was going to be late for her appointment with Moravia, a prospect that afforded her pleasure, although it would present him with the advantage of an additional period of time in which to think. His abstruse patterns of thought, punctuated by flashes of unnerving analytical precision, left one with little or no defence. But she could afford to be late; she had the photographs and an assortment of private correspondence. What would ensue would be a game of chess for empty stakes. He couldn't afford to lay claim to the knowledge that they had been stolen, for it would vitiate his bargaining power, while she had to assume the consternation of one who still believed that the photographs were in his possession. A dialogue between pretenders; the anticipation of the experience excited her. For once she was forearmed against his hold over her past, a hold that he saw as a weakness, and which she could now convert to a strength.

The girls were waiting for Diane to return; she had been their mutual confidante over developments at Blue Rock, and her extraordinary sympathy allowed her to view even Spike's actions with the rationale of objectivity. Pauline and Jan had been hynotised into staying there out of fear of Spike's threats of retribution if they left. But what had begun as a contract of fear had developed for both of them into a fascination with the man's propensities for the perverse, and by degrees an unacknowledged sympathy had been established between all three parties. Rather as a spar of driftwood is inexorably carried revolution by revolution towards the eye of a whirlpool, so they had found themselves at the centre of a field of experience from which they could not escape. Neither girl could properly explain her attraction to a way of life that was antipathetic to natural instincts. Their involvement in it was rather like falling downstairs in a dream. You arrived there but didn't know how.

Now that Spike was dead, and the circuit had been broken, they were free to think of the past with a perspective that had been previously denied them. Jan sat brooding over her wine. 'Was it really two years ago,' she said, 'that I first went out to the millhouse?' She looked around anxiously. Neither of the girls could believe themselves wholly free; they expected that he would return, that a rough, hairy wrist would suddenly grab their arm in a side-street, or that the van would pull up alongside, and he'd be leaning out of the window, smoking, not saying anything, just telling them with his eyes to get in.

'It can't be possible,' Jan resumed, extracting herself from a web of reverie. 'And the worst of it wasn't the ventriloquial fits; it was the agonised self-recriminations that succeeded these attacks. I suppose that's why we stayed. He'd be like a man imploring help, up to his neck in water, but when he was pulled in, he'd take fear at the sliding shingle beneath his feet, and go back out again in order to risk drowning. And, of course, the risk was stronger than the need for help.'

'I came back off the moor one day,' said Pauline, 'and I remember he was prostrate, stripped to the waist. I got into cover behind bracken and watched him. His body was contorted, and his hands continually beat the earth. Even when it started to rain he didn't shift his position. The rain was beating the earth bare. I ran for it.'

'We were trapped,' Jan reflected. 'He got you into that state of mind in which you hated Blue Rock, but every time you left you felt exposed, an outsider in the world, so you had to return. When I used to go home I thought my parents knew everything about what was going on. I imagined they could see my life inside my head, and I would break down.'

Claudette listened in silence to the two girls as they slowly unburdened themselves. It was as though they'd transported the tension of Blue Rock into Diane's flat with its white walls, and sparse furnishings. There were mauve and yellow autumn crocuses in a box by the window, each solitary flower wrapped in a delicate spathe, without any stem.

It was Jan who broke the silence. 'I don't think anything could have helped Spike,' she said. 'When he trespassed into the world

157

of human emotions, he applied the same instincts as a badger does on leaving its set. His suspicion attracted people, but it was used as a decoy to lead them into a trap. There were so many who came and went from that house; but never once did he express any fear of retribution. His own magnetism made him inviolable. He was permanently like a man scrutinising his own features in a shaving mirror.'

Pauline looked out of the window. 'We were luckier than most,' she found herself saying. 'At least we've come through; there were others who didn't. Whatever became of them, I wonder? The van would be gone in the middle of the night; you could hear it for miles in the still of the countryside. I would watch the headlights tunnelling through the black of the skyline until they disappeared over the ridge of the moor. Yellow beams probing the black lacquer.'

'He was cunning,' Jan reflected; 'the locals assumed he used the millhouse for periods of rest. He kept apart, isolation was his strength. He drew everything to his own centre.'

The girls lapsed into silence. Claudette sat in the blue-cushioned cane rocking chair, her legs crossed, her eyes searching out the striations of darkness in the mauve crocuses. Her eyes were made up in rich teal and orchid, her black satin gloves were frosted with *diamanté* stars. All of her life she had lived in the separation of mind and body, and if her emotions had become dulled as a consequence of being abused by others, she had never lost her compassion for all who suffer. The small room, the scruffily dressed girls, the evident poverty; all of these things reminded her of her childhood, of her initial struggle to live in Paris.

'I'm sure you're waiting to hear about how we retrieved your photographs,' Pauline said, recollecting Claudette's silent presence. 'It wasn't half a strange house; most of the furniture was antique, and the books, the house was lined with them, room after room, ranked from the floor to the ceiling. But it was unnerving, the silence in there was like a cave; you felt that faces were watching you from the mirror, and that at each step something might shatter. There was also a dog smell, as though an animal had impregnated the carpets with its scent. But it was spotless, there wasn't a mote of dust on any surface.' *But when I was upstairs I could have sworn I heard the panting of a dog; I could hear something sniffing around downstairs, going from corner to*

158

corner of the room. I thought he might have kept a watch-dog, but when I went downstairs there was nothing. I thought I was going to fumble things; each time I started to remove the photographic wallets, the pacing of paws running over a wooden surface would begin again. I couldn't find out what it was, so I put it down to a dog that was in a neighbouring house.

'But it was the smell which upset me more than anything else; you couldn't escape it, not even with the windows thrown open wide.'

Pauline suddenly looked old. Claudette saw her as she would be in thirty years' time, her face fleshed out and containing the skeletal imprint of her youth. Jan was meditative, she seemed to be reliving the big fog; she sat half listening and half preoccupied with a narrative that was her own. She carried the expression of someone reflecting upon a stream of running water. In the end you weren't even aware that you were thinking – it was the motion of the water which was thinking for you.

'I filled three sacks,' Pauline said, 'before I realised he was watching me.'

'Who was watching you?' Claudette interjected with a voice that relayed alarm.

'A boy was,' Pauline replied. 'He'd been sitting there all the time, buried in a big comfortable bedroom chair, with his back to me and his eyes looking out over the street. He was so silent I couldn't even hear him breathing; he just turned round with a single slow movement of his head and sat looking at me. I screamed, but he only smiled, as though it wasn't important to him who was in the room or what they were doing. There was something terribly wrong with him; he'd used a red crayon or lipstick to initial a red M on his forehead. The jacket he was wearing was too big for him. There wasn't any expression in his features. He toyed with an unlit cigar in his hand. When he stared at me it was as though he didn't see me. He went over to the window, and said, very deliberately, "Yes, you can bury my past life." It was almost as if he'd prepared his speech. "As the sovereign of this house, I'll permit that," he said.

'Of course I was immediately suspicious; he could have been anyone, a relative, a guest, a plain-clothes man . . .

' "There are letters you'll want also," he said; "they are in the lacquered cabinet to your right, the one with the oriental spray of plum blossom and a crane lifting into flight. I've kept them there

for longer than I can remember. But everything's neatly tabu-
lated; this house bears the signature of an ordered mind. I can
account for that."

'I still wasn't sure whether this was a game or whether he was
crazy,' Pauline said. 'I knew that Jan would be getting worried.
Fortunately there's a narrow lane behind the house, and we were
able to park Spike's van outside the back door. The lane's a
dead-end; no one can see you there from the road.'

'So what did you do?' said Claudette. 'Did you just carry on
emptying the wardrobe?'

'He got up at this point, and walked towards the door. "I'm
going to get a drink," he said, "and anyhow I have to consult a
book in preparation for my appointments tomorrow. But don't
worry about me. I'll be downstairs if you need me. Do you read
Burton's *Anatomy of Melancholy*?"

'Can you imagine my state of bewilderment?' said Pauline.
'His manner was so unsettling, so self-absorbed, that I couldn't
make out whether this was a sick joke or an act of complicity. I
worked quickly in his absence, unloading armfuls of yellow
wallets, and then I ransacked the cabinet he had pointed out to
me. I was working so fast that I couldn't recall doing anything;
my hands couldn't even feel the folders of letters I was transfer-
ring from one box to another. There were six black vinyl sacks to
be taken out of the house.

'I told myself that if it was a trap, why would he let me get this
far? The very fact of being in the house was an offence, without
allowing someone to go ahead and select the items they wished to
steal. There wasn't any reason in it.' *I could hear him downstairs
playing a piano in intermittent snatches; it sounded like he was giving
expression to his mood, rather than attempting to play music. The
notes were heavy, sometimes tempestuously sombre, and then I could
hear him pacing back and forth again before he returned to the piano
and resumed.*

'I decided to go downstairs with nothing, and to run out of the
house empty-handed. But somehow he must have calculated
this, for as I was coming downstairs in my socks, and on the balls
of my feet, he came out of the room downstairs and looked up at
me.

' "Let me assist you with your things," he said. "You've got
transport, haven't you; I saw it parked outside. Are you sure I
can't offer you a drink before you go?" ' *What was odd was that*

his eyes never shifted their focus. They weren't looking at me or anything extraneous within the field of his vision; they were preoccupied with something within. 'As you'd told us he was a psychiatrist, I wondered whether this was a mad patient who lived in his house. He was still toying with his cigar, and he had a folder tucked under his arm. He pointed to this, without looking at me, and said, "I've got to read up for a problematic case tomorrow morning. You go on ahead."

'He went back to the piano, and this time lit his cigar. His ponderous notes added to the melancholy of the house. He didn't show any sign of having detected the flurried pacing of a dog which seemed so close that I was looking for it in the corners of the room.' *He had his eyes closed, he played like someone orchestrating a dream, feeling for an inner silence that the music would animate.*

'I went back upstairs and shouldered two of the sacks. I still couldn't believe that he was going to let me pass without questioning me, but he did, and I walked out through the garden, and returned again.

' "It's no good anchoring oneself in the past," he said; *these things represent the shadow hemisphere of a life I should have renounced. The underworld of the wolf, the triumph of the fox. Can't you smell it? The animal scent that pervades this house, the stink of fox. And what if the wolf and fox couple? The conception is a hybrid outsider that is dragged down by dogs into wiry bracken and savaged.*

'I started to climb the stairs again, and he stood there watching me. "I'm the fox," he screamed, *and my past lies in the swollen belly of the wolf. Do you know what it's like to hunt by moonlight, that cold stony light which magnifies each detail in a night wood? No, you'll never know.*

'I came downstairs again carrying two more of the sacks. He was leaning into the hall mirror straightening his tie, playing obsessively with its knot. He didn't even see me as I walked into the sitting-room, he was so preoccupied with his clothes, and with distorting his eyes, pulling the skin down beneath them,' *as though he was searching for something inside himself that wouldn't come clear.* 'I managed to slip out again, and told Jan to have the engine running as the next journey would be my last. I didn't trust him; he had gone into himself so far that I feared he might explode with physical violence.

'He was talking to himself about someone called Robert

Blakestone, conducting a measured dialogue with this imaginary person for whom he improvised in a staccato baritone. If you hadn't known you would have been convinced the person was present, he answered him with such careful and varied provision. I got back upstairs and tidied the room, I didn't want to leave traces.

'All the time I could hear him conducting this intense dialogue with the mirror.' *He must have seen in it an imaginary room in which he sat on one side of the table and Robert Blakestone on the other. The bedroom was stifling. I heard the whine of a dog again while I was preparing to leave, something hot brushed against my legs, the leathery saltiness of an animal's tongue. I remember taking one of the cologne bottles from beside the bed and spraying a fine dust of perfume over my clothes.*

'I came down the stairs for the last time and he extracted himself from the mirror.' *You could almost feel his image peel away like adhesive from the glass.* 'For the first time he looked at me, a look that went through me as though he was witnessing some horror that had compelled him to stare. I remember his exact words. He said, "I'm going to die tonight; I'll be killed in a car at Chester Gate. I already know the driver; he's an executive who drives a white Jaguar. He has a dinner appointment to keep at 8.00. Neither of us will reach our destination."

'I got out to the van and told Jan to get away quickly. We came back here and waited for you.'

They were silent. Each of them was anticipating Diane's return, and when she came in out of the dark it seemed as though they had willed her presence into the room.

'There's been a terrible crash somewhere,' she said; 'there are police diversions everywhere, and fleets of police cars racing in the direction of the park. The traffic's paralysed, which is why I'm so late.'

'I have an appointment at 8.00,' Claudette said. 'What a long way we've come since those days when I first encountered you all at Blue Rock. Do you remember the tall foxgloves in the shade, and the flowers that I always knew by name? Wiry pink cones of Cornish heath, the pink daisy-like flowers of Hottentot fig, sea-campion and kidney vetch. I knew their names because as a child I read books about wild flowers. They were the only books my mother had, and some of them were illustrated with colour plates; I still remember the excitement of finding flowers that I

162

could identify by matching them against the hand-painted plates. It was like finding oneself, segment by segment. I would take a field and systematically set about naming each flower that accompanied the various seasons.'

'I have to go back there,' Jan said, 'there isn't anywhere else to go.'

'You could try to find a life in London,' Diane said; 'it would be hard, but not impossible.'

'What will you do with the photographs?' Pauline asked.

'I'll leave them here tonight,' Claudette replied, 'and tomorrow I'll have them burnt. I like the purity of fire; if only one could wash one's hands in fire and have them remain uncharred.'

Diane poured out a glass of red wine and said, 'I can't help recalling the oddest young man I met on the tube some weeks ago. I was reminded of him today by someone I had to visit – a boy who possessed a corresponding desperation, and who could only identify with animals. This one refuses to enter the house; he insists on living in a shed with the family whippet. Even his speech has become incomprehensible. His parents have been unable to persuade him to go to school at any stage in his life, and now that he's nineteen, they don't know what to do for him. He is devoid of the most rudimentary hygiene, but is completely without violence. He warmed to me as the other boy did.'

'And what was the other one like?' Pauline enquired.

'Totally withdrawn, and obsessed by the animal world. He had run away to London, and had only his psychiatrist's address. He stayed here a night, but in the early hours he underwent some sort of nervous paroxysm, and in the morning he was gone. He left me a note, and then came back one afternoon when my boyfriend was here.'

'What did he look like?' said Pauline.

'He's not easy to describe,' Diane replied. 'Tall, extremely slim, too nervous to allow one a clear focus into his person, shifting moods, gentle and, apparently the second time he called, immaculately dressed. Perhaps he has money? But it's not easy to describe his features because his acute nervousness made you respond to his vulnerability. In following his moods, you tended to forget about his physical presence.'

'It sounds rather like the boy we met this afternoon,' Pauline said. 'We accomplished what we discussed with Claudette last night. After we'd got over the initial fear, and the unreality of our

163

being there, we realised that someone had been watching us the whole time from an armchair. I was going to run away, but when he started to speak about the photographs belonging to him, I was convinced that he was as much an intruder as we were. How could we know who he was? He could have been a relation, someone staying there. He had to have some connection with Moravia. The clothes that he was wearing didn't fit. He had quite clearly taken them from the wardrobe in which the photograph wallets were kept. He had an obsession with his tie which he kept altering and rubbing between the forefinger and thumb of his right hand as though the texture of the material soothed him.'

'That sounds like him,' said Diane. 'How strange that we should each of us have encountered him. He was called David, and at first I noticed him because of his peculiar air of not belonging. It was this that made me approach him. He was a stranger to cities, like Jan, and at first I attributed his anxiety to his sense of displacement. But it went much deeper than that. He was removed to a degree that was painful to watch. There was a barrier within him that he couldn't cross; he'd come up against barbed wire and retreated into the safety of his inner world.'

'You're quite right,' Pauline said. 'I'll never forget the way he played that piano. Sometimes he'd strike the keys with all the strength in his body, and then suddenly the notes were scarcely audible. I think we were too shocked to realise the danger of the situation. It hit us afterwards.'

Claudette excused herself; she would return the next day for her bullion of photographs. She went out into the night, and listened to the traffic buzz like a hive in the bowl of central London. She waved down a taxi and took off across town to her rendezvous with Moravia.

From old habits the night always instilled in her a sense of imminent adventure. Those who slept by day walked the endless tunnel of the night. The stoned drag-queen collapsed in an alley, the tormented somnambulist who kept walking until dawn, the revenant, the fugitive, the vagrant, the nocturnal gathering of those consigned to the sulphur-blaze of the pit. She had known them all; the desperate, the hunted, the wolf slaking its thirst at a limed water-hole.

She had surmised that he would be late; her dramatic entrée set the bar in quiet motion. Eyes crept out of conversations to look at her like a family of badgers emerging from a set. She exacted this response from people and delighted in the corresponding stimulus it afforded her. Wishing to instate his superiority he would be late, he would enter cold-eyed, impassive, and order champagne with a superciliousness that relegated her to the ranks of low breeding. He would never let her forget that she had sold her body, and he could never forgive himself for having been her client. Caught in this vicious paradox, he treated her as the extension of himself he would have beaten with his bare fists if he'd been able to castigate his double.

She ordered a glass of Chablis, and chose a table in the corner; the light pooled itself with the glitter of star fragments. She had always possessed this solitary hauteur; people were fascinated but they shyed away from approaching her. She felt conspicuous; ill at ease. Her corner of the room was cold, a persistent draught transmitted a chill to her spine. To sit waiting beneath the city allowed her thoughts to slow to a deep pool. On the black face of the water she could see Moravia. He hung there with the jettisoned cargo of her past. She felt cold and unnaturally vulnerable.

To her right, a baggily dressed banker was attempting to get his short-skirted secretary drunk. He had rested the little finger of his left hand on the black snowflake pattern of her thigh, and balanced it there, uncertain as yet whether she had divined his intentions and would meet his advances with a sharp slap of disapproval. His finger balanced unmovingly on her leg with the isolation of a lunar module.

Claudette looked at her watch; he was already thirty minutes late, something of an aberration for a man who prided himself on his punctuality. She knew that he couldn't afford not to come, and attributed his lateness to the traffic. He was probably sitting in the insulation of his car, listening to Mahler, thinking of ways to enmesh her in his abstruse dialectics. She remembered how he appeared to have aged when she paid him that unexpected visit this morning, something she had put down to the strain of his conducting diametrically opposed public and private lives. Half of the men she had known in her Paris days lived like this; some had wives, families, diplomatic careers, professions, and all shared one thing in common – a sexual hunger that had them risk the foundations of their lives for the bizarre sensations of an hour in her apartment.

165

She would use the time in waiting to good effect. She took out a pencil and blue pocket notebook and made a résumé of her novel to date. In relating his experience of having died, Andy had initiated Martin into secret rites that the latter would assimilate and propound to the sect after Andy's death. Andy's apparent invincibility would carry greater mystery if he were to disappear for an indefinite time prior to his sensational death in a car-crash. The latter incident would come as the explosive denouement to the book; shards of glass would explode in a shower of sparks across the book's last page, while Andy was projected into the illimitable inner space that he had spent a lifetime exploring. She could feel the rush of words in her; they were building with an adrenalin stream, missiles homing for the attack. As the book existed in a fragmentary and still unchronologised state, it didn't seem to matter if she plotted his death out of sequence. Besides, she had learnt from experience that the way to neutralise the aggression of others was to engage oneself in total self-absorption. To read or write was a way of establishing invisible defences. A paunchy, ox-eyed man was already leering at her; she would dispel his intended advances by writing. Moravia shouldn't be very much longer; at any moment she expected to see him nonchalantly staring at her from the other side of the room, one hand on his tie, and the other in his right-hand trouser pocket. It had always been his manner to approach her casually, to pretend indifference to those around him, as though she was a curiosity or relative that he had condescended to meet, in all probability only to dispense a little charity.

Claudette started writing.

Andy had been driving for two hours; his face was silvered with fatigue. For a decade he had hung on to life, incognito, incom-municado, but all the time working to prepare his papers for the research of the cult he had so painstakingly founded. He had scrupulously avoided any intimation of fiction, verifying his experiences wherever he could by scientific research into death as a paranormal phenomenon. After a year of enquiries, friends had assumed he had gone missing or had in all probability committed suicide. He hadn't even changed his name; he'd travelled across the States for a year on a legacy left to him by an uncle, and then he'd come back and settled in a small cottage in Wiltshire, a place so remote that he had been able to work and think uninterrupted for the best part of a decade. He had no telephone and entertained no one from the village. He had grown so unsociable that he resented even the intermittent visits of a postman bearing the inevitable bills that not even the solitary are exempt from receiving. He had cultivated his garden, grown vegetables and flowers, and come to love the cycle of the natural world. He prided himself on his marrows, his purple aubergines, the crisp emerald of his lettuce, the tubular firmness of his courgettes, the ripeness of his yellow pears in September. He had trained roses on the sheltered garden walls – red and pink and biscuit; he lived within his walls as though they were the only habitable area of earth after a nuclear catastrophe.

The road was empty and he was abnormally tired. Another twenty minutes and he would be home; he allowed his mind to shut down intermittently, the flick-flack of the trees as he passed them was beginning to be mesmeric. He was reaching that state of inner vibration which allowed him to harmonise with the cosmic pattern. Lights were coming on inside his head – gold and blue and red and mauve, an intrinsic rainbow he would have to span.

He'd held the car at a steady 60 for the last hour. His blue Austin Montego sat comfortably on the road. A mackerel sky was banking in the west, blue and silver bars flushed with peach and green; another hour and it would resemble embers popping in the blue ash of a wood-fire. Relieved at the prospect of arriving home, he pushed his foot down on the accelerator and woke up to the engine's corresponding burst of energy. He was travelling at 75 mph, his mind preoccupied with that state of trance which usually precipitates astral projection. He could feel his psychic body triggering to lift-off, the web was unravelling to a single silver thread.

He was too dissociated to register that a car was travelling rapidly towards him, the first for at least thirty minutes. An Alfa Romeo Sprint was hurtling towards him with suspended anima- tion, the car appearing to lift in the air as it hung back in the instant before projecting itself veeringly at the oncoming car.

Andy couldn't rejoin his body in time to avert the crash; the headlights of the Alfa Romeo were powering into the back of his head, he was lit up by a white explosive radiance that gouged in as his hands made frantic contact with the wheel in a reflex action to haul the car wide before the detonating impact of metal exploded in his face.

167

He didn't feel any pain; he was already above it, cushioned by a spider's web that he projected into, the web ballooning out with the velocity of impact, endlessly resilient as he thudded into it, setting off twinkling lights that were nerve-flashes. He was being telescoped into a sky-lake of colours that he had never perceived before. He was motivated without the restraining anchor of his body; he had himself become a travelling rainbow of light gravitating towards his tutelary star.

When the first emergency vehicles arrived at the scene of the crash, they found the driver of the Alfa Romeo headless in a ditch. They couldn't find the driver of the Montego, the car crumpled like a leaf in a white fulmination of flame.

Claudette looked up. The bar had been steadily filling with people; a small party was excitedly laying claim to three tables to her left. The birthday girl wore red ribbons in her hair and was courted by ice-buckets of champagne. It was 9.30. Surely he would never come now; perhaps he'd been indefinitely congealed in traffic and turned around and gone home. She would telephone; after all she had nothing to lose now. She had the photographs, while he was in the unenviable position of being unable to take legal redress without risking his future career as a doctor.

Her old habit of clicking her heels persisted, and faces looked up as she snaked over to the telephone, her walk impeded by the tightness of her dress. There was no response at Moravia's end. She decided to wait another fifteen minutes in case he was genuinely delayed by traffic. Her sense of disquiet grew; the inconclusion of her affairs with Moravia was like the persistence of a sooty footprint in a field of snow. She was becoming aware of someone to her right, eyes trained on her with unflinching scrutiny. It was the heavy, coarse-featured, swarthy man who had menaced her with his eyes when she had first arrived. Instinct told her that the man's intentions were harmful; it was animosity rather than lust making him fix his eyes into her. He had moved his seat nearer to hers, and was positioned in such a way as to make it impossible for her to bypass him without his having to get up from his table to allow her through.

She re-read what she had written, going over it without comprehension. Her eyes slid over the words, running like tiny insects that couldn't grip a polished surface.

168

All the time she could feel the rigidity of the man's stare playing into her nervous-field like a flashlight used to blind an animal before shooting. He had turned round to face her full-on, his implacable affrontery was unshifting. The tension caused a sharp pain behind her right eye, that same intense flash that had preceded migraines in her childhood. She returned to her notebook in an effort to decentralise his fixation. She couldn't fit an identity to this man; if he had belonged to her former life in Paris, she would have recalled him. She forgot no one, and this was a part of her hell; the dance of wolves pervaded her dreams, face after face filed past like those paying their last respects to a coffin before the earth is shovelled over with a flat spade.

He had come closer; she could hear the scrape of his wooden chair on the tiled floor as he came to occupy the table next to her. He was drinking a red Chianti, and there was a flush to the coarse features of his face – the bird's hooked nose, the cheek folds, the heavy lips with their unsensuous twitch. He wore a maroon tie loose at the collar, his shirt and suit were badly creased, his black curly hair which had thinned on top was straggly with grease.

Under pressure, she found that she couldn't re-enter the notes for her novel; conjectured fragments of narrative broke up like pack-ice beneath her eyes. She found herself writing disconnected words, automatic phrases, variations of her signature but, despite her resolution to exclude him, he wouldn't retract. She nervously glanced around the room. No one was paying any attention to the evident hostility this man bore for her; the small party had become animated by champagne and an exchange of jokes concerning mutual acquaintances and, unrebuffed by any resistance, the businessman on her other side was in the process of stroking his secretary's shapely thigh.

Claudette was terrified by the war going on between herself and this indiscreet stranger. They might have been facing each other on a remote dust plateau, no habitation or growth for as far as the eye could see. He was closing in; his intention was to sit in the chair opposite her, and in a few seconds he would have arrived there. Nothing now could divert the crisis which was building. His eyes were locked in an immovable focus, black squid's eyes, thumb-pressing their way through the fabric of her defences. His eyes were heavy inside her like two musket balls that had holed her cranium. The metal was scorching. He poured himself another glass of wine and drank it without a pause. She had encountered this sort of menace before, but never so persistently, and with so intentional a desire to inflict harm.

She heard the heavy clatter of his chair as he got up and sat down heavily so that he was facing her. She quickly looked round; no one else was aware of her distress, no one seemed to have noticed the man's unsolicited intrusion. This was the isolation that crowds afforded; everyone inhabited a private isthmus and remained on it – if an emergency occurred they were unable to get back across the water to help.

'Ain't you going to speak, sonny?' the stranger said.

Claudette continued to look at her notebook; she knew that silence was her only defence under such provocation. She was a child again, gathering sea-pinks on the granite ledges of the Ile de Houat; blue and white butterflies formed double stars as they fluctuated above the wave.

She could hear the putter of a lobster-boat rounding the coast, the stern loaded with wicker pots. The fisherman was at the wheel in a blue and white wheelhouse, the sea was choppy, metallic blue and skeined with invisible currents that glossed on the surface where two currents met in a channel.

'You're wearing falsies,' the man said in a gravel-voiced whisper. 'Who are you? I know your sort, and I don't like you.'

Claudette still made no effort to speak or even acknowledge the stranger's presence.

'Want me to call the police?' he said, flatly and brutally.

She could see herself as a child again, too shyly sensitive to walk into the presence of strangers, delighting only when she was free to escape to a field and lie low in the mist. She could hear cow-bells in fog, the plangent wail of the foghorn that punctuated her summer vacations, red poppies and sanfoin in the corn, her sympathy with the tiniest of insects that helicoptered on to the gold hairs on her wrist. There was the crackle of sun-scorched holly leaves beneath her feet, the electric jab of a lizard zig-zagging for cover in the ivy.

'You better come outside with me, love, and we'll see who you are then,' the man was threatening. There was no echo to his voice; it met her square in the face, and didn't carry. His breath was acrid from the wine.

She feared the resulting scene, but she would have to make an exit and run for a taxi. She allowed a last childhood memory to colour her mind. It was the image of a rainbow, its primary colours diffusing to a vapourish mother-of-pearl, lilac and silver droplets dispersing into the blue ether. She had watched that rainbow, captivated by its luminosity and by the mint of warm rain that had abruptly silvered the hollows of her cheeks and, as the rainbow dispersed, she had felt it correspondingly pass through her. It was a sign, a token that she would live.

12

When he came back, I didn't recognise him. He'd been gone for six months, and most of us feared he'd either taken his life or simply gone missing. Time has that quality – it correspondingly dilates and contracts. Sometimes I'd go out to the old barn, and it was as though he was standing in a gold cone of light, hunched into himself as was his way, the light dusting his black singlet. But life's like that; you can replay an inconclusive conversation on the sensitive film of memory, and sometimes get the answers right. What he left me was a legacy of unfinished chapters and, when I picked up the thread where he had left off, it was like regaining contact with a current.

It was late spring in the countryside. The woods were purple with bluebells and massed with gold-eyed stitchwort. The cuckoo had returned; you could hear him pursuing a liquid arc across the fields. Yellow waterfalls of laburnum, willow catkins, the stickiness of elm buds, the pink and white snowstorm of cherry blossom – everywhere colour had reasserted itself. Swallows had just returned, punctual to the day; you could hear the whipcrack in the air as they flew past, their aerobatics anticipating the slightly later arrival of swifts.

He'd come back of his own accord, although the police wanted to speak to him in connection with his psychiatrist's death. I hadn't expected him; he was sitting on the floor of the barn, in a suit that was too big for him, and which had become torn and polished from continual wear. I knew without speaking that something was very wrong. He had his notebook with him and was chewing the stub of a turquoise pencil. He had tattoos on the backs of his hands – two 'M's needled in mauve and red ink, with a snake flourish embellishing the capital letter. He had reefed in his shirt sleeves in order to draw attention to these designs. I assumed that the notebook contained the script of the novel he had begun before he went away.

But it was worse than that. His eyes had gone inwards. There appeared to be a division between himself and what he saw, or rather had given up seeing, so you felt he didn't even know you were there other than by the sound of your voice. His skin had become discoloured; some radical alteration had occurred in his chemistry.

'You're Bunny,' he said, as though a third party had described me to him, and he was meeting me for the first time. 'I've changed my life,' he said, 'I've taken over another mind.'

'You'll always be David to me,' I replied, trying to coax him back into a recognition of his surroundings. 'Have you seen how the swallows have returned? They're nesting in the eaves outside.' *That scarlet splash against the white underbelly; remember how we watched them each dusk last summer, picking off insects with such electric voracity?* 'Did I tell you that Tommy Smith has decided not to go to university? He's going to stay home and work on the land. He'll most likely marry a farmer's girl.'

He looked down at the page on which he was writing, distracted, searching for a mental clue to which I had no access. I could see him turning his thought round and round, getting the pivotal balance right before he spoke. He seemed to have developed an obsession with his tie; he kept fingering it as though the friction of his finger on the material brought him some relief from his evident anxiety.

'I'm not staying long,' he said, 'I've got patients to care for. I'm just down for the weekend.'

'You missed the crocuses,' I replied. 'They were spectacular this year – a panoply of purples, saffrons and whites. And the snowdrops before them; they constellated the wood up past the farm. We picked bunches of them and brought them indoors for their bitter scent. Have you noticed how they smell of snow? And there was a robin all winter who tinkled at our window.

'I came out here even on the worst days. I'd scatter seeds for the birds, and even shy birds like jays alighted with temerity. There were fieldfares and redwings, and water-rail and Carolina ducks on the pond. I'll show you my notes in case you want to catch up on your own journal.'

But nothing I could say had any effect. It was as if he had never had a past, and yet he'd come straight out here on his return. Perhaps it was instinct that guided him. He'd heaped the straw into a mound, and sat there as though he was trying to

173

remember who he was. The light was the clear daffodil of early May; larks were going up into the windy azure.

'The girls are still around,' I said. 'Shall I invite them out one evening? They're sure to be excited that you're back. Now that the evenings are lighter, we could have a bottle of wine out here.' I spoke like someone cautiously tiptoeing over thin ice, waiting at any moment for a fissure to appear followed by a crack. I could almost hear the drum of snipe's feet skidding across a polished mirror of blue ice into the one area of steely water that had thawed.

'I won't be here long enough,' he replied. 'I've managed it this one time as a break in my busy schedule. My novel's written though.'

'Is it the one about Branden?' I said, hoping to draw the mollusc from the impenetrable shell. 'I remember how you frightened us that night with your narrative.'

He closed his notebook, and measured his words. 'Branden's dead,' he said; 'he and I exchanged bodies. It's me who has taken his place.'

I could feel the anxiety mounting in me, that sense of unease that occurs when you know the person you are speaking to is answering his own inner monologue. It was the isolation that chilled; I realised that he and I could no longer communicate by shared ideas. Words didn't reach him or properly register.

I suggested a walk. 'The woods are full of bluebells,' I said, 'and let's see if we can find a nesting chiff-chaff or whitethroat.' I thought this might revive his love of the natural world. I opened the old wooden door and let the clear air into the barn.

He followed me across the fields, dogged, walking with his head down, seeing nothing. I noticed he had black suede shoes on, and he was at pains to keep these from getting damp. Rooks were building in the beeches; they shouted at us as we went through a copse towards the pond.

'Shall we visit the keeper's gibbet?' I called back to him and, receiving no response, I directed my path through the pheasant wood and came to a clearing. He was lagging behind. The gibbet had its usual assortment of twisted weasels and stoats, jackdaws and crows but, to my surprise, nailed up to an upright by the bark was a fox, its body limp, the russet brush still beautiful in death.

I could hear him coming up behind, deliberately dragging his feet, conducting a soliloquy of which I could only catch occasional words. I waited for him, examining a jay's plumage for the vivid blue in its wing feathers. The feathers were stiffening to the same texture as tree bark.

When he came up to me, I could feel his eyes searching the carrion. For a brief instant he seemed to have regained his animation. His nostrils were sniffing as though he'd picked up a familiar scent. I didn't have time to tell him about the fox hanging up on the other side of the tree. I only heard him scream on discovering it. Then he was rolling over and over on the ground, attempting to push stones into his mouth. He'd undergone an attack of some sort, and I had to keep him from biting his tongue. I sat him upright with his back to a tree, and waited for the convulsions to subside. I thought he might have become epileptic, and that this accounted for the change in his person.

I knew I couldn't get him back across the fields, so I ran to the keeper's cottage. Fortunately there was a telephone, and Tommy Smith's father drove out from the village and collected us. That was two days before they took him inside. He went into a ward in the old square brick asylum called St Agnes's, ten miles north of Norwich in a flat wilderness of skylines and wheat. He wasn't allowed visitors for a long time; we heard he had been locked up in a violent ward.

I visited him in September of that year, by way of a valediction before commencing my university term. When you approached the nineteenth-century granite and brick façade of the country mansion, it had the air of something dredged up from the floor of a sunken lake. The inertia of the place was evident in everything. A groundsman was clipping a yew hedge, two or three men who could have been patients were spraying a rich burgeoning of pink roses.

Inside, the corridors smelt of stale air and antiseptic. A man in a chocolate double-breasted suit walked up and down the corridor, back and forth like a sentry on duty. His line never altered; he could have been walking dead centre on the fluorescent divide of a road, or conversely on a tightrope above a precipice.

David was in the large visitors' room, sitting alone in a corner by the window. Although he was dressed in a blue bathrobe, he toyed obsessively with a tattered bottle-green and pink striped tie that he kept passing from hand to hand. His face was walled in

175

by drugs; you could feel the coating of sedatives on his skin, and somewhere within, lost like a deep-sea diver in a wreck, was the animated spark of the David I used to know. He was like a stone that the sculptor has still to fashion into an image.

This time he looked at me, but there was no light in his eyes. It was as if he was looking up from the bottom of a well on an oppressively cloudy day. I gave him the various nature magazines that I had brought with me, but he professed no interest in the journals. He was aware of nothing outside himself, and one had no access to his thoughts.

He'd completed his novel and hoped to have it published; this much I gathered from the sister on duty. She said he called it *Branden's Book*. I didn't stay long; there was no point in the matter. Outside the window three men were punting a red plastic football into the air. The ball went up and lodged itself in a lime tree. I could see it there, suspended like the sun. The men threw sticks into the branches of the tree, but they couldn't unseat the ball. Eventually an attendant in a white coat came hurrying out with a ladder. The men greeted him with raucous cheers.

That night I went back to the wood before dark. An owl was hooting in the mauve twilight; not a breeze, not a footfall. The fox was still there, only it was eroded by the elements. It had become a stringy coil of fur, vermin-infested, and almost indistinguishable in shape. I cut it down, put it in a sack, weighted it, and threw it out into the pond. After the ripples had subsided, I looked up. The stars were brutally lucent; their mineral light transmitted from point to point of the galaxy. The moon was a pearl coming clear in the water.